A Smooth Driver

Cithara Susan Patra

Anuci Press

First paperback edition 2025

Anuci Press edition 2025

www.anuci-press.com

Cover Design by Adrian Medina

Fabledbeastdesign.wordpress.com

ISBN 979-8-9926529-6-3 (paperback)

ISBN 979-8-9926529-7-0 (eBook)

A Smooth Driver

Cithara Patra

For my writing group

Chapter 1

Kara glanced at the rearview mirror as a red car pulled up right behind her and stopped on the curb. Her blue eyeshadow smeared a little on the side, so she rubbed it back in to make her dark eyes pop a little. With how long she stood in this line, she could fix all her makeup. Her blush needed a touch up, she smeared her lipstick over her coffee cup, and her mascara clumped over some of her lashes. Not that she expected anything else. This was the usual traffic outside of Charlotte-Douglas airport. On a Friday night, the cars stood bumper to bumper with each other. Inching forward whenever another car before her moved, she struggled to find a lone spot to park into. She wouldn't come here except to drop off people or pick them up. So naturally, on one of the busiest nights, she had to pick someone up. She didn't know what convinced her to accept this ride, but nothing else going on in her life and the airport being close by, she took it. It wouldn't take long to drop this person off.

"Come on, come on!" She checked the place she needed to go. Not Downtown Charlotte for a change. Usually when she picked people up, they were going to a hotel over there, but this person was going to an unknown location. At least, for her it was unknown: McIver Drive. She never dropped anyone over there before, so it would be a brand-new adventure. There were parts of Charlotte she had yet to discover. Might as well discover them now.

"Please still be there..." She pleaded as she slowed down through the terminals. Her passenger, Thomas, asked for a ride ten minutes ago and she got in earlier than usual. The traffic on the way to the airport wasn't terrible. She got on the highway and off it within seconds. The moment she turned into the exit for the airport, that's when cars started lining up and slowing her down.

She turned her attention back to the big pickup truck that squeezed right in front, screeching to a stop. The baggage in its bed shook and fell over as the driver jumped out. She gripped the steering wheel as the driver let out his passenger. Fantastic. This guy was a rideshare driver too, though he worked for another company. She didn't spot the bright yellow Happy Riders sticker on his windshield, but a purple one. Jerk. He took up at least three spots, blocking people from getting in and, judging how he cut off his lights, he intended to stay there.

"Oh, come on!" She groaned as she stared at the map where her rider waited. Only a few feet to Terminal C. She needed the perfect moment to get out and zip over there. "Move it already! I got someone to pick up."

Naturally, the truck driver spent the next two minutes talking to the passenger, so she waited till she found her opening and drove away. There! She'd find her rider, a man named Thomas Whittle, coming in from Japan and ready to head home. At least, she assumed he was headed home. She knew nothing about him except that he'd be alone, and he would be waiting outside Terminal C. This was where all the international passengers came out of. Hopefully, he had a good trip and wouldn't worry about her weaving in and out of cars.

Just a few feet more...I can make it.

Looking in the back, she checked on the water bottles and snack packets she left for riders. Many of her colleagues didn't leave anything for their passengers, but she couldn't do that. With the weather growing warmer each day, most people craved water. It was one thing they praised her for in reviews: keeping water and driving within the speed limit. Now she eased around the airport lot, foot on break as people walked across with their luggage.

Be cool, Kara. This is the last ride you're doing tonight. Drop this guy off and you can go home. She only hoped this was the last person wanting a ride. If anyone else asked, she'd decline them. Her time was up around 8 PM and the night shift drivers took over. Hopefully, everyone she drove around enjoyed her company. Time was money as her company Happy Riders loved to remind their drivers. Happy Riders. She cringed every time she saw that sign taped on her window. While the company was nice and the pay was good, it wasn't the place she wanted to be in. It was just something she did while looking for work in between.

"All right, Mr. Whittle. Where are you?" She squinted as she finally found an older gentleman standing on the curb. He had two small bags with him, which he grabbed the moment she pulled up to the curb. No doubt, she found him. Parking the car, she cut the engine as he came over. "Let's get you home then."

He waved over at her. "I thought you'd never show up! I was worried you couldn't find me with all these people."

"Sorry about that. Hope you didn't wait too long." Kara popped up the trunk and got out to grab a few bags. The man stopped her as he put both in the back.

"Ah, you didn't need to get out. I can handle this from here." He closed the trunk for her as a car whizzed by. Kara leaned against the car door to avoid getting hit. Idiots. Only at the airport, someone would speed through and not care about who got on and off. "Ah, be careful! You better get back in!"

"Do you have anything you need help with?" Kara blinked at the empty sidewalk. Odd. He was coming from Japan with two tiny bags, probably fitting only three outfits in each plus the toiletries. Her family wouldn't go to India without a minimum of seven bags. Maybe this man was a better traveler than the people she lived with. He packed better than they did anyway. His bags didn't bulge out or appear to weigh a ton. Her mother couldn't zip up bags and often had to use the overweight baggage section, paying extra for all she brought along. Not this guy. She envied him as he closed the trunk.

"I'm good, thank you." He got in the back seat as she took her place in the driver's side, checking on his name. Thomas Whittle. That had to be him. "Are you Karishma Sinha? Sorry if I'm mispronouncing your name but..."

"It's all good. You can call me Kara though. Everyone else does. Only my parents call me Karishma because I was named after a Bollywood actress my mother likes. And I guess you're Thomas?"

"That would be me. Thomas is just fine, not Tom or Tommy. I wasn't named after anyone famous unfortunately." He buckled up as she took care of the rideshare information. "Thanks for being so prompt. I come across so many drivers that take too much or have no idea where to go."

"Ah, this place can be confusing." She confirmed everything before putting the gear into drive and slowly inching her way out of the lot. "That plus all the people that are coming and going...it can be hell to get around here. Fortunately, I drop and pick up people at the airport all the time. It's close by so I have no issues making my way around."

"Really?" His ice-blue eyes twinkled as she eased into the next lane. Now out of the crazy terminal, she could drive without worrying about hitting anyone crossing the road. He grabbed one of the water bottles she kept in the back for thirsty riders. His fingers slipped as he attempted to pop off the cap. After a few seconds, he got it open. "Do you mind if I take this? Being up in that stuffy cabin dries you up."

"Help yourself. You can have any of the snacks I keep too. I imagine you're very hungry after a long trip."

"Famished." He grabbed a packet of Goldfish crackers. "And these are the extremely cheesy ones. That's why you have some napkins on the side, huh?" His fingers trembled as he picked up a wad of them, dropping some on the ground. "Oh God, I'm so sorry! I'm so clumsy! You'll probably have to refill that."

"Don't worry about a few napkins. I got plenty of them. I figured my passengers might want to wash their hands. That's why I also have some hand sanitizer for you. I want to do everything I can to make sure everyone is comfortable." She flipped the blinker and changed lanes, gazing over her shoulder so no one darted out in front. The red car behind her had a nice distance, giving her enough room to move. "Ah, that was easier than I thought. Sorry if I get a little cautious here. The highway can be crazy at night."

"I believe you, Kara. You're doing a great job."

"Thanks." Kara brushed off the compliment. He wasn't the first person to praise her driving. Due to knowing the best roads and fastest ones, she often received good reviews from people who needed to go or come from the airport. Thomas' destination wasn't too far either, a quick turn onto the highway and she'd drop him off at the first exit. Still, the road wasn't one she recognized. McIver Lane. No one lived around there. Then again, she didn't know every single part of this town. Perhaps it was a relatively new area that Thomas moved into. She checked the clock and got on the interstate while he stared out the window like a child impressed with everything passing by. Most of her patrons usually spent time talking to her about pointless things or eyeing their phones. It was a little charming to find someone impressed with the drive. The only other time she found this was with little kids who liked counting cars or singing songs. Thomas did none of these things, just stared out. That excitement ended in a few minutes once traffic slowed and they ended up in a long line. Kara internally groaned at the bright red line representing the road. Red lines always meant heavy traffic and, as she scrolled to see how long it took, it appeared never ending. Her phone started blaring a warning, much to her annoyance. Fantastic. That sound only came when someone went missing. She glanced at it once traffic came to a stop.

Her stomach churned over every little bit of info she got. Every few seconds, she turned from the road to read it. Dangerous as it was, she wanted to know everything. A woman named Anne Lyle went missing two days prior. The only thing the police had was that she lived only a few miles from town. If anyone had information, they had to contact the authorities right away. Kara swallowed as she put the phone down. A missing woman in her town. That never happened. Granted, this was a bigger city, but Anne Lyle disappeared from a town that was a few miles away. People in Charlotte could stay on high alert from her. The smaller town would have a little harder time. The police over there wanted all the help they could get, all the information they could find. Her phone went off right then as the traffic began to move forward. She saw Thomas shivering, trying to stay still. Fearing he caught a cold in the car, she raised the temperature to a little warmer.

That's funny. I normally have a decent temperature. Her hand swept over the air, letting the cold blast hit her fingers. No one complained whenever they got into her car. Not too hot during winters and never super cold in the summer. If anyone asked her to raise or lower the temperature, she'd do without question. Thomas mentioned nothing, so she figured he wanted to be polite.

So how long have you been doing this?" Mr. Whittle broke her out of her reverie as the traffic slowed down. "Is this your only job?"

"For now, yeah. I've been doing it for three months while I'm looking for work. It's hard to find anything, even when you have the degrees and the experience to do the work." Kara cursed under her breath as a few cars got in front of them. "I'm so sorry, Mr. Whittle. It seems like there's a slight traffic jam ahead. I can't find an opening out of here."

"Ah, don't worry about it. These things happen. I'm in no rush, so take your time." He leaned back in his seat. "And you can call me Thomas. Mr. Whittle is a little too formal. As for the whole thing about jobs, it's tough out there. The degrees and experience no longer matter to the higher ups. It's all about who you know."

"Tell me about it." Kara slowly inched forward, craning her neck to find an opening. All the way to the front, she saw nothing but cars and trucks. No one gave her enough space to squeeze in. "They always pick the people who don't know anything. They're lucky that they're some higher ups friend or kid or some crap like that. I try explaining that to my parents, but they can't get it. They're boomers, you know? They're the kinds who think people aren't looking hard enough or working enough or doing enough to get by. Still stuck in their old ways."

"I get that." Thomas agreed. "I've dealt with my share of stubborn baby boomers. They're always right even when they're wrong. Trying to get them to see another perspective, even if it's the right one, is the same as pulling out teeth. They make every step harder."

"Oh, really? What do you do for work?" Kara grimaced as a Tesla moved right in front of her. "Goddammit! I'm sorry, this guy just cut me off before I could move forward!"

"It's fine, Kara. Like I said, I'm in no rush. Just stay patient and calm, all right? We'll get there." He chuckled as the traffic continued to move at turtle's pace. "I'm used to this type of travel. I do it all the time. Sometimes, I get where I need to be quickly. Other days, it takes longer. I've learned that over the years, patience is key. I'll get what I need one way or another."

"I see." He didn't answer her question, but she refused to press on. It wasn't her business anyway. The man wanted to get somewhere so she needed to shut up and drive. Let the man enjoy looking out the window as the traffic picked up. She inched closer towards the exit she needed. "All right, I think we're almost out of this mess. I can't see what's happening up ahead_"

"Car accident." He nodded to the corner. "Tons of cops lingering around. The damage is awful."

Kara followed his gaze and saw the mess ahead. Sure enough, one car was completely totaled while the other missed its fender. It appeared that all passengers were out of the car, and no one appeared severely hurt though most talked with the police. She glanced back at Thomas who stared blankly at the scene. Swallowing, she moved on and picked up the pace once the traffic moved. She turned towards the exit, checking on Thomas. Again, he stared at that accident with no uneasiness or interest. Just one blank look.

"Um...we're moving again." She reminded him. "I should have you at your destination in another minute or two."

"That's fine, Kara. Take your time and watch where you go."

She wrinkled her nose at that last line. Most riders never told her to watch where she went; they assumed she knew where she was headed. Hopefully, he wouldn't strike up another conversation in the next minute. Her shift was almost over. Once out of the exit, she followed the GPS towards McIver Drive, a dark road on the right. She bit down on her lip to ask if this was the right place. Flipping on the high beam lights, she slowed down and left her foot hovering over the break. She hated these inside roads with nothing but trees lining them. No sign of life around, yet if she wasn't careful, something could dart in front. It was the only reason she didn't hit the gas. Heart pounding, a small white house came into view, and she calmed down at the driveway. Good. She found his place.

"Here we are!" She exclaimed as her foot pumped down on the break. Leaving the engine running, she turned to find him still gazing out the window. "I'm...I'm in the right place, right?"

"Oh yeah, you are." Thomas laughed. "Sorry. It's been a while since I've been home. My lawn needs some work."

"I wouldn't worry about it right now. You just came home from a long trip. I hope you have a good night, Mr. Whittle. Get plenty of rest."

"Likewise, Kara. And as I said before, you can call me Thomas. We don't need to get too formal with the whole Mr. Whittle thing. Now can you do me a favor and open the trunk? I need my bags."

"Right! Sorry about that!" Kara unlocked the doors and the trunk. "Do you need any help getting your luggage?"

"No, I'll be fine. They're not too heavy." He unbuckled his seat belt. "Thank you for everything, Kara. I hope the next ride will be smooth, and maybe we'll deal with less traffic. Look on the bright side. You didn't have to drive through downtown Charlotte."

Kara checked on the clock, her head spinning at those numbers. Time. She usually didn't care for it because it threw her off. As long as she was punctual, she'd be fine. She got him to his destination a minute late, but they got there. Hopefully, he'd give her a decent tip for being so patient and driving carefully. "It's no problem at all. Maybe we'll run into each other later."

"Oh, I know it'll be soon. I'll be asking you for a ride before you know it." Thomas winked at her as she sunk into her seat. What was up with him? Between his friendly demeanor and quiet voice, he wasn't a threat. He had no qualms with her being a minute late because of traffic and he could hold a conversation. He wasn't supposed to scare her, being better than most riders she got. So, why is he giving me the creeps?

"I... I'm not so sure. Happy Riders has a lot of drivers out there, driving at all hours of the day." She bit down on her lip as he got out. "You may end up with me a second time, or you might get someone else. There's no way of knowing. It'll depend on who's free."

"Believe me, Kara. We'll be seeing each other again. You're gonna give me my next ride." He grinned at her as he slowly closed the door. "Thanks for this ride. Let's hope we don't get into a traffic jam again."

"Yeah, I hope not." As soon as he got his bags and closed the trunk, he waved to her while she started to back out of the driveway. That's just a little too weird. What makes him think he'll get me as his driver again?

The house didn't creep her out given its bright white sidings, long driveway, and two-car garage. Aside from being far from the neighbors, she didn't hate the area. He disappeared into the house, throwing another wave in her direction. Confirming the drop off,

Kara took off and shook her head of these thoughts. He wasn't a bad guy. He didn't do or say anything to make her wary. Yet the more she dwelled, the more he bothered her. Who was this man and why would he say these things? He truly didn't know if she'd be his rider again. If so, where would he go next? He knew something she couldn't figure out. She drove on, getting onto the highway, and relaxing once she saw all the bright taillights ahead. Without a traffic jam, she could go home with ease.

"That's it. That's all I'm doing for tonight." She checked the rearview mirror. He hadn't done anything to her backseat or windows. He wasn't a mess or a rude man. Why worry about him? She eased into the next lane for her exit. She'd be coming home a little later than expected, but at least she'd get there.

Her phone beeped at that moment as she squinted down the road. As soon as she hit the highway, she cut those high beams off and went where she belonged. No doubt her mother was texting her for the eightieth time today. Kara reminded her that the shift could go a little bit over, but she sent messages to make sure everything was all right. Somehow, she believed Kara was a little girl who still needed to tell Mom and Dad everything that happened in her life. They wanted every detail on where she went at night. Even if it was all for work, they made sure she didn't fool around.

I can't wait till I get my own place. Soon...at least I hope it's soon. God, I need a better paying job. She checked the rearview mirror as something blue glinted in the corner. Blue? Slowing down, she checked behind her. Nothing but endless roads and trees. Huh. That strange blue thing could reflect something else. Light blue like the color of...

Like his eyes. Once more, she whirled around and didn't see Thomas anywhere. He disappeared into the house when she left. He couldn't chase her down here. He took all his bags so why would he follow? Maybe her parents were right to be worried. Thomas appeared so nice. He didn't bother her or say anything that could be a threat. Why am I so scared of him? Why did I think I saw him? He's long gone now.

Her phone beeped again so she drove to the opening, parked the car for a second, and checked on it. If he followed her, she could hit the highway and get lost in the traffic. No one could chase her while she drove at 65 miles an hour. Home. She wanted to go home. Yet the message on her phone unnerved her, checking her backseat and areas around. Emptiness. No Thomas, no blue glints, nothing to scare. Ahead, she saw the cars zipping by, relaxing her shoulders. She checked the phone once more.

Thank you for the lovely ride. I enjoyed your company.

Kara pushed the gear into drive, pumped the gas, and peeled out of the darkness. Those two sentences calmed her but the one after gripped her soul as tightly as she gripped the steering wheel.

May our next ride together be as smooth.

Chapter 2

Kara clocked out around 9 PM once she parked in the driveway. Cutting off the engine, she checked her messages to find anything new from Thomas. His old message from the app remained, a promise to meet again since he was always needing rides. She couldn't brush it away anymore. She didn't mind the giant tip or great reviews, but the message tugged away at her nerves. Would he try to request for the next ride? Happy Riders didn't exactly have that option for riders. It was something the higher ups planned to implement in the future, but no one knew anything more than that. Thomas had no way of requesting her again. He'd get someone new, most likely someone else worked the hours she didn't.

Glancing at the phone, she found another message from him, reiterating what he said earlier. Why so many messages? Did he think she didn't understand? Did he expect a reply? Happy Riders didn't recommend their drivers write back to riders unless it was to thank them for reviews and tips. Their connection ended once the ride ended. Yet here was Thomas sending another message.

Thanks for the smooth ride. I hope the next one is even smoother.

That last line scared her as she read over it. Who wrote things like this? Even when she got messages from other riders, they were polite with a simple thank you. No more and no less. This man went a little too far. Annoyed, she closed her app and dumped the phone in her bag. He couldn't make a request for her. If they did cross paths, it would be nothing more than coincidence. He couldn't get her again. He could try requesting, but Happy Riders wouldn't oblige. Let him be someone else's rider instead.

Opening the door, she kicked off her shoes and sniffed the air. Dinner was long over, but her mother cooked enough to let the smell linger around. Cumin, coriander, turmeric, paprika...she already ate, yet her stomach rumbled. This was one of the things she hated about working the evening hours; she missed dinner with the family. Her mother could cook anything, making the entire house smell all night long. Not only that, but anyone could also tell what she made simply from one whiff of the air. Kara stuck her nose and sniffed. Chicken curry and vegetables. Most likely, they had rice with that and for dessert, she warmed up some gulab jamun that she bought from the Indian grocery store. Cursing herself for missing another great meal, Kara found her slippers and put them on. Time for another quiet night at home.

"Is that you, Karishma?!" Her mother called from the family room in the back.

"Yeah, Ma! It's me!" Kara put away her jacket and bag before heading to greet her. "I'm sorry I'm late! I got stuck in traffic! You know how it is around the airport."

"That's why I tell you to keep using the inside road." She entered to find her mother glued before the TV watching one of her Indian soap operas. Kara rolled her eyes at the dramatic music playing while the actors stood around with eyebrows raised and appearing constipated. She never understood why anyone in her family enjoyed this stuff. Granted, she watched her share of garbage but at least they weren't all the same stories. In these soaps, people either cried a lot on screen or screamed like banshees at each other. There was no in between these shows. Crying and arguing was what Indian actors did in these shows. Ignoring the latest kerfuffle on screen, Kara leaned over to kiss her mother.

"It didn't take me that long to get out. We got on the road, but then there was a small accident so that slowed things down." She stifled her laughter at the people staring dramatically on screen. "What's happening again? Did they find out who stole the money?"

"Not yet. They accused Tipu of stealing because he's desperate, but he is innocent. I know that." Her mother nodded as she shifted her weight on the sofa, pushing her long black hair aside. The golden stud in her nose sparkled as it caught the light. Kara's father gave it to her on their fifth wedding anniversary and she was never seen without it. "How did everything go at work?"

"Eh, it was fine. I did a few small rides around town." Kara sat down in the big armchair and propped her feet up. "I'm beat though. I wish I could find something that didn't require me going around town."

"Are you still looking for jobs?"

"I haven't stopped, Ma." Kara leaned back in the chair. "I look for stuff when I have my free time. Unfortunately, not even retail stores are looking for me. Anytime I think I find something that fits me, they move on to other applicants."

"Do you need someone to look over your resume?" Her mother lowered the volume as a commercial popped up. "Maybe you haven't written it out right. You should go over and add everything that you know."

"It's not the resume, Ma." A headache pounded as Kara struggled to find a way to get out of this. Her mother couldn't understand that jobs didn't fall out of trees. No one could wake in and get one like in the old days. "They just aren't looking for people right now. That's it. I can keep trying but I can't guarantee anything. For now, I've got to take rides for Happy Riders. I might even do some food deliveries. It'll keep me busy."

"Still, is this what you want to do your whole life?"

There it was. As soon as one of her parents brought up her current work, they assumed she wanted to do this forever. Since the money helped her out, they figured she had no more goals after this. Kara rubbed the back of legs as her mother turned back to the TV. "It's just temporary, Ma. I'm trying to get a full-time job, but there's no guarantee. The job market's way different from when you guys were looking for work."

"The job market different? Tell me something I don't." His father poked his head into the room. "I thought I heard you, Karishma. How was your day?"

"Hey, Baba. I got in a few minutes ago." Kara stopped rubbing her legs. A warm sensation draped over them, and she rocked back and forth in her chair. "It was a fun time. I made a good amount of money, and I went to a lot of places. The usual."

"Were you able to find anything in between?"

There it was. As soon as she mentioned making money, they wanted her to find something better and bigger. She wasn't trying hard enough to find a job, yet she couldn't explain why. The market wasn't great. Jobs weren't around and, if they were, they didn't pay well. She often brought up working retail, which they also scoffed at.

"You want to spend your entire life making hamburgers and bagging groceries?! That's not real work!" They'd scold her. "That's what people who have no education do!"

Kara gritted her teeth and always fought back, reminding them that not everyone who worked these jobs were uneducated. Many worked while in college or high school. Many people working in retail had a second or third job to make ends meet. And it was very much real work as they still got money. They argued it wasn't enough money yet couldn't fight the fact that it was work. Everyone worked these days to survive, no matter what the job was. Her parents conceded this point, yet the same issue started up again the following week. They still didn't get it.

"I wish you had a safer job." Her mother threw in. "I just heard about a young lady who was kidnapped from around here! The police don't know where she went. She lived all by herself, and no one's heard from her in days! I can't imagine what would happen if that were you!"

"Oh, that girl?" Kara's heart skipped a beat. Of course, they'd know about this. Her parents glued themselves to the news. Despite how stubborn they were on certain issues; they knew things before she did. "I'm sure she'll be found."

"She'll be found, yes. The question is if she'll be found alive." Her father squeezed her shoulders. "Look, Karishma. I'm not saying this to scare you. I know you like to be on your own. However, until we find out about this girl..."

"I'm still going to work, Baba." Kara cut him off. "I get the concern. Really. I hope that girl is found alive. And I promise I'm not taking any rides that might be too far away or in places I don't recognize. I'll stick to the stuff close to home. Really."

"So, you don't need me to come along?"

"Oh God, no!" Kara shuddered. Her father coming on her job only reinforced the idea she needed her parents. "I'm old enough to make these decisions, Dad. Good and bad decisions. I swear to every god out there I'm not going to take anything that'll be hard or scary. I promise."

"I still think you need someone with you. This girl that went missing...she had no one. She lived all by herself, no friends, no family, nothing! If she had someone..."

Kara shook her head. "Even if she had someone, there's no guarantee she'd be safe. People get kidnapped in broad daylight, Baba. They have family and friends and everything. You don't need to protect me. I can protect myself."

"All the same, I hope you get another job soon. If not, then maybe going back to school..."

"I just got out of school, Baba. That was hard enough as it was." She shuddered over the memory of long nights, pouring over books and notes. School was never her favorite place, going to it only because her family insisted on it. Getting into college gave her multiple headaches. Getting through it only intensified the pain. After being diagnosed with dyscalculia in high school, she created ways to understand numbers and make math a little easier. Those methods worked and somehow she graduated with her degree. That door just closed. Why did he think she wanted to open it again?

"It's only a suggestion. It could help." He motioned her towards her bedroom. "Take some rest for now. We'll talk about options later."

As her mother went back to that Indian soap, Kara played around with her phone and came across bits of information on Anne's disappearance. While she couldn't see well while driving, now she got tweets and posts with her photograph. A young girl with dark brown hair, a small spread of freckles across her nose, and a shy smile filled up her entire timeline. The same message went under her photo: if anyone had information, let someone know right away. She noted not one post mentioned calling the police. Just someone, anyone that could help her out. Checking the comment below posts, about fifty percent came from trolls wanting to show off their nudes in their bios. Another thirty percent were trolls who blamed Anne for getting herself kidnapped. The remaining twenty percent asked others if they had answers or fought with the trolls. None of them knew anything.

"Why did I even bother?" Kara turned away from the posts and went to the Happy Riders website. Thomas' review remained there with several people giving it a thumbs up. She got a message from her boss telling her to keep up the good work. Continuing being a good driver and driving smoothly. Of course, her mind couldn't stop wandering occasionally. Right now, she thought about her job, her desires for a new job, Thomas' review, and Anne's disappearance. She couldn't decide which to focus on first.

"Ah, it's time." She stretched. "When did I take my pills?" Glancing at her alarm clock, she got a reminder from the Alexa app to take those ADD meds. "Crap. I almost forgot. Thanks, Alexa."

With a headache coming on, she went to the bathroom where the medicine cabinet waited for her. Her father helped label her meds out as well as mark when to take each one. Opening the medicine box, she got her pills and poured herself a cup of water. Whenever the last pills wore off, she stopped concentrating and her mind went in other directions. Once she took those, she stared at herself in the mirror, squirming at the small zit growing on her chin. Of course, she still got pimples well after her teenage years. They happened around the time of her period, which didn't make sense, as it came last week. The period blemishes disappeared as quickly as they came. Now, she had another blemish without an explanation.

"Gross!" She poked away at her skin, hoping to pop the stupid thing. "Really? Where the hell were you last week?"

Fumbling in the cabinet for her medication, she took the pills and checked the name. Zoloft. Of course, her old friend. Swallowing the pill, she grasped the side of the sink and waited for the medicine to do its magic. She tried several other medications, but this one was the only one that showed her some results. The psychiatrist always told her that the medication took a long time for her to notice any change. At first, she didn't care for it. It gave her slight headaches, yet the anxiety didn't disappear. It didn't get better till a few weeks later. Anxiety didn't leave, but now she controlled it. She took it right before every drive but forgot it tonight. Oh well, she took it now. Maybe it could help her relax a little.

She began to clean her face, rinse off all the makeup and get rid of the greasy spots. Scrubbing those tough areas, she checked on the blemish after she washed everything off. It stayed there, but not for long. She wiped her face on the towel before heading back to her room. She was home. She had nothing to fear right now. She lived with her parents who were both puttering around in other rooms. To top it off, her house had an alarm system. Her parents set that alarm every evening right before bedtime. No one could get inside.

I live in a safe neighborhood. I live with other people. I'm okay. She reminded herself as she stared at Thomas' last message. He didn't say anything terrible, yet she didn't want to hear from him. He knew something that she didn't. He smiled at her with a secret hidden behind those blue eyes. Their next trip. He couldn't wait for it.

Sick to her stomach, Kara tossed her phone aside as it went off again. She didn't believe it. She didn't want to accept it as she picked it back up. Another message. He took time to send her another message, just as unnerving as the previous.

Thank you for being there, Kara. I'll see you soon.

Chapter 3

Kara woke up to her phone going off, setting her heart racing. Scooping it up, she only calmed down upon seeing the notifications were just reminders that her next workday was Sunday. Thomas didn't have her number. He couldn't send her messages even if he wanted to. Happy Riders didn't disclose drivers' personal information to the public. Every bit of communication happened through the app. Groaning, she dropped down on her bed and put the phone back on the nightstand.

Well, I guess I'll be okay for today. I'm not taking anyone around. She stretched her arms out, gazing up at the ceiling fan. Last night burned fresh in her mind. She normally forgot about riders, but Thomas Whittle refused to leave her brain. Something about him bothered her. He wasn't rude or creepy towards her. He didn't touch her, didn't say things that should make her uneasy, and he didn't push anything onto her. He was the perfect rider.

The perfect rider. There lay the problem; they didn't exist. Each rider had some issue with them. Some talked too much. Others didn't acknowledge her at all, stuck on their phone. Some wanted to smoke in the car, which she refused, yet they still reeked of nicotine. On some occasions, she got a few people passing gas and pretending it wasn't them. The smell didn't leave until they did. The worst was the person who brought their dog along for the ride. Though not a service animal, she allowed them to come on. It wasn't until after she dropped them off, she smelled that foul order and found that the dog pooped in the back seat. Since then, she became wary of anyone wanting their animals when they weren't service animals. The suspicions grew whenever those people didn't clean up after their pets.

Thomas wasn't any of these riders. She didn't mind his conversations, and his cologne was a welcome change to flatulence. That strong bourbon smell meshed with her pine needles and cinder air freshener. He didn't leave a mess in the backseat, he didn't waste time on his phone, and he agreed with her on certain things. That made him a little too perfect. The catch had to be in there somewhere.

"Come on, Kara! Forget about him. I'll get more people to drive around later." She pulled herself out of bed and lumbered towards the bathroom. Her parents were already up and downstairs while she hung around here. A part of her wished she had reasons to wake up earlier. A job would push her out of bed early and busy for the day. She wouldn't have to wait for work to come in, it'd be waiting for her. Yet a quick glance through her emails and notifications revealed nothing but rejections. Those were the better places since they informed her. Those who ghosted her hurt a lot more. She wasn't worth a simple 'no' for a reply.

Once she washed up and got ready for the day, she checked on the app to make sure no changes were made. Her schedule was mostly working the late afternoon and early evening hours of Monday, Tuesday, Thursday, and Friday while also working the mid-morning to early afternoons on Sunday. Hopefully, no one would change it for her. Happy Riders weren't the kind of group to drop notices without warning their drivers ahead of time. She crossed her fingers and checked the reviews from last night.

As suspected, they were positive with only one person complaining that she didn't have any Reese's Pieces for snacks and another wishing she kept veggie sticks as healthier options. Rolling her eyes, Kara scrolled away from them. In a warm car, chocolate would melt, and most veggies wouldn't last long in heat. Sure, she could add more pretzels and crackers but that was as far as it went. Head pounding, her eyes fell on the most recent review from last night. Him. It had to be.

"Oh God." She closed her eyes and opened them again. He wasn't leaving her alone. He wrote a review to remind her of his existence. Breathing in and out, she sat on the bed and went over it again. He left no threat in it, just praise for her. He liked her driving. He liked everything she did. This was what Happy Riders wanted from their drivers. Yet the more she read this, the more she hated it. "Calm down, Kara. He's doing what any smart rider would do."

She racked her brain over the other people she picked up, yet none of them would write like this. They kept their words simple. This new review clearly came from Thomas. She read it all in voice, pretending he talked about her to another colleague. *My driver was very kind and arrived at the right time. I came home from a long trip, starving and tired, yet she had plenty of snacks and water for her passengers. Even though there was a slight traffic jam, she never lost her composure on the road. Such a smooth driver. I hope our next trip will be pleasant.*

"He's so convinced there's a next trip." She rubbed her thumb against the phone screen. No, she couldn't get rid of it. If the company put up a good review, it stayed there. Oh well, it didn't do any harm to her. Maybe Happy Riders would consider letting her do more or earn a little more money. Anything to get away from home and find her way in the world. Much as she loved her parents, she wanted her freedom. She wanted to drive around without telling anyone where she went. Spend her money as she wanted. Be her own person.

Then again, Thomas Whittle's review didn't put anything at ease. He wasn't faking this kindness. He didn't write this to butter her up or boost her self-esteem. He meant every word, praising her to high heavens. That sent every hair on her arm standing on end. Why did he talk about her this way? She got plenty of reviews saying the same thing, complimenting her skills. Yet this one, this simple review, chilled her blood. She glanced behind her in case someone pulled up. Squinting, she spotted something in the corner. No, it couldn't be. He didn't know where she lived. He didn't know where she'd be driving today. He couldn't know that. Yet as she locked in on the shadowy figure, his icy-blue eyes popped into her head. Those eyes. Out of every body part, they got under her skin. He showed no sign of life or emotion in them. Ice-blue and empty. His words held more weight than his gaze. She shook her head to wipe and turned back to the corner. No one. Slowing down her breathing, she dropped her hand on the gear and shifted it into park. He wasn't there.

Get a hold of yourself, Kara. You're seeing things. You didn't sleep well last night because you keep thinking about him. Forget what he said. You deserve to relax today.

Downstairs, her parents waited for her as they made breakfast and checked the news. Her mother cooked over the stove while her father put coffee together for everyone. Kara helped with setting the table, hoping a simple chore like this could take her mind off Thomas. Not that it helped much with the news blaring around her. With their cell phones propped up, she caught a bit of a report about Anne Lyle's disappearance. So far, the police had very few leads and didn't know much about her except that she lived alone. She worked at a fast-food restaurant the night before her disappearance, the last time anyone saw or heard from her. Kara gasped as she grabbed a hot bagel out of the toaster and nearly dropped it when Anne's face flashed on screen. The girl couldn't be older than her. She lived alone and worked to keep herself afloat. Why would anyone take her?

"This is why we don't want you driving around at night." Her mother pointed her spatula towards the phone. "And we don't want you working at restaurants! This poor girl..."

"Working at a restaurant isn't a reason people get kidnapped, Ma." Kara spread cream cheese over her bagel. By now, it cooled down enough for her to pick it up. "The police don't know what happened, okay? It can happen to anyone working a fancy, well-paying job too."

"All the same, you should stay vigilant. I can't imagine what to do if you..."

Kara tuned them out as she listened to more about Anne Lyle's disappearance. Her eyes. She was so happy in the photos they posted, always smiling and joking around. If someone kidnapped her and kept her alive, where was she now? Kara pictured her locked in a dark room, tied up and terrified, praying for someone to get her out.

"Are you there, Karishma?" Her father poked into her thoughts. "I was talking to you."

"Oh! I'm sorry, it's just that..." Her phone beeped at that moment. Holding her breath, she saw the message from Happy Riders despite not being on the clock. Kara forced herself to smile at the name.

Thomas Whittle needed a ride, this time from a shopping center. He predicted this. "What a coincidence."

"What is a coincidence?" Her father wanted to know. "Is your workplace calling you? You're off today!"

"I know but it isn't a big deal. It's the same guy I picked up yesterday. He probably has no idea I'm off today." She struggled to laugh. This wasn't a funny situation, but she couldn't let anyone see it. Thomas hadn't done anything besides promise they'd ride together again. He might have predicted this, but it didn't mean he was harmful. "I could use a little more gas money with all the driving I did this week. I'll take it."

"Take it?" Her mother grimaced as she sipped her tea. "It's your day off. Can't he find someone else to take him? If money's what you need, I'll give you money. I just_"

"Ma, relax! It's only one ride. It's not too far from here so I'll drop him off and then I'll come home."

"Are you sure? You can reject the ride."

"Yeah, but he left a huge tip last time and gave me a glowing review. I guess it won't hurt to pick him up again. He wasn't a bad rider."

"That's fine and all, but it's unusual. You never get the same riders twice in a row." Her father narrowed his brows. "Kara, are you sure this is fine? He doesn't want anything from you, does he?"

"I don't think so. He just wants a ride like all the other riders."

"Still, doesn't he have his own car or someone else who can drop him off? Also, the bus station isn't far away. Couldn't he walk there?" Her father pushed on with good questions Kara had no answers for. Thomas could get public transportation anywhere here. There were other drivers and rideshare apps out there. How could he get her twice? It couldn't be a coincidence. "Are you sure everything is alright? Maybe I should follow you over there so we can be sure."

"It's fine, Baba!" She grabbed her keys from the table and her purse on the chair. "I will be back quickly! You don't have to watch over me anymore. I'm not a baby."

"Maybe not, but it's a father's job to worry. After your mother showed me that news story about the missing woman, I can't help worrying. She didn't live too far away from here! What if her kidnapper is still around?"

"First off, we don't know if she was kidnapped, Baba. Nobody said it was a kidnapping. Secondly, I'm not going to an unfamiliar place. I'll be in a well-crowded, well-lit area. That shopping center never closes. If anything does happen, I know what to do." She assured him. "You don't have to follow me. I'll be alright."

"Well, if you're fine…" Her father dropped the subject. "Remember though, you can call me. If you notice anything funny or someone makes you uncomfortable, you tell me right away."

"Right, baba." She checked the phone again before grabbing her wallet and keys. "I'll be home soon, okay? I'll just drop him off. See you soon."

As soon as she left the house and got on the road, Kara wished she kept her big mouth shut. Her father offered protection, yet she turned him down when she was on high alert. The moment she left the shopping center, it would be only her and Thomas in that car. If he told her to go down that dark road again, they'd be alone where he could do anything.

"Oh no, come on!" She cursed herself. "If he wanted to do something, he'd do it last night. It was dark. We were on an abandoned road. That was where he'd commit the perfect crime. Why would he let me live and call me for the next day?"

All the same, Thomas wanting a ride from her on her day off struck a little suspicious. He didn't know her schedule. He didn't know if she'd be available or not. Why would he ask for her specifically? She checked out everything in her backseat, making sure there were plenty of water bottles and snacks in case he wanted something. She appreciated him taking his water bottle and garbage when he left. He didn't even leave crumbs behind, so that meant no vacuuming the rugs and seats until the next person made a mess. He truly was turning out to be the most unproblematic rider she came across.

"Maybe he's just friendly. He's trying to make life easier for me and other drivers." She convinced herself as she got behind the wheel. "What am I complaining about? Let's just embrace it and move on."

Kara drove to the shopping center without running into any problems on the road. Given it was ten minutes away and close to a million other shops, she had no reason to worry about him stalking her. If he tried to get handsy or make her uncomfortable, she had places to call and run to. She could stop him with the help of others.

So why am I still terrified? She swallowed as the light flipped from red to green and eased her way into the shopping lot. Her eyes scanned for Thomas, praying that she missed him. It wasn't like the airport where he could mention the area he was waiting in. All he mentioned was standing outside of the kitchen supplies store. To her relief, there were three of those around. He never mentioned which one he waited at, just the kitchen store. Maybe he'd miss her. God, she hoped he'd miss her.

Driving around, she checked the GPS for his location. Yes, she was where she needed to be, yet he wasn't. Did he change his mind? No, he hadn't canceled the ride, and the app reminded her that he was waiting in the same spot. Slowing down, she eased along the side to get a look at him. He never mentioned what he was wearing, so it didn't help seeing several gray-haired men walking around. Not one of them gave her the creeps.

Maybe he did change his mind and I...

BAM! A loud rap on the window woke her out of her reverie and she jerked back in her seat. The hand pressed against the glass first, then came those familiar blue eyes. Thomas grinned at her as she rolled the windows down.

"Hey there! I thought you were gonna leave without me just like at the airport." He joked as she unlocked the doors. "I watched you driving around this place."

"You did?" Kara swallowed down a mouthful of spit. "Sorry, I was...you didn't tell me which kitchen supplies store you were at."

"That would be my fault, yes. I realized that as soon as I sent the request. I never put the name of the store." He got inside and buckled the seat belt, leaving his bag next to him. "I almost canceled the trip and then I saw you. Thank goodness I got your attention!"

"Yeah, that's a good thing." Kara checked everything, making note that he wasn't headed down McIver Drive this time. It was another area a few miles from the shopping center, another house without neighbors. "Are you headed home this time, or do you have more errands?"

"Ah, I have to make a quick pitstop." He explained. "There's some work to do, so I need to take care of it."

"So, that's where you're headed? To your pitstop?"

"You could say that." He leaned back. "Just drive, Kara. We'll be good."

"Well, I can do that. I've got more snacks in the back if you want some. I even replenished the water bottles and added some pretzel sticks."

"Always so thorough, Kara. No wonder you get good reviews." He grabbed one of the water bottles. "I think we're gonna have another good ride today."

Thomas went back to his usual stares outside of the window as Kara drove on. She couldn't bring herself to have any conversation as the previous one with her parents swirled around her head. They worried a little too much, but this time, it made sense. Anne Lyle didn't have any enemies that the police knew of. She couldn't find her on social media either, given that there were a few other women with that name. The only messages she found came from randoms on social media praying for her safe return. With each passing hour, Kara feared there was no safe return. A girl like her, a girl who worked at night like she did, disappeared from the face of the planet. She probably had people waiting for her to give them a sign; to let them know she was all right. Even Kara, who knew nothing about her, wanted to get some news from her.

Oh please, please, PLEASE be okay. If you went away for some reason, tell someone. Tell them you went on a trip, you need some time away, that you don't like what you're doing and want a break. Just say something so everyone, including me, can be at ease. That's all.

"Is everything okay, Kara?"

Thomas taking her out of thoughts revealed she stood before a green light with angry people honking from behind. Pushing her foot on the gas, she raced on while he jerked a bit. "Sorry! I'm so sorry! I just...I should have...are you okay? I didn't mean to hit the gas like that! I just_"

"Kara, it's okay." Thomas patted her on the shoulder, pushing her hair to the side. His fingernails grazed the back of her neck, leaving her sick inside. "You were daydreaming. I get it. I've seen other people do that. I'm just glad you hit the gas while the light was still green."

"Yeah, that's a good thing." She winced as drivers whizzed by, cutting her off. "I can't blame these guys. I took too long at the light."

"Let them be impatient. You focus on the road." He took his grip off her shoulder. "Relax, Kara. You are so tense today."

"Well, it's because I..." *There's a girl missing for two days and here you are, touching me and brushing my hair. Why wouldn't I be tense?* She almost snapped out at him. Given how close he got to her neck, she kept that thought locked away. "It's because I've never driven down this road before. I'm not familiar with it. Even with the GPS, I feel like I'm driving down to some brand-new area."

"Don't be so nervous. You'll get used to it soon enough."

Kara's hands slipped down the steering wheel as the GPS commanded her to turn right. "You're going to come down here again?"

"Maybe not this house, but this road...you'll know it like you know your family members. It'll be all too familiar." Thomas started unbuckling his seatbelt as Kara pulled up to another lone white house at the end of the road. This wasn't his home. He wanted her to take him to this house far from people and the busy streets. Before she could ask more questions, he jumped out of the car. "Keep the engine running. I'll be back."

"You'll be back? But I'm supposed to_"

"Keep the engine running, Kara." His icy-blue eyes glowered at her as she sunk into her seat. That friendliness left his tone. A chilly voice replaced his calm one. She couldn't drive off when he glared at her. "Remember, this is just the pit stop. You'll need to go back to McIver Drive. I won't take more than five minutes."

"I have to drop you off there too, huh? I don't_"

"Just keep the car running. It won't be long." He lowered his voice, which got all of Kara's attention. This was not a thing she could question. "If it will make you feel better, I'll give you a bigger tip for your time. After all, you're doing me a huge favor. You just have to wait. That's it. Wait right here."

"Wait, I just_" She stopped as he ran off. There was no more point in talking. He disappeared around the corner. To her shock, he didn't use the front door. That couldn't be right with a simple house like this. Some people who lived in gated communities opted to be dropped off at the main office. Others opted to drop off a few feet from where they lived. No one ever entered through a back door. Now her suspicions grew higher. No, he wasn't the perfect rider. He had his share of secrets.

What secrets does he have though? She glanced back to where he had been sitting. Spotless. He didn't leave a mess in the backseat save for putting the water bottle in the back coaster. Her heart raced as she drummed her fingers on the steering wheel. Some music. The one thing that could calm her down was music. Fumbling the dials, she found the pop music station and let random tunes by Sabrina Carpenter and Olivia Rodrigo run through. They'd help a little bit.

Be cool. He told you to wait. I don't think it's anything bad. If it were, he wouldn't drag you out here.

That thought only increased her anxiety. The music didn't help for very long, so she cut it off and waited for Thomas to come back. He never mentioned what this place was or why he needed to come here. In the corner of her eye, she saw the number on the mailbox. 1119. The GPS labeled the road as Donnelly Ct. 1119 Donnelly Ct. It didn't look too different from the other house on McIver Drive: small, old paint job, closed windows, and no neighbors in sight. He really liked these houses far from civility, yet she picked him up from busy areas like the airport and the shopping center. He was a good rider, but an odd person.

The more she pondered over Thomas, the more curious she grew. It didn't make any sense. Did this house belong to a friend of his? If so, why didn't this friend pick him up from the store? Who visited their friends for only five minutes? Even when her parents' friends came over, they stayed for tea and conversation. Only those who were dropping things off took five minutes or less. She didn't see him carrying anything to the house, so everything confused her.

Maybe I'm overthinking this. He said it would be five minutes. He's not gonna lie to me, is he? She grabbed her phone to waste some time on it. There was nothing decent on TikTok, nor did she have any important emails. A few other riders gave her good reviews, which raised her spirits. Thomas's review remained on top of them, which brought those spirits back down. There was nothing wrong with it. He said nothing different from the others.

Kara stared down at the GPS, noting that she still had ten minutes on the clock. Could he do whatever he needed to in five minutes? He ran around the back of the house as she locked her doors. No, she didn't want to hang around here any longer. Something about Thomas had her ill to the pit of her stomach. The kind nature from earlier to the coldness now? She didn't trust him. She didn't want to chauffeur him from random house to random house. She didn't get paid that well by Happy Riders to keep taking this man around. Her heart lurched forward as she gazed at her phone. No new rides for the next ten minutes. If she had one, she could use that excuse and get away.

Come on, come on...someone send me a message. Her fingers tapped away at the phone screen, scrolling through messages. Nothing new. Social media gave no new updates, her parents sent her nothing, not even Happy Riders checked in on her. Her foot slowly lifted off the break and inched over to the gas with her hand dropping on the gear shift. She could leave. If he didn't come out in five minutes, she'd hit the gas and get out. Every nerve in her body yelled to get out. Run. Drive off. Forget traffic laws, just speed out of the driveway. Drive, Kara. Just drive. Forget the messages, drive away and_

SPLAT!

A bloody palm hit her window as she dropped her phone. Gasping like a fish out on open land, she struggled to scream as the hand slid down her window, streaking red all over. Blood. That hand smeared the blood down her windows and then came Thomas' face in the middle of it. He pressed down, keeping his eyes locked on her, and motioned the door.

"Unlock them. Now."

With trembling fingers, Kara found the button to unlock the door. As soon as he opened them, she fell back into her chair and held her tongue from screaming. There he was, drenched in blood, making his way into her backseat. His hand clutched a knife also covered in bright red. The man she drove around no longer held that friendly demeanor in him. Those eyes told a new story, a chilling tale that didn't end with her in one piece. He held the knife out, pointing to the road ahead.

"Drive."

Chapter 4

Kara shifted the gear into drive as they got on the road while Thomas glared at her. She pumped the gas as the tires squealed against the gravel. The man in the backseat, holding the knife, was in control of her car. He had control of everything while all she could do was drive. She paid no mind to the knife or the blood, only on her breathing. If she breathed, she lived. She wanted to hear herself as proof she was still alive.

In and out, in and out. He's not doing anything to you...yet. Her hands sweat all over the steering wheel as she drove on. Her foot refused to move off the break. The bloody man sat there, blue eyes blank and hands folded on his lap. His body shivered and vibrated against her seats, so she lowered the AC. She put her focus on the road, praying no one peeked through her windows. She'd have no explanation for this.

"Keep driving." Thomas motioned her to watch the road. "Everything will make sense. Now that we're in this together, you'll have to follow a few rules."

"We? What do you mean we're in this together?" Kara suspected that, as she gazed at the mess he made, it wasn't anything great. "I don't want any part of it!"

"Ah, I'm afraid I didn't make myself clear. You don't exactly have a choice in this matter. You're my driver. You're taking me wherever I want to go. Right now, we're heading back to McIver Drive." His fingers trembled as he removed his hands off his lap. Kara checked the air conditioning, finding it at the right temperature. The car wasn't freezing, yet he shook like he was in a snowstorm. He pressed his hand against the door, leaving a bloody print along the door handle. "That'll come off with a good cleaning. Spray this place up too. Blood leaves an awful stench. You don't want anyone to complain about the smell."

She nodded without looking at him. She caught those blue eyes in her rearview mirror, letting her hands slide down the steering wheel. Escape. This creepy man in blood sat in her backseat while all she thought of was escaping the car. She couldn't grip that wheel anymore, letting her fingers hang onto it. The tires continued squealing she drove out, hoping he wasn't buckled in. In the past, she learned that if someone kidnapped her in the car, her best bet was to crash it. It didn't matter if the car suffered damage; no car was worth more than a life. This road didn't have anything she could crash into, just skinny trees that would snap the moment she hit them. She needed a curb to run up on, which this area had none of.

Stay calm. You have a passenger covered in blood. You have no idea what he's capable of. Don't let him smell your fear.

The calmness she wanted was nowhere in sight as he wiped the blood from his face. He grabbed a few more tissues from the same place she kept the water bottles. Rubbing them all around, he succeeded in smearing the blood more than removing it.

"What the hell happened?!" She gasped as he took off his coat, smearing more blood over her seats. "Are you hurt?! What did you_"

"Don't you worry your pretty head off. I took care of business. All you must do is drive." Blood dripped down his arms, pooling on the mats below. Drip, drip, drip. The stench of blood stung as she listened to it falling. Her father would kill her for ruining the car...provided this man didn't do that first. "We'll go back to the same place as yesterday."

"I, um..." Kara scrolled through the address and found McIver Drive. She didn't question this since he could plunge the knife into her any second. "Okay, we're going. It's only ten minutes away."

"Good." Thomas wiped his hands clean some of the napkins tucked between her water bottles. "I'm sorry to ruin your things here. You may want to get rid of all this."

Kara hyperventilated as her hands slipped down to the steering wheel. Blood. The man got blood all over her car windows and seats. He sat there with the bloodied knife, breathing in and out, leaning back in the back seat. He wasn't talking about anything. He held the knife as she peeled out of the driveway, wondering what to do now. She couldn't keep taking his requests.

"I...um..." She turned out of the driveway and headed towards McIver Drive. "I don't..."

"Listen." Thomas unbuckled his seatbelt and leaned in, still clutching the knife. "I have nothing against you, Kara. I have no intention to hurt. Don't give me a reason, okay? I realize you want an explanation though, and I'll give you as much as I can. I do things that are...a little unsavory for a reason. It's my reason and mine alone."

"What happened back there?" She focused on the road ahead, ignoring his breathing fanning down her neck. "You're covered in blood! You...are you injured? We should_"

"It's not mine." He cut her off. "I realize I'm leaving a ton of blood stains in your poor car. I am sorry about that. I never expected you to stay as long as you did."

"I stayed because you said so. I didn't know..."

"No, you didn't." He sniffed the air around her. "The blood will come out, okay? Your folks will never know a thing. You do as I say, take me where I need to go, and we'll be good. Keep your mouth shut. Follow my instructions. No harm will come to you."

I don't believe you. Yet she had no strength or bravery to say this out loud. Her eyes stung with tears as she drove on. Given that she drove on her day off, Happy Riders wouldn't reach out to her.

"Please don't hurt me." She pleaded as tears stung her eyes. The road now blurred before as she drove on. "I won't tell anyone what happened. I won't even go to the police or do anything. Just leave me alone."

"I know you won't tell anyone. You know what's at stake here." He breathed down her neck, his fingers twisting themselves into her hair. "You wouldn't do anything stupid to get yourself hurt. You or the ones you love. And yes, Kara, I know you have people that care about you. Not like that girl or the ones before her. You have people you'd die for and vice versa. If you keep driving, no one will die. No one you love."

As he gently tugged her hair, her mind flashed to her parents. Overprotective and nagging as they could be, she didn't want him near them. Not speaking to them, not touching them, nothing. If she had to follow his orders, she'd do it to keep them alive. "What do you want with me?"

"Now listen well. You don't have to do anything but drive where I tell you to drive." He held the knife close to her neck, the metal blade glinting as the sunlight landed on it. Thank God she took this morning ride. In the darkness, he could cut her through and give her no time to react. "Don't worry, I'm not doing all this for free. You'll get paid. Since you're off Wednesday and Saturdays, I know now not to drag you away from your normal. I had to do it today though. This little thing...it couldn't wait."

"Little thing?" Every piece of the puzzle fell into place. He wasn't hurt. He hurt someone and, the moment someone found out, the news about Anne Lyle would blare all around town. Social media would update with all the details people found. They'd demand more answers, something Kara had yet couldn't give. She was inches away and did nothing to stop the violence.

"You hurt her, didn't you?" Kara inched her fingers towards the door. If she could tumble out of the car, she'd be free. Sure, she'd eat dirt and concrete, but she'd get away from him. "You did something to Anne."

"It makes sense now, huh?" He laughed as he cleaned the knife. "She wasn't as smart as you. So beautiful but so naïve. She trusted me. I wish she saw it coming like you did."

"But...but why?" Kara's hand hit the door's handle. Any second now. Open the door and roll out while he stayed locked in the car. "What could she have done to you?"

"It had nothing to do with anything she did. She's like all those girls: quiet, unassuming, extremely gullible. You can't understand if you're not in my shoes, Kara. You grow angry at them, being so simple and wasting their lives away. They're not worthy of what they have. Working, toiling away at some job that doesn't respect them. They've got no one in their lives. Okay, maybe they have a pet or two, but that's not the same. They're little girls just living and doing nothing."

Kara gritted her teeth as she changed lanes, getting closer to the curb. "It's not up to you to decide that. You don't get to kill because you don't like how they're living their lives."

"That's not all, Kara. They're wasting away...not like you. You go out every night to give people rides. That's why I liked you out of all the riders I've had. You drive well. You normally pay attention to the road. You aren't planning anything stupid like jumping out of this car." She pulled her hand away from the door. "Good girl. I knew you'd come to your senses. Now drop me off and I'll call you again."

"Me?" Kara glanced at the clock. He was the last drop off. The moment he left her car, she'd drive away despite all the bloodstains over her seats. "Come on, why are you dragging me into this? Can't you drive yourself? Can't you_"

"DON'T!" He snapped as he grabbed her shoulder, pulling her back. A car in front swerved away from them. Once it sped off, he let her go. His bloody palm stained the top of her shoulder and shirt. That rotten smell now messed with her head. His wet mark soaked through her top, hitting her skin. He touched her with blood-covered hands. Anne's blood. She couldn't go home in this state. One glance back revealed blood stained over the drinks and snacks she left for other riders. He tainted everything in her car. "That lunatic nearly ran into you! It's a good thing I pulled you back."

You're one to talk about lunatics. She ignored the blood stains taunting her as she finally got towards McIver Drive. All that red. Even if she cleaned this car from top to bottom, that smell lingered. Her air fresheners couldn't mask that hideous scent. He left his mark on her, a reminder she belonged to him. She followed his bidding. As she slowed to a stop, he gave her one more pat on the shoulder, caking more blood over her. Her brain screamed at him to get out. *Get out, get out, get out of my life! Don't do this to me!*

"I had another pleasant ride with you, Kara." He leaned into her driver's side window. How he got around so quickly, she couldn't figure it out. Not that it mattered. She wanted him out. "Those reviews were right; you drive well. You and I are gonna have some great rides together. You'll keep your free time though. Next time, I'll get you only when you're on the clock."

"Next time?" She squeaked out. "There's a next time?"

"Oh, there will be a lot of next times, Kara. This job is nowhere near finished. Keep an eye on your phone. We might be in the same car together." He patted the side of the car. "Get some rest, sweetheart. This ride's only beginning."

She couldn't reply to that. He sauntered off, throwing a wave over his shoulder. She didn't bother checking to see if he went in. Her hand went to the phone, finding a million text messages from other people. Happy Riders reminded her of her next working day along with reviews from the last few riders. She couldn't read them now. Putting the car into drive, she drove away and struggled not to break down. The scream couldn't leave her throat. She wanted to cry and yell and beg someone to help her. Given she was in the middle of nowhere, that scream burned in her throat. The car's tires squealed as she peeled out of McIver Drive. Home. She only wanted to go home now. Forget about anyone else. Forget about work or the messages or anything. She wanted to be home, sitting in her bathtub, and trying to scrub that bloody smell off her body. She didn't kill anyone. She didn't hurt them, yet she was responsible for this. She took this man around. She knew his truth.

He had her life in his hands, and she had his. The only way either of them were getting was through drawing blood. With her veins pulsing, she drove on as her blood pressure rose. A nightmare. She was stuck in a nightmare now.

"God help me." She prayed out loud. Not that she'd get an answer. She put herself in this situation, not God. She got stuck with Thomas. He knew it. He knew how much it bothered her. He knew how to get her on edge even without being in the same room. He had her.

He wouldn't let her go so easily. Not without ruining what was left of her life.

Chapter 5

It took Kara at least two hours to clean up the car along with herself. Thankfully, she kept plenty of cleaning products along with an extra pair of clothing in the trunk. She could no longer offer these water bottles and snacks to riders, so her best bet was to leave them, now all cleaned up, in the trunk. They didn't deserve to eat snacks stained in blood. For those two hours, she scrubbed and wiped every inch on every surface. Even with cleaning herself, she scrubbed off anything that resembled blood. Red or brown, she got rid of it. Her hands turned rough with each scrub, yet she went on till she no longer spotted a drop of blood. Heaving and shaking, she stepped back to check the car out. No blood. She didn't see his blood or anyone else's. The smell lingered yet it would pass once she turned the car on. Her gas tank now hovered near empty, which meant a quick stop before home. With her phone going off every few seconds, she knew her parents would hit her with an earful. Why didn't she call? Where was she? Didn't she know someone went missing?

Well, Anne Lyle was no longer missing. She was dead. Thomas killed this girl, and God knows what he did with her body. A part of her wanted to drive back and find Anne, get her out and let someone else take her home. Let the whole world know what happened to her. Yet with him still holding onto her and no clue if she could dig around that house, she opted not to. There had to be another way to get the message out. Sending it viral on social media could work, but it could get authorities suspicious. They'd track her down and take her in as the killer. Even worse, Thomas could find out and she didn't want to be at the end of his wrath. Those eyes sent out a message: cross me and die. Whatever Anne Lyle did to him, she no longer existed. He made sure of it.

Once she cleaned up and put everything away, she glanced at her phone. Eighty percent of the messages came from her mother and father, demanding to know why she wasn't home. She promised to come back early, yet she spent too much time outside. Their messages went from concern to anger and then right to fear. Both began expecting the worst, that she'd been kidnapped by the same person who hurt Anne. Well, they wouldn't be entirely wrong. Thomas might not have kidnapped her, but he held her under his control. She was his driver, taking him wherever he wanted, no questions asked. The message from him remained clear when she found it.

Remember: No police, no social media, nothing. No one will believe you anyway. Don't make it hard for both of us if you know what's best for you.

Swallowing, she scrolled away and sent a message to her parents, lying about a traffic accident. She was unable to reply solely because she was stuck on the road. It wasn't her best lie, yet she couldn't give them the story about driving a killer around. They wouldn't believe or, worse yet, they'd get involved. With Thomas threatening them, she'd stay silent. She wasn't ready to lose them, no matter how obnoxious they could be. Sobbing and sniffling from the smell of cleaning products, she got into the driver's seat and headed towards home. Despite the cleanliness, Anne's blood never went away. She saw it in every corner, bright red and blooming against the seats. Anne's voice started haunting her as she drove on. She never heard Anne speak before, but there it was. Pleading, crying, wanting to be found.

Get me justice, Kara. Only you can do it. Get me and the others the justice we deserve.

The others. Thomas mentioned others like Anne. What had he done with them? Would anyone find their remains? The missing person's bulletin wouldn't help much as people went missing every day. So far, she couldn't track Thomas' pattern. He didn't appear close to Anne in any means. He only killed her because he thought she wasted her life. She was a girl who lived alone and worked in the fast-food industry. To him, that was wasteful so maybe he targeted people who didn't have anyone who'd notice they were gone.

Except people did notice Anne went missing. They've talked about her online and in the news. So, someone out there is looking for her. Someone deserves answers. Shaking and cold, Kara pulled into her home's driveway. She couldn't let Thomas win. He couldn't keep killing the people he deemed 'worthless' just because they weren't well-known. She'd get everything taken care of as soon as she got a plan. Right now, her head throbbed as soon as she opened the door, and her father scooped her into his arms.

"There you are!" He boomed, squeezing her body, and rocking her back and forth. She muffled into his chest, trying to get out an apology. "Where were you?! Are you alright?! Did you get hurt? Sick? Did something_"

"I got stuck in traffic thanks to an accident, Baba. This one was bigger." She pulled away from him as her mother came in. Then it started up again with her mother hugging her and crying into her shoulder. "Ma, Ma! It's okay! You can let go now! I'm okay! I'm home!"

"But why are you home so late? That accident took you two hours to get back?"

"Well...yeah. Someone died in it." Kara sniffled. That bit was true. "It was...it's...it's a big mess, Ma. Everything is a mess." She draped her arms over them, burying herself in between. As the tears came, she dropped down to her knees. "I'm sorry, guys! I didn't mean to! I didn't_"

"Hey, Rishi! What's wrong?" Her father rubbed her back. "You're home. That's all that should matter. Did you get hurt?"

"...No." She wiped her eyes. Her parents only called her 'Rishi' when things got emotional. "I'm okay. Really, I'm not hurt or anything."

"You're crying." Her mother wiped the tears off. "Did someone say something to you? You still have your job, right? Did they fire you?"

"No, I still have my job." Kara held up her hand to get away from both. They swarmed over her while she took her place on the couch. "The accident was...I've never seen anything like it. I swear the guy was dead. I didn't mean to look but..."

"Shh! Don't say anymore." Her father took his place on her right while her mother sat on the left. They both held her, moving back and forth to calm her. "It happens. Death is something that happens, and it can be sudden. It's not always pretty. Remember the conversation we had when your grandmother passed away?"

The tears flowed again at that memory. Her grandmother passed away when she was eight years old, unable to grasp that death meant forever. She asked questions on why she couldn't see her grandmother anymore. Why did she have to go? Now that she was older, she understood death, but violent deaths still baffled her. She didn't understand how a person got to the point of hurting another person. Thomas looked at this girl and decided to steal her life, letting her bleed out. He stood there as life drained out of her. Worst of all, Kara didn't help. She knew nothing of this, so she didn't help save Anne.

Well, next time wouldn't be the same. If Thomas planned more killings, she had to plan well ahead of him. Figure out where he went, save who he wanted to kill. If lucky, she could get out of his little deal without a scratch on her.

"I'm glad I'm working the morning shift tomorrow. I can't do another night right now." She pulled herself off them. As much as her heart ached, she wanted time alone. Thomas' warning rang in her head the more she clung around them. He knew about them. He knew she lived with them while looking for work. Unlike her, they'd never survive his wrath. They weren't as strong as her.

If you tell anyone what happened, if you refuse a ride, I'll be very upset. You don't want to make me upset, do you?

She got the message and continued to step away. "I need...a quick shower. It's been a long day, and I stink." She sniffed her underarms to prove a point. Despite the lies, she truly did reek of sweat and fear. Maybe some blood leaked through her shirt and went down there. "Oof, yeah! That's gross!"

"Do you need me to bring you anything?" Her mother reached to grab her hair as Kara pushed it away. "Karishma, please...I see your hair is..."

"My hair is fine!" Kara insisted as she played with it. The blood dried up in it, sticking all the strands together. Hopefully, it didn't reek of blood too. The moment her mother touched that hair, she'd have all the questions. Kara pretended to comb through it with her fingers, ignoring the pain of yanking on the strands. Pulling apart bloodied hair took a bit of work. "Let me just rinse myself off, lather up, and I should be good. I need this."

"How about lunch first? I figured after a long shift of driving, you may be hungry so I'm thinking of making reservations to Jade Rose. What do you think?" Her father grabbed the car keys, jangling them before her eyes. "I'll be driving this time to give you a break."

"Uh, make the reservation in an hour, Dad. I need a little rest first." She began walking backwards, heading towards the stairs. "I'll be down in a bit, okay?!"

She raced up the steps before they asked more questions. Thank God she avoided anything about the drive itself. Thomas couldn't hurt them because of her stupidity. She picked him up on her day off when she could say no. She knew nothing of him until now. She could remind this wasn't her driving day, to get another driver or take public transportation. Yet if she refused, he could attack them when she didn't expect it. No, she was trapped with him for now. Until she got her escape plan together, he held her life and those around her in his grasp.

Inside the shower, she let the water get warm before stepping under it and letting her hair soak in it. Blood swirled at her feet as it left her body, running down the drain. Anne's blood ran into her tub. Grabbing the shampoo and conditioner, she ran them through those thick black locks, straightening them out. Bit by bit, the strands untangled themselves and all the dried blood rinsed out. Lathering up, she scrubbed the smell off her body. The fact that Thomas touched her after killing Anne burned her up. He treated her like they were friends, used to close contact, when she didn't know him until yesterday. He wanted more from her than just being a chauffeur.

We'll have a lot more rides together. The moment I call for you, you're going to come. No questions asked. If you ignore me…well, let me give you some advice. Don't ignore me.

Once all the blood and dirt left her body, Kara cut off the water and grabbed a towel. The warm fluffy cloth wrapped around her body provided comfort she craved. Sniffing it, she inhaled the lemony scent from the laundry detergent and dryer sheets. Her mother laid it out in the morning, leaving the whole bathroom smelling like lemons. Kara dried herself off as the tears formed. What had she done? How could she agree to any of this?

He's using me. He knows that if he gets caught, he can blame it on me. The fear mounted as soon as she left the bathroom and her phone buzzed. Grabbing it, her shoulders relaxed upon seeing it was nothing but an article about young people growing more stressed. Not that she needed articles for that. Job hunting added extra years to her life, and Thomas took a bunch more away. She couldn't go through her phone without reading his messages. He didn't post anything new, yet she waited.

Anytime I ask for you, you come. I'll tell you where I'll be. I'll expect you there.

Her heart twisting in fear, she now turned to information on Anne Lyle and possible other victims. Most social media accounts hadn't updated with the discovery of her body, but those who knew Anne spoke up. They called her quiet and sweet, the ideal employee at her work. Always punctual and polite to customers. She didn't get angry easily, nor did she rile anyone up. Her coworkers admitted she kept to herself but had no issues with her. She stayed out of their way; they stayed out of hers. Even in looking at customer interaction, Kara found nothing that matched Thomas' description, so he clearly didn't find her at work.

The Traveler. Perhaps he found her waiting outside for her ride or caught her walking on the sidewalk. He could drive up alongside her, ask for directions, then pull her into his car when she let her guard down. The moment he went away with her, whether she was forced to go or not, he had her. What happened between the abduction and the murder, that remained a mystery. No one figured out how long these crimes took place. They ended when the bodies popped up.

Kara stayed alert by her phone, waiting for Thomas' next messages. The man unnerved her without saying a word. He appeared normally, talked to her like they were old friends, and held her in the palm of his hand. Anytime that phone went off, she grabbed it in fear that he would send her something. Ninety percent of the time, those messages were either spam, political texts, or coupons for various places. These were the days she wanted some friends to get her through this. In college, she couldn't keep in touch with any of her classmates. Most of her friends from high school cut her off once they went their separate ways. They were having a better time without worrying about her, wondering how she got through each day. Kara blamed herself for not being a better friend to them. They understood she had ADD. They knew there were certain things that were challenges. They didn't care about those, yet she couldn't keep a hold of them. Even in high school, she ended up behind everyone else. The girl at the end of the line whether it was academics, popularity, athletics, or a combination of all three. Kara Sinha was a ghost in those halls. If they saw her, maybe they'd say hi. If not, they walked right past her like everything else.

Once in college, the struggles started up and she never got the time to make new friends or hold onto the old ones. Not even people from her hometown asked how she got through each day. She tried to make friends with professors and TAs to no avail. They weren't there to experience college life with her; only to help her get through it.

They offered up plenty of options when she needed it: club meetings, parties, various get togethers where everyone got to know each other. When she went to them, she hid in the back with her cup of soda and stayed there the entire time. No one approached her for a dance or conversation. They were having too much to care about some girl sitting in the back, wanting to jump in and be with them. She craved to be like other students, enjoying their time and learning their names. Maybe from there, they could all start something new.

Yet desire never led to getting off her butt and walking over to the groups. It never got her to open her mouth and start conversations. She couldn't bring herself to ask if she could sit with a group, let alone find out anything about them. For those reasons, Kara stayed alone the entire time she was in college. She never went into a dorm to save money, never stayed out too late, never got the right experience like the others. Hence why she was driving people around, but not making friends with them. This was a job, nothing more. It wouldn't lead to anything except money to keep her afloat. Even still, it wouldn't be enough to live on.

Then again, do I really want to burden someone else with this problem? Thomas could have hurt them too. She went back to read his comments again on Happy Riders main page. Oddly enough, he never left any reviews for the other drivers. Only her. He praised her to high heavens and wanted her to drive him around town. He didn't leave any downvotes on the other drivers but whenever someone else made a great comment towards her, he upvoted them. She prayed he wasn't going to stalk any of the reviewers who posted less than five stars. Nothing the three- or four-star reviewers said was anything particularly horrible. Some pointed out she was late, though she got them to their destination in a timely manner. They weren't rude about it, understanding that traffic in Charlotte got brutal during the peak hours. Since these reviews were mostly protected, he couldn't find out who left each one. He didn't know every rider she had. Unless he knew how to track these people down, they'd live to see more days.

Leaving the Happy Riders sight, she found a few pop-up articles on The Traveler. Everyone in Charlotte now spoke about this guy, warning people not to be out too late. She picked one of the articles and started reading up on how Anne Lyle could be the next victim of The Traveler. Just in bits and pieces, she learned he was a serial killer who didn't have much of an MO. He attacked whenever he wanted to, and his victims were random though the majority were on the younger end. She shuddered over how some parts of him sounded too much like Thomas. The police warned that he was a charming person who could ease his way into any conversation. He worked alone except for one thing: he needed someone to take him from place to place. They could never trace a vehicle back to him.

He doesn't have a car at all. The lump in Kara's throat grew with the tiny bits that the police pieced together. They didn't get it, but she feared the worst: Thomas was The Traveler. He was the one everyone dreaded to come across. Those who didn't cross his path were the lucky ones. They didn't have to worry about losing their lives because they didn't catch his eye. The ones like Anne Lyle were his favorite prey: single, young people who didn't have too many friends in their lives. These were people he could manipulate and whisk away with his charms.

"People like me." She concluded. "God, why didn't I make any friends when I was younger?"

Because it's hard. An unfamiliar voice broke through as she dropped her phone. Glancing up, she found herself face to face with the bloodied face of Anne Lyle. This girl, someone she knew nothing about except what articles told her, stood in her bedroom. Her mouth opened and closed like a fish gasping for air out of water, but she didn't scream. Anne couldn't hurt her. She was dead. She didn't open her mouth to say anything, yet her words rang clearly. *When you're older, it's much harder to make friends. Everyone knows who they are at this point. They know what they want.*

Kara nodded though unable to reply in agreement. This girl, bleeding from her head, made her way into her bedroom and now stared at her reflection. Kara got up and pushed the phone to the side, unsure whether to call for her parents. They'd never believe any of this. A girl who died, the same girl everyone wanted to find, stood right before her. Anne crossed her arms, cocking her head on one side.

I've looked better. Without the blood, I'd look more like myself.

"What...What happened to you?" Kara managed to get out. "Who did this?"

Isn't it obvious? He did. Anne brushed back the bits of hair falling on her forehead, revealing the thick jagged scar. *I hoped he didn't hit me hard enough. I guess I was wrong.*

"Thomas." Kara confirmed. "I should have known. If I had known..."

You couldn't stop him. No one's ever been able to stop him. She found a spot to sit on Kara's bed, crossing her legs and leaning back. *You would end up just like me. He hates it when the victim tries to fight back.*

"Is that...Is that what happened? You fought back?"

It was pointless though. He overpowered me before I got a chance to leave. He may not look like much, but his strength...it doesn't take long before he's in control. He'll mess with your mind first.

"Yes." Kara didn't want a reminder of how charming Thomas was. How he messed with her head, appearing all friendly and polite. Deep under that smile and nice talk lay a monster who could flip his temper in a second. "How do you...How can you get him out of your head? I'm scared."

Don't worry. You'll know what to do.

"Rishi?!" Her mother called for her. "What's taking so long? We're waiting on you."

"On me?" It hit her then. Lunch time. Her parents were taking her out to eat now. "Oh crap! I'm sorry, Mama! I'm coming!" She whirled to face Anne. "Sorry, you're gonna have to_" She paused with clothes in hand. Anne no longer sat on her bed. She no longer bled on the carpet or talked to her. Typical. She came and went without leaving anything behind. "I...I guess I'll deal with this later."

After a quick change of clothing, she left the house and found her parents waiting in the car, engine purring. She locked the door behind her and hopped into the backseat. Putting her bag next to her, she buckled up as her father backed out. Having been in the driver's seat so much, it calmed her to be in the back. "Sorry, guys. I...I'm still so shaken by everything. I keep reading up about it."

"Well, don't read about it." Her father suggested. "The less you look at it, the less stress you'll get."

"I can't escape it, Baba! It's all anyone talks about! Even if I try to curate my likes to what I want, something about it pops up. It doesn't help that this girl is close to my age. She's a young girl who doesn't have many people in her life." Kara peered out the window as they started to roll down the street. She missed those moments where she could lean back and enjoy the view. Her riders got the best part of the ride: they got to see where they went. As her stomach growled, she remembered all the good Chinese food that waited for her. "Anyway, I don't want to talk about it now. I want to eat my weight in dim sum and veggie lo mein if that's okay."

"You can order everything and anything you like from there. I'm paying for it." He made the turn out of their neighborhood, getting onto the road. "And maybe if you're up for it, we can get some ice cream. How about a cheesecake from that new place that opened last week?"

Kara perked up on the sound of a cheesecake. "Can we get the chocolate and peanut butter cheesecake?"

"Eh, ask your mother."

She snorted as she folded her arms. Whenever her father had no answer, he always deferred to her mother who'd have the final say in everything. Given that her mother didn't enjoy either chocolate or peanut butter, the chances of picking up that cheesecake went straight down to zero. The only kind she'd accept was a plain old cheesecake with no fruit toppings or syrup. The most basic cheesecake, which Kara also enjoyed but it was boring.

To her surprise, her mother shrugged. "You can take whatever you want."

"Really?" She blinked. "Are you really my mother right now or a robot replacing her?"

"It's me, Karishma. You can take whatever you like as long as you finish it. I don't want to see a ton of cake wasted away in the kitchen. Then I'll have to throw all of it away."

"Yeah, well, I won't waste that." Kara turned towards the window as something caught her eye. Blue glint. Not again. He couldn't follow her out here. He didn't have a car. Unless he found another driver, he wouldn't know her address, let alone who her family was. He never watched her leave, nor did he know which turns she took to get back. He didn't know where she lived.

I don't have my address lying around in the car, do I? She focused in on that blue glint, expecting Thomas to pop out and brandish that knife. God, he couldn't be here. He couldn't do anything to her. She closed her eyes, trying to push his image out. That bloody man who sat in her backseat, demanding she drive, promising to put that knife through her if she screwed up. She opened her eyes to find nothing hiding in the trees. No Thomas, no knives, no blood covering the area. Anxiety shooting through the roof, she clutched her head as the car picked up speed. Not now. She didn't want to think of him now.

You can't escape me, Kara. You and I are tied down. You picked me up, and now you'll do everything I say. You have no choice.

She heard him taunting her as her breathing picked up. How could her parents not hear her hyperventilating? They weren't talking loud enough to block her off. They were in their world, going on about their problems while she struggled to push Thomas out of her mind. "Go away…Go away…"

Once again, her parents didn't check up on her. Her mother played around with the radio, slowly putting up the volume and tunes from multiple Bollywood movies now filled the area. Her heartbeat slowed down thanks to the fast-paced dancing tunes. In a way, her mother helped her out with this music. She understood none of it but welcomed it all the same. It wasn't long before Thomas' image faded out, replaced with the images of dancers and bright colors of Bollywood movies.

He's not here. I'm rattled, but he's not here. He can't be here. Taking a few minutes to count to herself, she cradled herself while parents focused on the road ahead. They didn't turn around to find her inches from a panic attack. Slowly, she pulled her head out of her hands and gazed out the window. No Thomas, but Anne stood off to the side. She didn't scare Kara, not even with the blood trickling down her face. She didn't open her mouth or react to anything, just stared at Kara.

The message remained clear: stop Thomas. By any means necessary, Kara had to stop Thomas from killing again.

And then, only then, would she be free from driving.

Chapter 6

Kara tossed in her sleep the entire night, waking up every hour to check her phone. It wasn't her time to drive, yet that phone haunted her. She couldn't miss Thomas' messages for the sake of everyone around her. In a way, no messages from him gave comfort. That meant someone out, someone he had eyes on, survived for another night. She put her phone down with the screen away from her. The less temptation to go through her messages, the better rest she got.

Her heart ached over the previous attack. She never stopped thinking about Thomas' blue eyes even when they were in the restaurant. Her parents ordered everything she wanted: dim sum, veggie lo mein, and some warm tea to soothe her soul. Her father even got her that chocolate and peanut butter cheesecake she wanted. Yet even after downing two slices, she never got Thomas off her mind. She hated those evil eyes, always zeroing in on her. He didn't make it to her house. He couldn't search for her address unless he happened to be good at hacking things. Even if he knew, he couldn't go anywhere without a driver. All of this was swimming in her head. He got in deep, and now he wasn't getting out.

I don't want to think about him. I can't let him eat my mind. She sat up in bed, rubbing her head as it ached. Ever since he slammed his bloody hand on her window, he left his mark in her life. This was what he aimed for: rope Kara into the point where she couldn't twist her way out. He wanted her to think of him at every corner, see him wherever she went, hear him mock her for being so weak and helpless. Was this what he did with his other victims? Did he mock Anne right before he killed her? Men like this thrived off taunting powerless victims. He probably found Kara to be like Anne: powerless to go against.

"He wasn't there." She kicked the covers off the bed. "I'm thinking about him, but he's not there. If he was, he'd have attacked us a long time ago."

Nervous to the point where she couldn't sit still, she got out of bed and went over to where her parents slept. The bedroom door stayed closed, but she cringed over the sounds of her father snoring away. Go figure he refused to use that sleep apnea machine despite paying a good amount of money for it. He hated that thing, avoiding it when he got the chance. Somehow, her mother dozed off while Kara struggled not to laugh. It did offer a little relief. They were alive in there, or at least her father was. He snorted behind the door, so she gently pushed it in and checked on them. There they were both resting away. Thomas didn't come here. He didn't touch a hair on them.

Why would he come here? I haven't done anything wrong. I waited on him like he asked. I took him everywhere he wanted to go. I haven't gone to the police or told anyone about what he did. He's got no reason to go against me.

One more snort from her father, and she closed the door. Maybe now she could get a little bit of rest. She'd forget about what he did for the next few hours. When she was off the clock, he wasn't going to use her. He understood that her time cost money too. He vowed he'd never call for her when it wouldn't get her any money. If it happened, he'd pay her from his own pocket. This wasn't the way she wanted her money. Driving some maniac around wasn't her idea of a good job.

Driving him around. The one thing that still lingered in her mind was Thomas not using anything besides Happy Riders to get around. The places she picked him up from had other public transportation. Granted, the taxi service was a little pricey and the buses only traveled a certain route, but he could use them. He could use another rideshare app or get a friend to help him around. In a town where many people still drove themselves, he didn't have a car. He clearly paid for his rides, but who supplied his money? He never mentioned his work, only gave vague nothings.

"Okay, let me start from the beginning." She closed her eyes to drift back to the first night. Thomas wanted a lift from the airport like many others did. Nothing about him appeared suspicious, though he seemed well-rested coming from Japan. Having only two bags surprised her, especially since they were small. Did he really go to Japan? If he did, why was he there? Was it truly whatever business he did, or was he finding more wasteful people to remove off the planet? She still couldn't understand qualified Anne as a wasteful person. If anything, she was the one wasting away.

Then there were the others. She found nothing that tied Anne to any other victims. Thomas' methods of killing probably weren't the same. If he butchered Anne with that knife, what did he use on the previous victim? What would he do next time? The more she dwelled on him, the more questions popped up. His shaking body after killing

Anne also got to her. He shivered violently in her car, grasping the sides to stop himself. Clearly, it wasn't from the murder. A man that cold didn't crumble over a murder. It didn't stop until she came to a stop. Something in that house spooked him to the point of shaking.

"I wonder if…" She searched for shaking symptoms, coming up with several responses. Several medical conditions had shaking for a symptom, so Thomas could fit into them. If a doctor diagnosed him with something, it explained some of his behavior. Not all of it, but some of it to give her an idea behind his thinking.

Her phone went off and she grabbed it to find a buy one, get one free coupon for ice cream. Groaning, she silenced it before pulling the covers over herself. By now, sleep kicked in, so she spent the next hour drifting in and out. In the little dreams she had, Anne Lyle and many other dark figures loomed over her, demanding why she didn't help. She sat in the car while he killed them. She did nothing: no calls to the police, no attempts at rescue, no stopping him.

You let The Traveler kill us. You let him do this. You let him take our lives!

"No…" She breathed out as the dark figures danced around her, moving in so they covered her body. They chanted as they swayed in the darkness, up and down. Kara sunk in deeper, covering her ears to drown out accusations. "I didn't mean to…"

You let The Traveler kill us. You let him do this. You let him take our lives!

Round and round, they circled her with arms waving. These dark figures slowly became one with the shadows, blending into darkness. She found Anne in the mix, her head split open and blood seeping out of the wounds. Anne grinned at her, worms and slugs crawling out of her mouth. Kara opened her mouth to scream, but the shadow dancers taunted her.

You did this! You let us die! You did this! You let us die!

"What...what can I do now?" She squirmed as all the insects crawled over her body. Holding in her disgust, she went on. "How can I help now? How can I stop him?"

Stop him! Stop him! Stop him from killing again!

"How?!" She demanded as flies swarmed her head. "How can I stop him?!"

Stop him first! Stop him before he kills! Stop him NOW!

The flies continued to buzz around her as she swatted away. The dark dancers laughed as she writhed on the floor, still demanding she stop Thomas. Bony hands poked out of the ground, grabbing her and trying to pull her in. At the center was Anne's grinning face, half the flesh gone to reveal half her skull. She sat there as the bugs and skeletons from the ground devoured Kara, all making fun of her and demanding she do more.

"Okay, I'll help you! I'll stop him! Just tell me how!" She pleaded as the skeletons pulled her away. "Tell me how to stop him! Tell me!"

"Rishi! RISHI!" Her mother's voice cut through as she broke out of the slumber. Kara gasped and lurched upwards, grabbing away at the air. Breathing hard, she went for her phone to find more free coupons and tiny messages from relatives overseas. Her mother turned on the light and put her hand on her forehead. "You're so hot right now. Is this a fever?"

"Hot?" Kara put her phone down. Thomas didn't reply, and Happy Riders had nothing for her now. Of course, they wouldn't. "I'm...I don't think I'm sick."

"You were screaming a lot. Here." Her mother pulled back Kara's hair, untying it and re-braiding it. "You kept saying you would stop him. You wanted them to tell you how to stop him. Who is this person?"

Kara glanced at her phone, then back at the foot of her bed. She sweated up a storm all over her sheets, her comforter tossed onto the floor. She didn't have skeletons coming out of the ground or dark figures dancing. "I guess...I was dreaming about that girl...she's not much younger than me, you know."

"Oh." Her mother finished with Kara's braid. "I can see something is bothering you. If we bring that up, it makes you nervous. Maybe your father and I need to stop talking about this."

"No, it's not you. It's all over the news, so I'd hear about it anyway. I'm sorry if I bothered you." Kara got out of bed, putting on her slippers and robe. "I had a hard time these past few days. You guys are right to worry. I won't feel okay until someone finds out what happened to Anne Lyle." *Except I already know. If only I could let you guys know without snitching on myself.*

Her mother patted her back. "You'll be fine. If you do want me or your father to come along, maybe follow you_"

"No!" She walked over to her dresser, leaning against it to keep from stumbling. "I'm driving people around, Ma. I'm sure most of it is uneventful. Maybe we'll talk a little bit, but that's all. I'd rather you both stay at home."

"Still, if you're in trouble..."

"Who said I'm in trouble?" Kara's soul dropped all the way to her stomach. "I know I've come home late, but there's no trouble. It's nothing I can't handle. If any trouble does come along, I'll let you know. I just need some sleep, that's it. Hopefully, I won't have too many rides to make tomorrow. You should rest too."

"Do you want to come into our room?"

"No, Ma. It's all good." Kara helped her mother up and towards the door. "I'm feeling a little better now talking about the dream. I know it's not real, so I think I'll rest easy. Hopefully, I won't dream about that."

Her mother picked up the message, unlocking the door. "Well, if you're fine, then I'll leave you. I'll see you in the morning, Karishma. Good night."

"Good night, Ma." Kara caught the time on her dresser. 3 AM shone bright red back at her. She pulled her covers back on, lying onto her side and shutting off the light. "Well, it's now morning so good morning. I'm still gonna get some sleep though."

"Please do. And if anything happens, just tell me." The door closed as Kara got comfortable in bed. Her poor mother remained clueless about the deal. A part of Kara wanted to call her back and spill everything. Get the police involved. Show them where Anne's body was. Maybe find Thomas' other victims. Take everything one step further. Become the hero of her hometown.

I wish I could tell you what's been happening, Ma. Her heart ached over this secret. Knowing what happened to Anne, know there were more victims, holding it all in. She had no choice but to play Thomas' chauffeur until he chose to let her go. Either that or she had to force him to free her. *Then again, he forced me into this. He started it all. So maybe, it's time to force myself out.*

Force herself out. Save future victims. Get Thomas out of her life forever. All of this determined her survival. As her phone went off, she paled over Happy Riders posting something new. The color returned once she saw it was a reply from her boss asking if she wanted to take on a Monday shift instead of driving Sunday morning. Since she took a Saturday shift, she could move her break. Knowing Thomas vowed not to call on her on days off, Kara sent a 'yes,' she'd take that time off. That one day could save someone's life. A wasteful person as Thomas referred to them got to live to tomorrow.

And when Thomas called her for another ride, she'd give that person a few tomorrow to live through. One way or another, she'd save them all.

Chapter 7

As grateful as she was for the day off, Kara checked the phone constantly for calls. The only notifications were news and stores offering her coupons and good deals. Without the ringtone, she didn't panic as much, but it didn't keep her away from the screen. At the table, she kept the phone on the seat next to her, waiting for him to send a message. She grew sicker over Thomas plotting to kill someone new. Who would he go after next? Was it another girl like Anne, a poor soul just leaving their shift? Was it someone a bit older who needed help, and he'd lend a hand only to hurt them? Did he even know his victims, or were they all random picks? The more she dwelled on it, the worse her headache got.

Get out of my head! I'm not driving today! Her mind screamed at her. *You can't let that creep take over everything, especially not your time off. Do something else for a change!*

"Well, since you have no shift today, how about you run some errands for me?" Her mother handed over a list of groceries. "I would have gone yesterday, but you took so long to come back home, you didn't look well, and you weren't in the best mood. Of course, if you would tell me what went wrong..."

"I can go." Kara turned her phone over and grabbed the list. She thanked every star in the sky that her mother had the perfect distraction. Doing groceries was her favorite chore. They took time to complete, and she enjoyed standing in aisles and checking out prices. The longer the grocery list, the more time she got to spend in the store. "I hope you don't mind me borrowing your car though. I just...well, with the yellow sticker over my windshield, someone might think I'm on the clock."

"Of course. I don't want them to get confused." She handed over the keys. "Try to come back quickly, okay? I know you can't predict anything, but with all that's happened..."

"I'll be back." Kara put the keys in her pocket and grabbed the phone. No message from Thomas yet. He'd keep his promise for the next few minutes. Her mother's list contained the simple things: eggs, milk, bread, all those typical groceries. She'd grab them, make sure everything was priced properly, and get out. If Happy Riders requested her to pick someone up, she wouldn't take them at this moment. Every now and then, they would reach out to her to see if she could pick someone up on her days off. Most of the times, she didn't oblige, but they continued to do it. Hopefully, they wouldn't bother her today. "I would like less driving today. I want some rest."

"You'll need it. I heard you screaming in the middle of the night." Her father put down his newspaper. "What were you dreaming of? You sounded scared."

Kara dropped her phone on her lap. "You heard me too?"

"Heard you? I'm the one who told your mother to check on that." He chuckled as he grabbed his teacup. "Don't worry. She was already half-way out the door since you were screaming so much. I think the neighbors heard you."

Kara quickly put together her explanation, careful not to bring up Thomas or Anne. "I'm sorry, guys. It was a dream of bugs and ghosts and dead people crawling out. It was…" She shuddered. While not true, she still couldn't stand bugs and certainly not the idea of them crawling on her body. "Yeah, they were all over me. Gross."

"Definitely gross." Her dad shuddered and checked his own body for any insects. "I can see why that made you scream now. Are you sure you won't have bad dreams tonight?"

"I hope not." She hugged both before getting her purse. "Hang tight, guys. I'll get all your stuff from the closest supermarket, okay? Maybe that Walmart which is like five minutes from home. They should have everything on your list."

"Remember, go to the store and come back." Her mother tapped her foot on the ground, a reminder that Kara had to follow these instructions. "If you do get into trouble, call me. Send a text. Don't leave us wondering what happened."

"I won't. I'll send you a message if anything happens." Kara prayed she could still send messages if she ended in the worst situation. When she wasn't in her car, she cringed at how clean everything appeared. Thomas never got in this one. He never left blood on it, yet everywhere she looked, she saw spots of red. As she slid into the driver's seat, she couldn't shake Thomas' blue gaze on the back of her head. Checking the mirrors, she expected him to pop up and take his place in the backseat. Sit quietly, glower at her, hold her to her promises. Glancing back, she didn't find him. Not his steely glare or sharp blade. Not his shaking body. Not that silver hair and cold voice instructing everything.

"Stop it. He'll call when he's ready." She backed out of the driveway, hands tight on the wheel. With Thomas, she lost her grip but here, she clung for her life. Her first rider turned out to be someone needing a lift from the Amtrak station to a hotel. Thank goodness that was only a ten-minute and said hotel was in the middle of downtown Charlotte. She didn't enjoy the traffic, but for once, she wanted to be down a road full of honking cars and people crossing when it wasn't their right of way. She missed passing by giant buildings and strange sculptures while people moved around her. The bright streetlamps, the crazy people yelling at her, the exciting events taking place in downtown Charlotte...she no longer knew of what concerts or festivals took place.

Glancing on the phone, her heart sank at the reminder of restaurant week. Charlotte always had great restaurants where she could go for either lunch or dinner to have a three-course meal for about $30 or $40. In the past, she'd call up some old friends to try them out or she'd take her parents when no one was available. Right now, she couldn't go anywhere. She couldn't talk to people about the things bothering her. Her money went straight to gas money and her own expenses. She didn't carry $30 for three-course meals.

At the grocery store, she took only a few minutes to get all the things her mother asked for and even picked up a jar of Nutella for herself. She got a bigger jar for today. The last two times she got Nutella, her father downed the smaller ones in a single sitting. By the time she got around to tasting it, she found nothing but empty jars. This time, she'd hide them where he could not see. This was for her and her alone.

"Sorry, Baba. You gotta get your own." She bagged up her groceries and left with a nod farewell to all the employees. Quickly checking the receipt, she crumpled it up and headed towards the car. The entire time, she checked over her shoulder in case she spotted him. Thomas didn't stay at home forever. He had to eat as well. He had to shop for his food, so if he found her here, he'd warp her mind. That steely blue glare burned in her as she popped open the trunk. Not now. Not here. Thomas couldn't make her do anything. He couldn't force her to drive in a car that wasn't hers.

"You're fine." She placed the groceries in the trunk, slamming it and taking in her surroundings. No dangers so far. A few people walking around, others loading their groceries, and no one causing a scene. She got in the driver's seat, revved up the engine, and shut the door. Given that she had a different car, he couldn't spot her in it. This shopping center was also far from McIver Drive. Without someone driving him over here, he wouldn't get here without a good reason. She breathed in through her nose, buckled up her seat belt, and let the breath out of her mouth. Times like these were the ones where she wished she followed her yoga lessons on a regular basis. Since taking the job at Happy Riders, she never had the time to sit down and stretch out, let alone breathe. Now every part of her ached as she drove out of the parking lot, trying hard to ignore her beating heart.

"Slow down, slow down." She reminded herself as she left the shopping center. "He's not here. You're not driving him."

The entire drive, she stayed on point with her driving. She didn't run any lights, didn't cross lanes without using turn signals, nor did she blow the horn at anyone cutting in front of her. Glancing in the mirror, she half-expected Thomas to pop up there, keeping his eye on her. Instead, she got a shot of Anne sitting there, looking as emotionless as ever. She didn't scare her, only broke her heart. This girl couldn't be seen by anyone anymore. She sat in that car, quiet and waiting for Kara to make moves. Kara put her focus on the road again, ignoring everyone zipping by her. She lost her sense of direction during this time, unsure where she wanted to go. Staying on the speed limit, she paid attention to familiar areas, but nothing sank in. All she saw was Thomas everywhere she turned. His face, his eyes, his cold demeanor ended up in every corner. It wasn't until she saw the turn for her neighborhood that he disappeared. He didn't haunt her as soon as she got into the driveway.

Hopefully, he never finds this place. She parked the car, leaning back and taking in the warmth around her. She made it. Despite her head stuck in the clouds and her heart racing, she drove home without causing an accident. She sat for a while, letting the warm air circle her. She never wanted to leave this place. These seats never got covered in blood or carried a dangerous person around. This was her parents' car. It was the same one she rode around in for years. She didn't smell death in this car. She waited for a minute before getting out and opening the trunk. The grocery run took no more than twenty minutes, yet every second dragged on. She didn't bother making eye contact with her mother when she brought everything in. She wanted some time for herself after she put the groceries away.

Be cool. She's going to ask questions if she sees you panicking. She put the milk and eggs in the fridge, avoiding her mother moving around in the kitchen. Her stomach growled though she couldn't bother to put anything together. Her hands shook as she placed the food where it belonged. Pantry, fridge, counter...she stifled a yawn as she finished dropping the potatoes in the vegetable crisper. With everything where it belonged, she excused herself under her breath and ran to her room. Home. She was home, and she was running like he was right behind her. She didn't start relaxing until she got in her room, closed the door, and powered on her laptop. Information. She hungered for every detail about him. She plugged 'Thomas Whittle' into the search engine, which brought back nothing of substance. There were plenty of men named Thomas Whittle, none sounding like the man she drove around. She didn't even find pictures that fit his descriptions. All these other men with the same name didn't have those evil eyes. They didn't smirk or radiate the cold energy. He wasn't online.

Well, finding Thomas by himself was a dud. What the heck did they call him again? The first google alert gave her the answer: The Traveler. A fitting name given that she found him at the airport. There wasn't a whole lot else besides that, but everyone agreed on one thing: the killer was just one person. He never used accomplices. He never dragged anyone into his crimes. He never trained anyone to take over. He did it all by himself. *Well, that was in the past. Now he's got me to drive him from place to place.*

That was the other thing standing out to her. The Traveler never stayed in the same place for very long. As soon as he killed someone, he moved away before the police got a whiff of him. He left nothing behind except devastated families, dead bodies, and towns left with a million questions. They never knew exactly where he went, just that he wasn't around. As she read on, Kara discovered a long list of victims of The Traveler starting all the way back in 1990. This victim was a young man named Rodney Wallace, living off campus and working at a fast-food restaurant to pay for college. He disappeared after a night shift, never calling in the following day. His teachers or peers didn't see him in class. After two days, he was found in the back of an abandoned house, hands and feet bound. Kara shuddered upon reading about the abrasions on his neck.

Strangled to death and bound. The same was the case with another victim in 1995, a young girl named Cara Price. Another young retail worker leaving her job and never coming back. Found two days later all bound, gagged, and strangled. Then again, the same thing happened in 2000. Every five years, he strangled and bound victims. However, the year before, he stabbed victims to death. Always binding them but stabbing them. No one found the correlation between all this. The only reason Kara came up with was Thomas trying to throw police off. Change his methods, change directions, leave them stumped. These were the ones everyone knew of. They figured The Traveler killed over a hundred people of various ages and races, simply for being worthless. That word boiled Kara's blood as she pictured these poor victims, scared and tied up, unsure if anyone could save them.

"For a guy who's called The Traveler, he doesn't drive himself." She found another article on a new victim who stood out above the others. Dr. Tim Moseley worked in a hospital, helping patients with chronic illnesses. He lived alone, yet that was only due to his wife's death and his children growing up and leaving home. He had a family who wasn't in the house. Yet when he disappeared after a night shift, all of them called the hospital for answers. He never showed up for his next shift, and none of his coworkers or patients heard from him. Then, like the others, they found him two days later bound, gagged, and throat cut. The Traveler changed his methods yet again.

"He killed a doctor. That doesn't make sense." Kara murmured as she read up on Dr. Moseley. Nothing about the man gave her a bad vibe. Even old reviews praised his methods and kindness towards others. The entire community mourned his passing, raising enough money to create a memorial garden in his name. The police knew The Traveler struck again, leaving no clues to his identity and whereabouts. He never left a clue where or when he'd strike next. "Well, jackass, I know. You took a few lives, so it's up to me to help these guys out. Give them some peace."

"Karishma?" Her father knocked on her bedroom door as she closed her laptop. "Is everything okay?"

"Everything's peachy, Baba!" She got up to unlock the door, letting him in. "Sorry! I was...I was looking around for jobs and updating my resume. You guys were right. I've been...I haven't updated that thing in ages."

"I told you. You need to have that resume up to date if you want people to call you." He handed her a plate of fruit. "Your mother cut these up for you. She's worried that you're not eating much lately. Are you sure everything is okay with you? You still have that job, right?"

"I'm okay, Baba." Kara grabbed an orange slice. "And yes, I still work for Happy Riders. There's nothing wrong with it. If anything, my boss is pleased that I took on a few extra rides. Apparently, not everyone wants to drive those evening hours because it's getting darker now."

"You could change your schedule too, you know. If you feel better driving around in the morning, then you could_"

"I'm keeping my schedule." Kara bit into the orange, the juice dribbling down her chin. She wiped it off with her sleeve before her father handed her the napkin. "That would have been useful ten seconds ago, Baba."

"Sorry. Like you, I'm very nervous lately. Your mother keeps watching the news and all they show is horrible things happening to girls. Over here and in India, she watches the same thing repeatedly about men hurting women. It has me worried about you."

"Can't you tell her to turn it off?" Kara's skin prickled over those sentences. Men hurting women was sadly nothing new. The Traveler got his kicks hurting anyone he wanted. "I mean, unless some new information pops up and the perps are arrested, watching the same thing won't make it easier to endure."

"Tell that to her." He took off his glasses to wipe his eyes. "I know I've been worrying a little too much lately. I keep asking to help you on your rides, but you keep saying no. I get that. I get you wanting to do this alone. Yet with all this news, I stare out the window wondering when you'll get home. You haven't come back on time lately."

"That's my fault. I lose track of time these days." That wasn't an entire lie. Being around Thomas froze time for her. She never glanced at the clock while he went on his spree. Time no longer mattered if he sat in her car. "I should call or text back if I'm going to be late. It's just..." She stopped herself from revealing the rest. *It's just that this serial killer has me in his grasp and he's not letting go, Baba. I'm afraid of when he finally leaves me alone...I may not be alive when that happens.*

"What is it, Rishi?" He pressed on. "What aren't you telling me?"

"I can't talk right now." She rubbed her eyes. "I'm just...I'm always so tired when I come home. I know I'm working the shift I want, but I still wish I had something else. I try so hard. You guys think I don't do anything, but I do. I put everything into the applications and how many interviews did I get? Like two! And then...all of this, all that you guys watch...I don't even know..."

"Shh!" He calmed her down, letting her rest on his shoulder. "Forget about all that right now. I know you're tired, so you rest for now and clear your head. Once you've gotten rid of all the negative thoughts, come back to this again. I promise you that you can take your time. No matter what we say, keep working hard." He squeezed her shoulders. "It will happen to you. After all, people with less education get work all the time."

"I...I don't think so, Baba. If they do, they pull strings behind the scenes." She cut the conversation right then by rubbing her forehead. "Listen, Baba. I want to get some rest right now. I've got a little bit of a headache, and I need to..."

"Naturally. This is your time to rest, so do that. Take this moment to enjoy the things around you." He turned around, waving his arms to prove a point. "I don't know the last time you went out for fun. When was that?"

"Probably last year…or maybe three years before. Life was a lot easier to understand back then. I was in college, so I had to get that college experience. I wasn't a working person then. Now, I prefer resting by myself and having fun alone."

"Whatever works for you." He got the cue to step back. "I'll leave you to have your fun by yourself. If you need anything though, I am still here. Your mother might leave later to get some fruits for our prayer room and for our temple visit. It turns out we have no oranges." He laughed to himself. "I told her that the gods probably don't care about having citrus fruits, but you know her."

"Yeah, she needs three different kinds of fruits because the gods prefer variety." Kara glanced at her phone. No message from Thomas. "All right, Baba. Let me get to sprucing up that resume and maybe watching some TikTok videos."

"Do what you want. Just don't stress out."

Once he left the room, she began to scour through TikTok videos about The Traveler. To her shock, there were quite a few resources discussing Anne Lyle's disappearance. Most content creators decided that Anne was dead. With the little clues about her whereabouts, they didn't expect her to come out alive. A few creators thought they saw her in various places including Starbucks, the movie theater, and Tahiti. Another few were under the impression that Anne was working alongside The Traveler, being trained as his accomplice. Kara moved away from those videos, knowing very well these creators remained misinformed. Anne was dead. She wasn't a new accomplice, she wasn't in Tahiti or Starbucks, she was dead. She was hidden somewhere people couldn't find, but she was dead.

"Come on, guys. Give me something that I don't already know." Kara grumbled as she went through the videos. None of them held anything brand new though a few creators brought up the strange coincidences with other cases. The Traveler slowed down after some time. He took a long gap between years before killing. They only knew it was him because of his style of killing. Taking someone away, bounding them, and then killing them by stabbing or strangling. He wanted them to suffer, but for what? She watched plenty of crime shows and listened to enough podcasts to know he didn't kill for the heck of it. If it was a death that he wanted, he could easily get a gun and shoot these people. He could kill them without dragging them away. These types of killings meant something personal.

"Just who are you, Thomas?" She went to check some images of The Traveler. The only things besides bad sketches and fanart were some blurry camera shots. The victims were clear on screen, but a shadowy figure in the corner revealed nothing. Just a giant black blob. Yet the more she stared at that blob, the colder the room grew. Him. She didn't need to see his face to know he was right there, eyes locked on his victim. How did the other victims not get that same chill? She closed the screen down and opened TikTok instead, searching for videos on The Traveler. There were plenty of content creators babbling about him, throwing out all their theories. None of them came close to his real identity though many nailed the same things she did: he killed for personal reasons. He killed these people to make them suffer. If not them, he wanted someone else to suffer. He wanted them to pay.

Who hurt you? She closed everything down, wanting to forget his entire existence.

The phone went off right then, sending her that message she dreaded. He wasn't calling her for a ride. He wasn't sending reviews, or demanding she do anything for him. He texted her simple messages, including one that gripped her around the throat. She couldn't read the letters out loud, but there they were, big and bold and screaming in her face. She set the phone down, shivering as she checked it again. A simple reply, a kind one. How could one sentence break her like this? Yet the more she stared, the tighter her throat grew. He kept tabs on her. He knew everything.

I hope you had a good day, Kara. Enjoy your rest and be ready for tomorrow. Things are gonna get interesting for you soon.

Chapter 8

Tomorrow. Interesting for her. The more she stared at those words, the crazier she grew. Kara deleted a bunch of Thomas' messages to keep her sane. She only replied 'thank you' to the latest one before wiping it clean. He couldn't expect anything else besides that. He sent no other messages that night, so she put the phone on silent and opened her laptop again. Her parents hadn't called on her for anything. They didn't ask her to come eat or run more errands. Instead, she found them in the living room, drinking tea and watching old movies. Neither asked her about her troubles. They couldn't get it, even if she wanted to tell them. The less she divulged about Thomas, the safer they'd be.

Don't ask me about anything I'm doing. She propped her feet on the footrest and began her search. The previous message from Thomas unnerved her, but she got enough strength to research now. She opted not to go for TikTok theories, opting for some written articles instead. The written articles, as long they weren't in AI, would give her more facts than some idiot babbling and dancing in front of the camera. The TikTok crew didn't get it: this wasn't a game. This wasn't a movie they could sit in front of and critique for the crowd. They were the kind of people Thomas would hunt down if he had the chance. For their sake, she hoped they wouldn't find out about him.

"Home invasions...huh?" She went to the next article. This bit hadn't come up earlier. Some of the victims were taken from their houses, and there was always a struggle though nothing had been taken. Thomas didn't take trophies like many serial killers. He stood out to her yet baffled the police. They wanted everything to come together. The bits and pieces they received weren't enough to pin down a suspect, let alone convict anyone. "How are you getting in their homes? You don't drive...at least, I don't think you do."

The more she read about these home invasions and deaths, the more convinced she became of his guilt. Every place she picked Thomas from wasn't far from a previous victim's home. He made these parts his hunting ground. Find the weak, worthless ones and end their weak, worthless lives. Police dubbed him "The Traveler" for never staying and killing in one place. She marked that anytime the authorities discovered a victim, Thomas wasn't around. He ran to secure his alibi, wipe his trail clean and replace it with a new one. That was his pattern. He kept that because he knew no one could trace the crime back to him.

The only victim who didn't fit the others was Dr. Moseley. A doctor wasn't exactly a worthless person. He had a job, saved lives, and helped many people. Prior to death, no one had a bad thing to say about him. He diagnosed people quickly, and if possible, cured them just as fast. If he couldn't, he helped them find someone who could. Thomas holding hatred for this man didn't make sense. Everyone in town didn't accept this man's death. They vowed to find out who killed him and make them pay for the crime. That had been years ago, and so far, no one paid for a thing.

Kara didn't stop thinking about any of this even into the following day. When she woke up, she got that reminder of a shift starting at night. Yet Thomas sent her a message after she brushed her teeth and got changed. ***I know it's a little early, but I want to remind you that I need you again. Be ready to drive.***

He didn't give her a choice. Texting an 'ok' to him, she finished getting ready and stared at her phone until his next message came. ***It's time, Kara. I'm waiting at the same shopping center as before. The same store. Let me know when you're coming.***

Despite it being a little early, she agreed to meet him at the shopping center and take him where he needed to go. Saying goodbye to her parents, she vowed that she'd be back as quick as possible though every word out of her hurt to say. Lies. All she pushed onto them were lies. She wrapped her arms around herself as she headed to the car. Even when she got the engine purring and turned on the air conditioner, she couldn't shake the cold out. It followed as she drove towards the shopping center where Thomas stood in the same place as before. He held only one shopping bag today as she slowed down at the curb.

Opening the door, he placed the bag by the side. "Hello there, Kara. Right on time. I hope you don't mind leaving a little early."

"It's okay." She checked the GPS. Home was only a few minutes away. If she dropped him off, she could go back. "Did you...did you have a good day shopping?"

"Oh, it's the usual. Nothing was on sale." He got comfortable, buckled up, and nodded at the GPS. "Let's not go to McIver Drive yet. I need to make one stop before I head home."

"Right. What's the address?" He handed over a piece of paper with an address only ten minutes away. She plugged the new address into the GPS and eased out of the shopping center. "Is everything else okay with you?"

"Oh yeah, just fine." Thomas smirked. "The day's only starting for me though. I assume it would be the same for you."

There it was. He charmed her away with that small talk, acting like he wouldn't put a knife in her back at her first wrong move. Her mind went to his other victims. What was their first wrong move? What was the one thing that they did to anger? Maybe he found the younger victims annoying and loud. She could understand that given that she found a lot of people her age to be way too immature. It wasn't an excuse to murder them, but she grew frustrated whenever they got near her. Maybe his anger towards them went beyond mere annoyance. Yet it didn't explain one victim: Dr. Moseley. This doctor was much too old to belong to be in Gen Z. He probably didn't run around, hit up parties and bars, and make a lot of noise. He was a quiet man according to those who knew him. He kept to himself and looked after patients. He didn't fit the description of the other victims.

What did that doctor do to you? I know it wasn't because he was being annoying. Did he give a wrong diagnosis? What is it? She glanced over at him, sitting and watching trees go by. He shivered a little bit but stopped once she got on the right road. "We...we should be there soon."

"I know." He didn't bother changing the cold tone in his voice. That friendly mask no longer existed. Thomas Whittle, the real Thomas Whittle, got into her car for a mission. "You're doing just fine, Kara. No problems with the traffic."

"Yeah, none." Kara let a white van pass by them, its taillights flashing for help. Any other time, she'd slow down and try to help them. The van ended up on the curve while Thomas waved at her to keep going. "He seems to be in trouble."

"Someone else can help him. You drive on."

She turned towards the stereo system, getting her hands on the dials. "Do you...Do you want to listen to music? Any preferences?"

"You play whatever you want. This is your car, after all." He leaned back in his chair. "I'm only here for the ride. Never forget that."

The line didn't sound as sincere from him. Yes, she drove around, but he wanted more than a ride from her. He chuckled to himself as he checked the contents of his shopping bag while she fiddled with the radio station. Some soft classic rock began to play, getting her to focus on those words. She sang various songs in her head as they drove on. Thomas kept watch on her, approving whenever she used her turn signals or slowed down for stop lights. He also glared at the drivers who sped by her, honked their horns, and acted like damn fools on the road.

"I don't know how you can drive with these maniacs, Kara." He shook his head. "They don't have any respect for anyone."

"They're probably in a hurry." Kara suggested as she got onto another lane, checking both ways before easing in. "It's not a big deal. I'm used to it."

"Well, you shouldn't tolerate it. You should be allowed to drive down a road without worrying about who's trying to mow you down." He snorted as another car drove by. "Look at that idiot. Where's the fire? I doubt he's going anywhere important."

"It doesn't matter. I'll get you to your destination." She cut off the conversation there. Thomas kept scowling at everyone around them, so she opted to stay on the speed limit and get him to the new place. In her head, she worried about how lived here. He made no mention of what this area was. The only thing she knew was that it was another neighborhood, most likely far from humanity. God, she wanted the ride to end soon. Save this person. Save the one who lived in that house.

Keep Thomas away from them, give them another night to survive. The pressure for all of that tumbled on her shoulders. Anne and the other victims wanted her to do this. Not just for them, but for every victim out there. They deserved a little justice.

Kara slowed down as they got to the new house, another one hidden away from the busy Charlotte life. Hell, it was hidden away from any quiet town life. She glanced at the numbers on the old mailbox, memorizing each one repeatedly. 1980. That couldn't be hard since she had a cousin born in August of 1980. If she remembered that, she'd remember this. Now came the part where she warned the person inside. Her breathing slowed down as her mind ticked away with different plans.

Without any social media or phone number, she couldn't figure out who lived here. She didn't want to go through her phone in the event Thomas caught her. He watched every move closely, those steely eyes never leaving her sight. He knew she wanted out. Her desperation came right off as his stare bore into her back. He didn't want her to move. Taking a glance at the GPS, it announced they had arrived, and she needed to drop off Thomas. If only it ended right here. Drop him off and never see him again. With him now inches from her neck, she didn't dare make a move against him. He had the weapons and strength. All she had was herself to fight off. That wouldn't be enough to beat him.

"You keep the engine running, Kara." Thomas patted her shoulder, leaving his cold mark on her. "I won't be very long. And while you're at it, can you turn up the temperature in here? I'm a little chilly."

She nodded as she turned up the heat. Warm air quickly hit the car, turning the cold to hot temperatures in seconds. She fiddled with her collar, waving her hand before her face. Both nerves and heat got her sweating up a storm. "What are you doing here?"

"You don't need to know that. You drive me around. You're doing a great job of that." He whispered as he pulled her hair back. "Those reviewers were right; you're one of the smoothest drivers out there, always caring about the people in the back. You even refilled all those snacks and water bottles."

"I still have to take other people around." She gulped the phlegm forming in the back of her throat. "Once we're done, I have to get others."

"You'll have enough time to pick them up. Be a good driver and stay right in the seat." His hands ran down her neck before pulling away. "I know you won't do anything foolish. You wouldn't get away with it."

As he stepped out and headed towards the house, Kara waited until he went around the back before unlocking the driver's side. The car's engine hummed as she stepped on the dead leaves, careful not to crunch too many under her weight. If someone lived in this old house, she could send a small warning to them. Some small pebbles lay in front of her, and the windows were wide enough to hit. Crouching down, she put a few pebbles in her pocket and tiptoed towards the house. Trying not to step on leaves, she walked on the few wet patches in the ground and got close to throwing the pebbles.

If you are inside, you can hear me. Her hands dug into her pockets for a pebble, smooth and hard. *If you hear anything at all, get out of the house.*

She flung the first pebble towards the window, which hit the windowsill. The second one hit the siding, not loud enough to make a sound. The third one got the glass, making a small tapping sound. Unsure if the resident heard that, she tried again. "Come on, come on! Get out of that house! If you're in there, get out or hide!"

With the fourth pebble hitting the glass again, she turned her heel and ran back towards the car. Flinging the driver's side open, she got in and slammed the door shut, leaning back to catch her breath. Sitting there for a few seconds, she basked in the new heat within her car. This heat wouldn't go unless she refused to turn on the engine for a few minutes. She closed her eyes, enjoying the silence around her. He couldn't come in. He wouldn't_

"You cut the engine off."

She jerked back at Thomas' voice, turning around to find him in the back seat, still pristine and free of blood. He didn't stain her newly cleaned seats tonight. Her trembling hand went to the ignition as he buckled up, mind frantic for a good explanation. "Well, I don't want to waste gas. I must pay for that out of my pocket. Happy Riders doesn't cover that at all." That part was true, a part that she wished Happy Riders would change. Gas prices went through the roof in the last two months, and her paycheck paid for all these trips. As soon as she got paid, she lost it thanks to filling up the tank. "I want to conserve as much of it as I can, so that's the only reason I cut this off. That, and it was getting a little too warm in here."

Thomas accepted this excuse. "I guess I forgot about how much gas costs. I haven't checked it since…" He trailed off as his shoulders tensed up before relaxing. "Never mind. It's time to go back."

Kara began to pull out of the driveway. "You're…you're…"

"You can breathe easy, Kara. No one was home today. I guess I got the wrong information, thinking they'd be in at this hour." His eye twitched as she began to roll down the gravel. "Go easy down here, Kara. I'd hate for you to get a flat tire when there's no one for miles."

There was no one home. Oh God, there was no one in that house. Kara didn't know whether to breathe relief or fear. Whoever lived in that house went one step further than Thomas, protecting themselves for another night. In addition to that, Thomas didn't know about the pebble-throwing. He understood that she couldn't leave a car running for long now. Her foot hovering over the break, she eased on down the road, wincing whenever her tires drove over rocks. *Oh God, please don't puncture a tire here. Not with him right behind me. I can't fix anything in the dark.*

"You're getting better at this." Thomas approved of her easy driving over the bridge. "You're doing exactly as I want you to do."

"You didn't give me much of a choice." She pointed out. With no weapon in sight, she figured she could say something. "I have to know one thing though: why did you come back if you didn't find the person you wanted? Why not wait the whole night for them to come back?"

"I don't have a whole night to wait, Kara. Just like you don't have the whole night to drive around. The temperature's gonna drop, I'll get tired, I might..." Once more, he trailed off as she got onto the road. "Well, let's just say waiting is hard, but it must be done. Some people wait a long time for a bit of news. And sometimes, the wait is good for you. You know that old saying, 'no news is good news?' I believe it."

He's throwing hints at me, but what kind of hints? He wants me to discover something about him. Kara got onto the highway, now putting all her focus on the road. Thomas twitched and squirmed as she shifted lanes, yet it wasn't from driving. She wasn't going any faster than anyone else there. *He shakes a lot even when I'm not moving. Do the police know about that part?*

None of the articles about The Traveler mentioned any tics, which proved nothing. Thomas shook at random moments. Even now, as they slowed down thanks to traffic, his hands trembled on his lap. She couldn't help it anymore. "Are you okay? If it's too cold, just tell me and I'll put on the heat."

"I'm fine." He intertwined his fingers, dropping them back on his lap. "I'm a little disappointed to not finish my job, but there's always tomorrow or the day after. You work Thursday evenings, don't you?"

"Uh...yeah, I do. I tend to get a lot of requests then. I can't guarantee that I'll..."

"If I make a request, you take it." He cut her off. Kara fell silent as she switched lanes towards McIver Drive's exit. "I don't care if you want to pick someone else up or you're in the middle of a drive. You run my errands first before anyone else. If you have someone, you drop them off and come straight to me. I thought I made that clear last time."

"Yes, you did." Kara counted her breaths as she got off the highway, heading towards McIver Drive's dark road. By now, she could drive down it blindfolded and know exactly where to park. Thomas never told her if this was really his house, or a place he picked as a hangout. With the mailbox nearly falling off and weeds grown all over, he didn't keep up with the yardwork. "I'm sorry. I didn't think..."

"That's right, you didn't think at all. If you did, you'd remember something so simple. I hope you aren't rambling that pretty, little mouth off at others." He lowered his voice. "You didn't tell anyone anything, did you?"

"No." She whispered. "Your secret is safe."

"*Our* secret is safe. You're in this too, doll, whether you want to accept it or not. I picked you for a good reason. Have you figured out why?"

Kara gulped. "It's because I was the one who accepted your ride?"

"Well, that and one other good reason. Let's see if you can put this picture together. You're perfect for me, Kara. Not like the others. You listen and make sure that my ride is smooth and comfortable. I mean, look at you on a busy road! People pass by you, and you don't honk at them. They flip you off, and you don't get angry. You're the perfect human being."

"Um, thank you?" Kara calmed down as soon as she got to the house, putting on the breaks. She got a message of a pickup only seven minutes away, her finger almost pressing it as Thomas got out. "Well, we're here. If you don't want me to_"

"You can take another ride, Kara. I'm done for now." He leaned into the driver's side window, stroking her cheek. "God, look at you. You shake out of fear."

No shit. I'm terrified of you, asshole. She moved away from his hand, nodding towards the clock. "I really do have to go now. I still have some time, and there are probably other people who need a ride_

"Of course. I wouldn't keep you out too late, Kara. Your folks worry about you. I mean, you're an adult but as all parents, they think of you. You're lucky in that way. Someone in your life cares for you, thinks of you, notices you."

She almost snapped away at him. His little comments dug under her. He knew she had a family who wanted her safe. He knew others would worry if she suddenly fell off the face of the Earth. Gripping the wheel, she didn't let the uneasiness appear on her face. "I'll wait for your next call."

"I know you will. You're always on time. I like that." He stepped away. "Enjoy the rest of your night, Kara. There are some big days ahead of us. I hope that you'll be ready for them."

"When will I see you again?" She wondered out loud. "You know…in case I have to make any changes to my schedule or let others know I'll be late. I'm already driving outside of my shift as it is."

"Which I will compensate you for. That reminds me." He reached into his pocket and handed over a wad of hundred-dollar bills. She had no time to react as the cash landed on her lap. "For all your trouble. Don't tell anyone where you got it from. That's for you alone."

"But…"

"Don't question it, Kara. I'm helping you out. Keep that money to yourself and use that for things you need." He warned her. "Go. I'll let you know when I need another ride."

Kara didn't wait for more instructions. Shoving the cash in her glove compartment, she began to drive away. He had all that money yet spent his time killing people and driving around with her. He was the biggest mystery of all for her. Who was he? What did he truly want from her and his victims? He couldn't hurt his person, but they couldn't get as lucky next time. What was his next plan?'

Her heart ached as she left the area, wanting to drive far away from him. As desperate as she became to leave him, she couldn't do it right now. She had no answers behind his crimes. She knew nothing about him. He kept talking in his cryptic language, speaking a language she knew but offering nothing of substance. This was his game. He liked toying with her the way a cat toyed with its food. God, she was his prey right now. She was the one he wanted to kill and devour. The more he spoke, the more twisted her soul became. He wanted her to be like him, soulless and uncaring when someone died. Lose every bit of sanity she had in her. Eventually, lose all her humanity to it. He was killing her as well.

And at this moment, he was succeeding.

Chapter 9

Kara slumped into the house at nine-fifteen, pleased she made it before ten. Her parents both sat in the living room, watching their soaps together. At least her mother focused on the TV. Her father kept checking his phone to see what the cricket scores were. Taking off her shoes, she put her keys in her purse. "So, what did I miss?"

"You came home." Her father pulled away to find her taking off her jacket. "I thought for sure you wouldn't."

"Why wouldn't I? I've come home late, but I always come home." She joined them both on the couch, trying to figure out the latest debacle on TV. "So, did they figure Tipu is not the thief? Or is he the thief?"

"He's not the thief. It's his identical twin brother that no one knew about." Her mother lowered the volume as it went into commercials. "We do need to talk, Karishma."

"About what?" Kara's knuckles whitened as she clenched them. Her mind turned to the car that she cleaned out, praying every spot of blood went. She checked it from top to bottom, getting rid of the smallest drops. "If this about me staying out too late for work, I can_"

"It's not that." Her mother cut the TV off to signal how important everything was. Kara's face whitened with her knuckles. She didn't want to watch the end of her show. "I know we keep talking about that girl. Well...they found her."

Kara's eyes welled up. Her worst fears came into light: the truth was out in the world. "She's not alive, is she?"

"I'm sorry, Rishi." Her father pulled her into a hug. "No one knows who did it, and the police think that this isn't the first time this happened. They mentioned similar cases from years ago that fit this one. That's why they are putting in a curfew. No one can leave after ten at night. It's also why so many stores are closing early."

"Even the twenty-four-hour ones?" Kara stared at her phone at all the new notifications. Sure enough, the news mentioned the new curfew along with several places mentioning their new times. "What about the drivers who drive in the middle of the night or early morning hours? Some of them have this as their only source of income."

"You might have to see what Happy Riders is doing about that, but I'd like you to change your hours if you can. The early afternoon is fine, but when it gets dark...that's where I start to worry. Can you move it up a little bit? Maybe from 10 to 1 or something like that?"

"I...I don't know. I'll have to ask." Not that asking Happy Riders for a time change would help her out. Thomas knew her work hours, expecting her to be free then. If she changed her schedule on him, and didn't show up when he asked, then what would he do? That steel knife blade inches from her neck played back in her head. Any second, he could have plunged it in. The moment she messed up, he would put it into her. "I can't promise you anything, Baba. I can try, but don't expect a change."

"I know." Her mother joined in the hug. "It's not just because of that. You've been stressed out lately. Every time you come home, you appear scared and pale. You don't eat as much. I'm not even sure if you get enough sleep. After the last nightmare, I'm worried this job is taking too much from you."

"You don't know half of it." Kara slumped into the cushions. She imagined Thomas right behind them, moving back and forth, contemplating which one to kill first. Which one would Kara need more? Who would suffer harder. Or maybe he could save them the trouble and kill her off. A part of her wished he would end her suffering. Keeping this secret, knowing so much and being so helpless...it stung worse. She buried her head into her arms, letting the tears flow. They didn't get it. No one got it.

"Oh, Karishma! Oh, I'm sorry! I wasn't trying to hurt you, I..."

"It's not you, Ma." She murmured into her arms. "You guys did nothing wrong. It's me. It's all my fault I can't find work." She got off the couch as tears streamed down. "It's my fault for not being good enough for any employer. It's my fault this is...this is..."

Her words caught in her throat, keeping her from blurting out the truth. Thomas' presence loomed around her, waiting for her to slip up. A good girl. A perfect human. The best driver he ever had. He wanted her to stay that way, so she zipped it up. "It's my fault things are going wrong for me."

"Karishma..." Her father got up, helping her to the bedroom. "That stress is taking over your life. I think you need some quiet time to yourself. Forget about applying for any jobs right now. Rest, and come back to that later."

"But you guys..."

"It can wait." He squeezed her, turning on the lights and taking her over to her bed. "Go change your clothes, take a shower, and lay here.

Forget your phone too. You get glued to that all the time. What's so important about it?"

My whole damn existence depends on it, Baba. She pushed the phone away. "Well, I get my news from here all the time. I don't really watch TV anymore for that. Most stuff gets updated on social media."

"All the same, I think you can put it down for a little while. Watch some TV. Read a book. Go for a walk although don't do that now, it's too dark. Maybe if you want, you can go back to the gym and get some exercise. Do it for your mental health, not just the physical. It'll take your mind off things. You need that."

"I'll think about it, Baba. Right now, I want some rest." Kara grabbed her food, nodding to her father before he could go into how important other hobbies were. She didn't need that right now. She knew being on the phone all the time wasn't good for her emotionally or physically. Unfortunately, it was the best way for her to keep up to date with everything. News hit social media a lot quicker than it hit anything else. She didn't have to wait for the TV news to bring it when someone online brought it to her. She didn't believe everything from it, of course, accepting the social media information once she did her own research. There was no way to escape it in this time and age. Even if she did take on another hobby, her mind would be on the phone and wondering what bombshell would drop next.

He always thinks going to the gym will solve everything. That part got her the most. While there was truth behind it helping her out mentally as well as physically, she had neither time nor money to spend in a gym. The gym wouldn't keep Thomas from sending her texts, nor would it keep him from killing others. The most it would do is help her health, but that wasn't the main issue. She wished her father wouldn't jump straight to exercise as a solution. It wasn't the only thing in the world she could do.

"God, I need something." Putting the food down, she went to take her medicine. Somehow in all the chaos, she remembered to take her meds on time. She was late on some nights but still managed to take them. Her psychiatrist gave her enough meds to get her through the next month, so she wasn't ready to make changes to them. They all worked right now, keeping her calm during intense situations. Her heart still pounded in her chest, but she no longer had that added dizziness or nausea from earlier. She didn't have another appointment with her therapist until the following week though she wanted to postpone that. With Thomas holding her down, she couldn't talk about everything bugging her. She'd say vague nothings about her stress from work and her parents. They'd want to dive deeper, but she'd hold them at bay for now. Thankfully, she had time to come with answers.

Swallowing her pills, she left the bathroom and began to fiddle around with the phone. This was the other thing about hobbies: many people learned how to do things simply from watching videos. Classes were too expensive and often required people to buy their own materials from their stores. Here, she could get whatever she needed from a place nearby and for much cheaper. Most videos had easy, understandable instructions that suited all kinds of people. Why did she need to do a hobby without the use of her phone? Why did she need to do anything without? Her poor father still didn't understand some parts of the world. Even though he himself had a Facebook account and cell phone, he didn't see how much it changed on him. Then again, that's what she got for having Baby Boomer parents. They didn't have half the things she had when growing up. They reminisced about the days where they'd play outside and learn things from watching others, not watching TV or playing on the computer. For those reasons, Kara often struggled to see them eye to eye. Their own stubbornness kept them from opening their minds to new ideas. They were a little better about things now than in the past. She was able to get them to see the importance behind certain political issues and how they affected everyone. Even though their old Indian ways sometimes crept into conversations, they were willing to listen to her.

At the same time, she still wanted to leave home. She loved them, of course. She knew they always wanted the best things for her and gave support when she asked for it. But they weren't always understanding of all her issues. At home, she wasn't free to do anything she wanted. She still had rules to follow such as being home before midnight, letting them know where she went, and answering her phone when they called. She reminded them that she wasn't a baby anymore, she didn't need them for everything, yet that bit hadn't sunk in. Kara was their only child, their baby, the one they lived to protect. It didn't matter how old she got. She wasn't going past that infant age in their eyes. They were going to help her and get into her life whether she asked for it or not.

Bzzt...bzzt...

God, there it was. Her phone started blaring off messages with several coming in from different sources. Three were restaurants offering a buy one, get one free meal. Tempting as they were, she no longer had urges to stop by during her shifts. Some of them came from updates on social media, reminding her of things going around the world. Two were appointment reminders for next week as well as a reminder to fill out her questionnaire beforehand. One came from a voting poll, demanding donations for their campaign. Another one was a message from a cousin reminding her how much they loved her. And then there came the one message from the one person she didn't want.

Hello there, Kara. I know you're not driving now. You've got no reason to drive.

What makes him think that? She squinted and closed her eyes, hoping the message would go away. She never gave him her number, yet he got it. He texted her outside of work hours, always wanting her attention. Worst of all, she had to give it to him. He already vowed to bring harm if she dared disobey.

BZZZT!

Not a text now. Her phone's ringtone, a strange scratchy sound, blared through the room. Thomas was calling her. No more texts, just a straight up call. She peered out of her bedroom window, catching sight of her mother and father talking in the hallway. Good, they were alive. Then she turned back to the phone, her thumb wavering. What did he want? If it was urgent, why call her instead of texting? Walking on tiptoes, she checked every inch of her room in case he opted to hide. No, he wasn't there. He wasn't lurking in the corners. Thomas didn't lurk like this. He planned everything from start to finish.

Holding her breath, she pressed her thumb down and answered. "Hello?"

"Don't sound so hostile there, Kara. It's only me." Thomas snickered on the other end. Even his laughter went under her skin, pulling away at her insides. "I just wanted to compliment you on a good job today. You drive like a dream."

"You told me that earlier. You told me that a lot of times." Kara ran to her window, pulling the blinds apart. Darkness covered the neighborhood, but that didn't mean she was safe. "Look, I'm off my time and you promised..."

"I'm aware of my promises. You remind me all the time. You can't get paid if you drive outside of your normal hours. You don't like driving late at night. You have to pay for your own gas cause Happy

Riders doesn't give you much. I know that already, Kara. I wouldn't dare bend the rules that Happy Riders installed."

Kara couldn't remember how many times she told him all that, but her mind lost count ages ago. Other things bugged her more. "You know there's a curfew, right? They're not letting anyone stay out after 10 PM."

"I heard of that as well, Kara, but that doesn't concern us. You work until 9 PM, remember? We never drive so far that you don't make it home before 10 PM. Maybe I can't linger around shopping centers for long, but that doesn't affect the work I do."

"And that's another thing; you never told me why you did any of this." Kara choked out. By now, her curiosity and fear hit the roof at the same time. "Can you at least give me a reason? Why her? Why any of them? What are you going to get out of killing someone besides sick pleasure?"

The pause on the other end gave her the message; she caught him, but he wasn't about to tell her. Likewise, she wasn't about to stop pressing. Her eyes back on the windows, she stared into the dark streets expecting to find him lurking by the lamppost. "Well, maybe I like sick pleasure. Did that occur to you?"

"No, that's not it." She squinted through the blinds at something rustling in the bushes. Some rodents popped out and scurried across the grass. She clutched her chest as it disappeared, before going on. "You have a bigger reason than that. All these people are like me, alone and working these simple jobs. There's a ton of us like that out there. Don't you remember the first conversation we had? The one about how hard it is to find work?"

Again, he left her with a long pause as she listened to his ragged breathing. This wasn't the slow, quiet breathing she got in the car when he sat in the backseat. He breathed rough on the other end, so she pressed a little further. "What makes me different from them?"

"You're still trying, Kara." He rasped out. That cold voice turned into one of a smoker puffing away at the end of their cigar. "You want something better out of life. You don't want to drive people around for the rest of your life."

"Well, no, but at the moment, I don't have many options. I can try all I want, but that doesn't mean I'll get anything. What made you think none of them tried? You don't know everything about them."

"...You still don't get it, do you? I've been throwing the answer in your face, and you still don't get it."

"No, I don't." By now, her patience hit its limit. "Maybe I'm not as smart as you think. Maybe I care too much about the reasons behind things. You don't have a reason to hurt anyone. You don't know Anne or anyone else out there. You don't even know me!"

"I know enough. I've seen enough. People like Anne, like all of them...they get complacent in their menial jobs. They'll die stuck in their same old hole. I'm only helping them along." He cleared his throat to stop rasping. Then came the cold, familiar voice. "That's not the reason I called you, or the reason you replied."

"Then why are you calling?" She checked the hallway again. Her parents no longer stood in it, but their voices rang in the kitchen, talking about how to help Kara find work. Cringing, she pulled back into her bedroom. "What do you want if it isn't a ride?"

"I'm just checking up on my favorite driver. Is that such a crime?"

"No, but murder and kidnapping are crimes. Look, I don't understand who you are or what you really want. I don't know why you're doing any of this, or why I'm dragged along. I'm not that great of a driver for you to keep requesting me. What will it take, huh? Why can't you leave me alone?"

"And miss our fun times together? You wound me, Kara." Then his voice lowered, rough like ground gravel. "I'll let you off tonight for all that talk. After all, I called you, not the other way around. Next time though...don't use that one with me. And don't try to pull anything else on me. You won't succeed, sweetheart. It's you and me through the whole thing."

"When you're done, then what?" She sat on her bed, now violently shaking. This was never about these victims. Thomas got a thrill from killing, but his greater thrill came from pulling Kara into his game. "What will you do?"

He stopped for a long minute before replying. "It never ends, Kara. That's the thing. It won't end until one, or both of us, is done playing. Now which one that will be...we'll have to wait and see. Have a good night and get some rest. Your next ride is coming up soon."

He hung up, but Kara got all the answers she needed. This game wouldn't end until one of them died. Thomas didn't intend to go down, so her chances of survival dwindled with each hour. The quickest way to win would be to get the upper hand on him. Reading the articles on The Traveler could help. Laying on her bed, she began to search for more clues on him. Did anyone survive and get a description? Going through each one, she came to one of the victims who was found alive yet died shortly afterwards in the hospital. While her identity remained anonymous, the police were able to get a little out of her.

"A male...older male..." Kara nodded despite that description fitting a million people. The one thing that stood out were the words 'brown' and 'wine,' which didn't fit Thomas at all. The entire time they drove around, he never once asked to stop at a bar or liquor store. He never bought any alcohol either. Police figured the brown wine must have been something she drank, yet no trace of alcohol was in her system. Thomas didn't get the victims drunk before killing. Going through other articles, they all read the same: every victim was sober. Not one drop of beer or wine ran through them. In addition to that, no victim was sexually assaulted. No one was robbed. Just kidnapped, bound, and killed.

"So, if not for sex or money, why go after them?" The question kept burning in the back of her mind. The victims needed her to solve their cases. She still saw them in her dreams, all reaching for her with flesh falling off, revealing their bones.

Stop him, Kara. Stop him before he kills again. Only you can do it.

"Stop him how?" She stared into the air, wanting the answer to fall into her lap. "The only way I can think to stop is to kill him. But...But I'm not like him! I can't kill! I can't..."

You can stop him, Kara. He's in power now. Take it from him.

"Take his power?" Kara rubbed her eyes. "I know he's in power, but how do I take it away? I'm just a rideshare driver. I do this to make money while looking for work. I never asked to be part of it. I never wanted to..."

Only you can stop him now, Kara. You'll find your way.

Find her way. The analogy burned her given that it was one of Happy Riders mottos. No matter where they went, everyone would find their way. Well, she needed to rely on that motto now. She had to find her way out of this situation. Grab the wheel and drive right out. Happy Riders sent her another message of her next workday, as well as a reminder of her payment. She got her money, all right, but her comfortable life was now at risk. She would lose everything with one wrong move.

Thomas sent her another message, big and bold, with a sentence that she couldn't forget. Even hours later, it stuck in her mind, burying itself deep. She wasn't getting out easily.

Buckle up, baby. We're in for a couple of bumpy rides.

Chapter 10

Kara's next ride with Thomas came not long after his creepy phone call and text. She was already out and dropping off other people, none of them giving her the creeps the way Thomas did. They were friendly with her, making small talk and keeping her mind off The Traveler's escapades. They didn't ask her for her opinion on his killings, which she was grateful for. She didn't want to divulge anything that she knew. All the previous riders thanked her for the ride when she got them to their destinations. Some reminded her to be careful while driving. One of them even promised to give her a good review, which set her heart fluttering. Good reviews from these riders kept her going.

Then came Thomas' ride, only a few miles from her previous drop off. Without checking his message, she accepted it and checked the clock. Still an hour before her shift ended. She could drop him off at home or wherever he wanted to go. Hopefully, he would be in a good mood today. She held her breath the entire drive towards a shopping center. He'd be right in front of a bed and bath store, which wasn't his style. What could he want in that place?

Then again, these places do sell cutlery sometimes. I've seen knives and kitchen sets all around. She sniffled as she drove into the parking lot. With plenty of people around, he wouldn't be stupid enough to cause any troubles. He didn't want anyone's attention especially given that Kara had the car. If he tried anything, she hit the gas and drove out, ignoring him in the process. Biting her bottom lip, she found the bed and bath store where he waved at her, holding a plastic bag. Funny, it didn't look big enough to carry a knife set. She couldn't make out the shape of a knife in it either. What did he buy here?

Unlocking the door, she parked on the curb as he climbed in. "Good afternoon, Thomas. Did you enjoy shopping?"

"Oh, I didn't shop much today, Kara. I saw all those sales and deals, but nothing really appealed to me. That's why I'm going to a different store. Go figure it's about fifteen minutes away." He glanced around the seats before tuning back to her, blue eyes twinkling. "Do you have any room in front of you?"

"Um, yeah?" Kara stared down at the empty passenger seat. She didn't let people come on this side unless there was a big group of them. Right now, Thomas was by himself. "Is there something you need?"

"I hope you don't mind if I put this in the passenger seat. No one is using that." He didn't wait for a reply before dumping the bag next to her. "I didn't know where else to put it. Since it's so small, we don't need to pop up the trunk."

"Okay." Kara gulped as the bag shifted when she moved forward. "Is this something you bought that you're returning?"

"No, I have to buy some more stuff actually. That's the main reason I'm calling you today. I'm missing a few things. I tried looking for them here to no avail. Worst of all, no one's around to help you out. I can't blame them cause the economy is in the pits. Still, it would be nice for a little help" He sat back, nodding at her to pay attention. "Watch where you're going, Kara. I would hate for you to have an accident because you weren't paying attention."

"Right." She went back to the road, only glancing once or twice at the GPS for where to turn. She knew this shopping center well, which baffled her. If Thomas stalked his victims, why do it in broad daylight? Unless this was his way of creating alibis. If people saw him, they could say he wasn't The Traveler. He was shopping like everyone else in the area. She pictured him friendly with the staff, politely asking questions and making small conversations. Like her, he'd win them over with his friendly demeanor. He made them all happy like cows right before they headed to the slaughterhouse.

That fifteen-minute ride to the other shopping center went on for a long time thanks to so much traffic on the road. She kept her watch on the other drivers, trying not to cut anyone off. She drove at a rapid yet steady pace, careful not to get caught by the cops. The only time she ever received a speeding ticket was when she went 30 in a 25-mph speed zone. She hadn't noticed the speedometer going up, yet the cop caught her and handed her the ticket without hearing her side of the story. Since that day, she hadn't screwed around with them.

Catching sight of Thomas, she wondered about the contents of his bag. This wasn't a bag from the Bed and Bath store, which usually were orange in color. This bag was gray, so he clearly didn't go there. More importantly, the bath store had stronger handles so people could carry the heavier items. This was a shopping bag from a grocery store, and as far as she knew, this shopping center had no grocery store. Some things were not adding up, but she didn't question it as she drove into the next parking lot. Thomas leaned back in his seat, stretching his arms towards the top of the car.

"Another quiet, easy drive. You are a natural at this." He waited until she began to slow down. "You can just drop me off at the curb, then go park.

"Why are we here now?" She couldn't help asking, shuddering at the lack of cars. "I don't think this place is open."

"Oh, they opened at 8 AM today. They're going out of business so that's why you may not see much." He pointed to the signs hanging all over the windows. EVERYTHING MUST GO and STORE CLOSING screamed back at her. The emptiness only intensified the fear in her. Thomas got out, making his way to her driver's side, and leaning into the window. Those blue eyes glinted, scheming away at something awful. Kara left her hands on the wheel while his face moved in. "I'm gonna buy some stuff. It'll take about five minutes, maybe ten at most. You can cut the engine, even walk around a little bit. No one's here." He nodded at the empty lot around them. "Talk on the phone. Play games. Listen to music. Do anything you like, Kara, except don't look in the bag. It's nothing of importance to you."

Kara nodded though she feared the worst. She could make a million guesses on what was in the bag, none of them good. Years ago, she watched an old movie called *Seven* with her family. Her parents squirmed at some of the deaths, all of them influenced by the seven deadly sins, but the final moments with Brad Pitt yelling about what was in the box stood out. That along with Morgan Freeman's reaction gave away that nothing good came out of the box. Here she was in a similar situation, with a plastic bag. The difference was that Thomas failed to tie it up. The handles stood up in the air, tempting her to pull them apart and peek. The contents didn't appear to be the size of a human head, but she wouldn't put it past him to stuff some other body part there. She moved her hand towards it, then pulled away. If she touched that bag, she'd leave her DNA over it too. Should the police finally discover who Thomas was, they'd find out about her too. Her parents spent nights watching plenty of crime shows to know that criminals always left a piece of themselves behind. The less she got involved, the less trouble she'd end up in

Oh, what the hell am I doing? I'm screwed no matter what happens! Common sense no longer mattered here. She didn't need to touch the bag, but one quick glance wouldn't hurt. She wouldn't dig through the contents, just check it out. Leave it on the seat while peering inside. Letting her hands fall to the side, she leaned in to get a look. Something orange...no, a darker orange. A thing close to red poked out of the bag. Thomas couldn't blame her for this. He was the careless one with his things. He left this bag on her seat, slightly open for the whole world to see. He couldn't blame her if she saw it, no matter how much he warned her. She inched closer and yanked back once the horrible smell hit her.

"Oh God!" Waving her hand over her face, she began breathing through her mouth. This was no human skull, but she still didn't want to drive it around. He did something last night or even earlier this morning. Someone got in his way, and now, the remains sat in that plastic bag. "Oh God, what did you do? What did..."

No, she couldn't ignore any of this. What made Thomas think it was okay to dump this bag of human remains on her chair?

Her passenger side reeked of death from the bag. Plugging her nose with a napkin, she gingerly pushed the plastic bag open to find clumps of red hair matted with thick, dark blood. Not Anne's hair who was a brunette, but another person. Someone else either died or suffered that night with Thomas yanking chunks of thick, red hair out. The bile from her stomach ran up throat and hit the front of her mouth.

That rotten smell. She couldn't forget the blood on her backseat, and this hair had the same one. He killed again. He killed someone and never called for a ride. The long red strand couldn't give away the gender, yet Kara could figure out this person was much like her. A person living alone and working a boring job. He found out about them, buttered them with kind words, snatched them up, bound them, and then bled them out.

"I THOUGHT I TOLD YOU TO STAY AWAY!" Thomas' hand yanked Kara's hair, pulling her back. His grip tightened as she whimpered from the pain as his other hand covered her mouth. "I said don't look, Kara. That doesn't mean you do the opposite of what I say."

"I'm sorry..." Kara attempted to muffle through his palm. She tried to force her teeth out so she could bite him, force him to let her go. His hand pushed harder as she bit down on her tongue. Since he silenced her screams, she thrashed around in hopes someone noticed this. As empty as the lot was, someone had to see this and call for help.

Come on! Help me! He's killing me!

"Bad move, Kara. I thought you were smarter than that." His knife flashed in the sunlight, pressed close to her neck. "I thought I could trust you to follow the simplest instructions. Clearly, I was wrong. You let your curiosity get the best of you."

"Let me go..." Her tongue pushed against the back of her teeth, trying to get him off. If he loosened his grip, she could attack. Her hands splayed around her, trying to grab something to attack him. Nothing sat inside the glove compartment that could make a decent weapon. With him yanking her hair, her arms went up to the ceiling, fingernails digging at the top.

Oh God, I'm gonna die. I fucked up. I'm going to die. As her flailing slowed down, Thomas loosened the hand on her mouth, patting her on the lips. His rough flesh brushing against her left her vulnerable and broken. No wonder he kept telling her it was foolish to fight back. He didn't let her go, nearly ripping her hair out of her skull. Shivering, she dropped her hands by her side. She didn't dare fight now that he brought out the knife.

"You're lucky that you're you, Kara." He whispered. "You're a little naïve and that works in your favor. Being curious doesn't. Granted, I realize part of this is my fault. I left the bag open, so naturally you could see inside."

Kara winced as he tugged on her hair though tried hard not to cry out. "What did you do? Who did you hurt?"

"You'll learn soon enough. Now normally, I'd have cut your throat out for disobeying but, since you know my secrets and you've followed directions well, I'll let you go. I made a mistake by not tying up that bag. That's why I'll let you live. You and those you love, that is. However, I can't have you mess up like this again so..."

With the knife, he began to cut away at her hair, clumps of it falling. Kara couldn't scream as it fell all around her, wanting him to stop. Why her hair? Her parents would demand to know what she did if she showed up like this.

"Stop...please stop..." She pleaded as he dropped more hair around her. "I got the message. I won't do this again!"

"Of course you won't do it again. You know better now." He finally pulled away, so she got a look in the mirror. The right half of her hair was now shorter than the left, looking all jagged and frizzy. The left side of hair fell to her shoulders while the right side stopped right at her ear. "You can do what you want with that later. For now, we're going back. I have what I need."

Kara bit down on her bottom to keep from crying. She didn't care for the hair as much; in time, it would all grow back. She could style and fix it, so it didn't appear crooked. Her frizzy bits were long gone. Her skull burned from his pulling, almost setting off a migraine. The fact that he got close to her, he yanked on her hair, and cut it off? This was his warning. The only warning he'd give. If she crossed him again, she'd end up like the victim in that bag, whoever that was. She buckled her seatbelt, started up the car, and began to drive out of the lot. No one arrived in the whole time he held onto her. He had every opportunity to kill her, dump her body, and run off like before. He didn't.

He's still not telling me why he does any of this. She pushed away the remaining long hair, focusing on her driving. Thomas didn't say another word after that though he held onto the knife. No blood this time around, but it frightened her all the same. *Or maybe he is telling me everything. Maybe I really am naïve like he thinks. I can't figure out his methods or goals. The only clues he's thrown out are these people are worthless. But how are they worthless for working jobs, and why doesn't he consider me that way?*

Then she recalled what he said about her trying. He knew she looked for work in between. Luck wasn't on her side, yet she kept trying. He admired that about her. He liked that she didn't give up, and didn't resort to this as her entire future. He knew she wanted out one day. Well, she still wanted out of this mess. She couldn't quit working with Happy Riders yet. The moment she found out his next victim, she'd get there before he did.

As she pulled into McIver Drive, he leaned over and gazed into her mirror. "You really should have someone fix that hair of yours. It was always a bird's nest."

It took fear to keep her from pushing him back. He already took things too far, now he wanted to insult her appearance. Her hair was never perfect, but she prided herself with how wavy and long it was. Everyone gushed that she got hair from her mother, so silky and strong. They envied her for having no gray hair or needing to dye it. No one ever mocked it for anything except being a little unkempt. Now, it was a complete mess thanks to Thomas. She held her tongue as she parked the car. "I can fix it myself. It won't be hard."

"I'm sure it won't." His eyes scanned her neck where bits of hair lay. Brushing those off, he gently pulled back the remaining long. "Make sure someone straightens this out. You can't go out like this."

No shit. I didn't lose my mind...yet. She restrained herself from being sarcastic. The more time she spent with him, the more desperate she became to battle him with something. Words, knives, anything. Next time, she vowed to have something ready to fight. If he grabbed her, she'd claw at him, dig his skin, bite him, leave some mark behind. She remembered several self-defense classes back in the day where the instructors told the students to leave their mark. That little bit they left on the perp could be all that was left of them. The remains of her hair itched the back of her neck as she started to put the car in reverse.

"Wait!" Thomas slammed the window as she hit the break. Rolling down her window, she sucked in her breath as he came closer and flicked a bug off her shoulder. "That thing was on you the entire time. Watch your body please. You don't want anything to crawl on you and bite when you least expect it."

"No, I don't." Kara waited till he backed away. "I'll wait for your next call then."

"Good. Enjoy the rest of your night, Kara."

As she drove off, she kept glancing behind her and then in the mirrors. She had plenty of hats and headbands in the trunk to hide the lopsided mess. The harder part would be getting rid of her hair. Racking her brain, she remembered the kit with several tools and items in her trunk including scissors. Her father gave it to her, reminding her that it had everything she needed if she were in trouble. She scoffed at it, believing she had no use, but now its day had come. Once she left McIver Drive, she drove a few miles down and got off at the first exit. She knew this area since many other riders came here to shop or eat. Pulling into the lot of the first shopping center, she parked far from others and popped open the trunk. There was that kit tucked all the way in the corner. She reached back and found it half open, the scissors sitting on top.

"I'm no stylist but I'll do my best." The box contained a small mirror, which she propped up to watch herself. They weren't the strongest scissors in the world, not meant for cutting hair, but they'd do. Carefully, she chopped the locks off, gathering the bits in one area. She cut until both sides appeared similar. Grabbing the mirror, she checked it all out. That could do for now. Grabbing a headband, she wrapped up the bottom part, tucking her hair into it.

"This will have to do." She tied up the headband before grabbing the clump of hair and tossing it in the trash. Checking the clock, she still had a little time before getting home and one more ride waiting for her. The rider was only five minutes away, so she accepted it, got revved up the engine again, and drove. Checking on the rider, she breathed easy at this being a woman and not Thomas. She was driving someone else.

"God, I've been driving him around that I forgot about everyone else." She pushed back some loose hair that fell out and checked all her seats. No hair or stains in sight. Getting into the parking lot, she found three teenage girls waiting for her, loads of shopping bags on each of their arms. Pulling to the curb, she opened the trunk and doors before getting out to help them. "You guys need me to put that stuff in?"

"Nah, we got it." One of them put the bags away and shut the trunk. "Thanks anyway. And thanks for picking us up. I kept getting a million messages from my mom telling me not to be out so late."

"Because of the curfew?"

"More like a creepy killer." Another girl shuddered as they all got inside and settled in. "She thinks he's going to come after us."

"And you're not afraid?" Kara checked her mirrors before moving away from the curb. "I would be. I get why your mother's calling. This curfew got everyone scared."

"Yeah, I get that. But he only goes after people older than us, right? That's what people said all over social media. Only older people are in trouble."

Kara fell quiet as she focused on the drive ahead. All the victims were older than these girls, but that didn't mean Thomas wouldn't change his mind. If he didn't get them today, he'd get them later. She eased down the road, hoping that the conversation about the murders ended here. The moment she turned the corner, she switched the topic. "So, did you enjoy shopping?"

"Totally. I upgraded my wardrobe." The third girl replied. "Can you believe I have clothes from 2021? Ugh, I almost puked when I went through my closet. Thank God I can toss some of that crap out!"

"Yeah, I totally need to upgrade my wardrobe too." That was a partial truth. Kara found herself growing bored with her old outfits, wanting one day for shopping for new clothes. Her free days were supposed to be for her to do what she wanted. Yet each second that passed by, she forgot all about her desire for new threads. She didn't even know what was in style this season. "Tell me, is it boot season already? I got a pair that I've barely worn."

"Boots are still in. I wanted some boots with sturdy soles in case I have to...you know, if I've got to run from him. I don't want anything with super high heels or any heels. In case they break or, on the worst-case chance, I fall...I just want a chance to get away."

"I see." Kara's words stuck in her throat. This girl wanted boots without heels, not for fashion, but for fear of running into Thomas. She wanted shoes she could run for her life. The fact that she even thought of this messed with Kara's head. How could Thomas live with himself? He had every single person on high alert, thinking of escape plans. Even when she went on TikTok, she found numerous videos about what to do if The Traveler caught them. Everyone mentioned not giving too much information about themselves. Keeping safe distances from strangers. Never accepting a ride from strangers. Being alert of their surroundings and never going out alone. Thinking about all of that watered her eyes. No one deserved to live this way, wondering if this was the last time they'd do anything.

"Hey, you okay?" The girl frowned upon seeing Kara's tears fall. "I didn't say anything wrong, did I?"

"No, you didn't." Kara wiped her eyes as they slowed down to a red light. "It's just...it must be my allergies acting up. I should probably take my medication before my next ride. I really hope they get this guy. He's been doing this way too long."

"Oh, yeah, I want that too. I want to be able to go out at night and not worry about some creep stalking me. It's really freaking annoying." The girl fanned her face before reaching up to wipe her brow. "Do you mind opening a window? It's getting hot in the car."

"Sure." Kara opened the window a crack. "Is that good or do you want it lower?"

"That's good. You're doing fine." The girl reached over to grab some of Kara's snacks but stopped for a second. "Look, don't worry about it. I don't think this guy's coming after you."

"What…What makes you think that?" Kara grabbed a tissue to wipe her eyes. Thankfully, the first light she came across turned red so she could slow down and clean herself up. "He might change his mind."

"He won't. You're tough. You would never let a guy like him take you down. I can tell. It's just your aura."

Her aura. The girl was doing her best to cheer her up, but it didn't remove her fear. She knew Thomas. She dealt with him. She wouldn't escape him until one of them died. In spite of this, she couldn't reveal a thing. Kara finished crying as she drove on. She wanted this girl to go back to her normal life. She wanted her own life back too. She wanted to drive in the late hours, pick up food without worrying about who watched her, and wear boots with heels without wondering how to run in them. She wanted all of that back. No Thomas to haunt her and make her do his bidding. She got it all as she drove the girl to her destination. She wasn't just fighting for her life. She fought for her future riders. She had to beat Thomas for their sake.

Soon. She took a turn towards the destination. *We'll get off this ride soon.*

Chapter 11

Kara thanked her stars when she got home to find her parents back in the living room. Neither asked about the hair change as they talked to relatives back in India. Her mother caught her as she talked on the phone, motioning Kara to come over. Kara breathed in as she approached the sofa. On the other side, she heard her grandfather speaking. Good. She had a lot to ask him, but not enough to ask the important questions. Getting on the phone, she greeted him while laying down on the couch. If there was one thing her grandfather would tell her, it was the future. He had some skill in predicting how someone's life was going. He paid attention to birth charts, the planets, and stars, seeing how they aligned. Right now, she wanted some good news for the future.

"There are dark clouds, Karishma." He began. "The stars...it seems that you are in some trouble. It will disrupt your life."

Of course. It's already happened. Kara kicked her feet into the air, stretching her legs out. "How long are these dark clouds going to last, Dadu? I, um...is there any sign of them going away?"

"They'll go, but...you will get caught in so much turmoil. Your heart is in pain. You are confused about what you need to do."

"...Yeah, I am." She let her feet drop, then sat up. Her hair remained back in the bun, much to her relief. No one knew of the messed-up locks. "I'm in so much...turmoil, Dadu. My head's spinning. There's so much going on, and yet there's not enough happening in my personal life. Tell me there's something good coming. Will it be soon?"

"Well, your turmoil will end quickly. The stars are shifting in your favor. However, it won't happen so easily. You won't get rid of the trouble until you face it head on. The moment you push back, the clouds will go away."

"Face the problem." She cringed inside. It wasn't the first time she received that bit of advice. The universe told her to fight back. Now her stars were telling her grandfather that it was time. Thomas had to go. Get rid of him, get rid of the clouds. "Okay, Dadu. I get what you're getting at. My whole future depends on it."

"It does. Be careful with everything you do, Karishma. I want you to be happy. Stay healthy and wise."

"I want that too. I want a better life than this. Do you have any idea when that will happen? Please say it's soon."

"You'll get it. If you do the right thing, everything will be fine. Now you can give it back to your mother. Take good care, Karishma."

"Likewise, Dadu. I'll talk to you soon." Kara handed the phone back before heading to her room, shutting the door behind her. Thank God her grandfather didn't want to hear about her day. Somehow, he predicted that she only wanted to talk about the future, not the present. She couldn't tell him a whole lot anyway. Her parents would be close by, hearing whatever she spilled out. At least with the predictions, they'd stay too vague for anyone to figure out.

Dark clouds on the horizon, huh? I wish he could give me more than that.

She went back to the last rider who bought clothes that were practical for escaping. The girl made it home in one piece and left yet another good review. The only thing of note was that Kara started crying, which she figured must have been allergies. That was the perfect excuse. If anyone else caught her crying, she'd tell them it was allergies kicking up.

She puttered around the house, mind drifting off, before going to bed early. Her new hairdo bothered her. No black locks spilled down her back. She couldn't tie it up anymore, braid it, or do any fancy styles. Her hairbands were useless. Tossing around in bed, she took at least two hours to fall asleep. Her hair spilling around her, part of it shorter than the other, couldn't make things comfortable. Even in the morning, as she got out of bed, she still expected the other part of her to roll down to her shoulders. Only one part did.

"Shit." She held out the part with the jagged cuts. No, she couldn't live like this. She couldn't pretend it was a cool new hairdo. Even if she got away with hiding it yesterday and this morning, she couldn't pretend like this forever. Her mother often liked to style and dye her hair, calling Kara over when she had a moment to do so. She had to fix this before her mother touched it. A quick style and cut could be explained.

Tucking her hair into a small bun saved her from revealing the new cut. Given that Thomas hadn't called her for another ride and her mornings were free, she quickly scheduled a hair appointment to get the cut layers fixed. Her mother bugged her for ages about taking care of the split ends; now she got her wish. Checking her face in the mirror, she quickly fixed the mascara and tried on some soft green eyeshadow. These days, any color but red gave her comfort. It didn't matter what the shade; all shades of red, including shades of pink, reminded her of blood. She never got rid of that image of Thomas smashing his bloodied print against her window. He didn't forget about his soaked clothing, hair and cheeks streaked with red, and his blue eyes. God, those eyes held so much hatred. Day after day, his glares intensified. Even when he yanked her hair, she feared that steely blue stare burning into her.

Checking her phone, she got the notification of her appointment at 10 AM. Confirming that and tucking the last strands of hair in, she grabbed her coat and jogged towards the kitchen. Neither parent was there nor the news blaring on the TV. The message taped to the fridge revealed they had gone to temple for some early morning prayers. She sent them a quick text to let them know her plans. Hopefully, they'd pray for long and hard, for her health, her prospects, and getting out of Thomas' grasp. She turned towards the prayer room in their house, a small area where her mother set up all the pictures and small statues of deities. Hanging right above it was the garland of jasmine and other small flowers with a tiny 'om' painted on top of the door frame. Kara rarely went into this room except for special occasions. She prayed away from the house, keeping everything silent and to herself. The sweet scent of jasmine tempted her towards the door, so she caved in and pushed it open. In the corner stood the small altar of deities and their photos. Some flower petals lay right by them along with fresh fruit her mother laid out this morning. The offerings. Kara gazed at her empty hands before walking over, kneeling, and bowing her head.

"I know I don't come here much anymore. I'm not sure what to say. I don't know where to start." She clasped her hands. The gods understood English. Her mother told her the language didn't matter;

they knew everything. "And I can't believe I'm here now, but I'm scared. I don't know how I can get out of this. That man is either going to end up killing another lonely person or my family or me. Everyone's telling me to stop him. I know I should, but I'm afraid he's going to find out. When he does, well...look at what he did." She untied her bun to reveal her now shortened, jagged locks. "I'm just lucky it wasn't my neck he shoved that knife into."

The gods stared back with their empty eyes, but they heard everything. Kara lit an incense stick and let it burn while she continued praying. *Please, God. If you are out there, if you have an answer, give it to me.*

The incense burned down as she raised her head and clasped her hands. "Please..."

As she left the prayer room, she found the pad where her mother wrote the message. Messages on paper. She didn't have the phone numbers of potential victims, but she could still get a message across. The pebbles were one way even if the person wasn't home. Maybe adding a little extra something could save them. After all, people didn't always have texting and phones. They came up with other ways to send the word. Grabbing a pen, she began writing a few warning notes for the next time Thomas tried hurting someone.

YOU ARE IN DANGER! GET OUT OF THE HOUSE! NOW! GET OUT OF YOUR HOUSE! SOMEONE'S AFTER YOU! CALL THE POLICE AND LEAVE! DO IT NOW!

The all caps and thick bold letters could grab anyone's attention. Thomas never saw her handwriting so he couldn't figure this out. The moment he left for whatever he did, she'd send the warning out. Leave it by the windowsill, in their mailbox, throw it through the window or at the door. Give them enough time to get away from his grasp. That was her first chance. The second part would be getting the police involved. With her knowing so much, they wouldn't accept her explanations as easily. Even if they believed Thomas was The Traveler and arrested him, they'd take her in too for aiding him. Granted, this wasn't something she agreed to on purpose, but what cop would believe that? Even a so-called good cop wouldn't let her off scot-free. As long as Thomas lived, she stayed free.

Then there were her parents. They'd never live if they learned about her aiding and abetting a criminal. Not only was she a failure in a professional setting, but she was also a criminal. She might as well have been the one holding the knife. No, nothing good could come out of this, so why hesitate anymore? The incense wafting from the prayer room sparked something new in her. She had nothing more to lose at this point. Might as well go out doing the right thing. Gazing towards the prayer room, she prayed towards it one more time.

"Thank you. I really hope I'm doing the right thing for all of us."

With no new messages save for her parents saying they were stopping for lunch with friends, she put out the incense and headed towards the beauty salon. Given how early they started, she was amazed that the receptionist at front had a spot for her. She didn't comment on Kara's messy locks, so Kara was happy to take the appointment and wait her turn. Her hair would return to normal.

Her stylist came over to get her, checking on everything, and leading her straight to a chair. A girl with pink streaks in her hair, nose ring in her left nostril, and arms with colorful tattoos going around her body. As she took out the bun, she examined all the ends. "Whoa! What happened here? Did you lay down next to a lawnmower or something?"

That would have been less painful. Kara almost snapped back but stopped herself. The poor thing meant no harm. She reacted like any normal person would over this. "Nah, I had a little accident. I was messing with the incense and candles in my parents' house, my hair got a little too close to the flames, and well…"

"Ah, you don't have to say it. You tried to fix it, and this was the result. You're not the first person to burn their hair." The girl pulled her hair back. "So, you need this even out and shaped up. I can do that. Do you have any specific style you want?"

"Not really. I just need my hair looking…well, not so wonky, you know? If you can think of a style that won't freak my family out, that works."

"Yup, I got an idea on what to do. You just sit back and relax. I'll work my magic." Kara leaned back as more women walked around them. She couldn't help but envy how carefree they appeared, chatting and sipping drinks that the salon offered them. If they knew about Thomas, they weren't walking around in fear of their lives. They went about their day without worrying about who could be watching them.

The hairstylist played around with Kara's hair a little longer, checking out the cut strands. "Jeez, you did a number over here! Hand a hard time doing it yourself, huh?"

"I'm not a stylist, so I did what I could." None of those were lies. Kara cut her hair with the small scissors to even the sides, not to give herself a makeover. "This isn't too much of a problem for you, is it?"

"Nah, I've seen a heck lot worse than this. I do think you could benefit from shampoo and rinse though. Will make it a little easier for me to cut."

Kara agreed to it, following her to the hair washing section. Pushing her head up to the sink, she closed her eyes as hot water ran through those strands. The moment a bit splashed on her forehead, she whimpered from the burn. "Please make the water cooler. That's hurting me."

"Oh, sorry." Cold water mixed in, letting her calm down. "Is that better?"

"A lot better, thanks." Kara pulled herself up higher to support her neck, clasped her hands together, and closed her eyes. "Just let me know when you're done."

"Will do. Just sit back and relax." She began to collect all of Kara's hair, holding it out and playing around with it. "Yeah, I think I know what I can do. It won't cost you extra either. Let me just look around..."

As the girl continued to play around, Kara focused on the scene around her. Given that most of the stylists were students, many of them often called for instructors to help. This one didn't bother asking for help. She narrowed her eyes on the cut strands, nodding to herself and shaking when something didn't make sense. The smell of shampoo and hairspray started to shake up Kara's mind. Maybe the fumes messed with her, but her mind ticked away while a bunch of styles walked by her, giggling and gossiping, not caring about anything else.

Sit back and relax. She could truly do only one of those things. As the girl messed with her hair, the bag of orange strands caked in dried blood returned. So far, she got no news on who that could be. No one mentioned another missing person especially with the curfew in place. If Thomas killed this person before curfew, no one would look for them late into the night. They'd all wait till morning to do any searching, and by then, it would be too late to save them. What if they were like that previous victim who lived, muttering the words 'brown' and 'wine'? Brown wine still stayed up in the air regarding Thomas. What could he have that resembled brown wine? Did brown wine even exist? She knew of red, rose, and white ones, but not brown. Maybe they imagined beer and mistook it for wine.

Come on, Kara. You're wasting too much time on the small things. You still haven't figured out Thomas' motive. If you can tie these other victims together, you can get to the next one before he does. Okay, here are your clues: these are people living alone, working jobs like retail and fast food, there's something about brown wine, and Thomas' shaking. Her eyes flew open at that. She completely blanked out on that bit since it happened so often. Thomas always shook even when the car was warm. He wasn't cold or scared. Something made him tremble deep down. Even when he got close to her, the way he grabbed her hair, his entire body shook. He trembled as he clung to her, the knife moving in and away from her neck. That wasn't him taunting her; he couldn't control it.

There it was: the missing piece. Thomas Whittle trembled at random moments, sometimes to the point where he couldn't stop. She knew tremors were the result of some illnesses though getting him to tell her which one would take time. Yet what did his illness have to do with these other people? They weren't the ones who gave it to him. Her mind went to Dr. Moseley, the one victim who stood out from the others. The pieces swirled around in her mind. If Dr. Moseley had him as a patient and told him the truth, Thomas would get angry over it. She could understand him struggling to accept this. She could see him lashing out at the poor doctor, his rage mounting, hating the diagnosis, and wanting a cure. However, killing a doctor who could cure him didn't fit in.

You're almost there, Kara. Anne's voice kicked in. She squinted through the water and shampoo dripping down her face and ears. No Anne in sight, but her voice rang out. *You almost have the whole picture.*

"I do?"

"What was that?" The girl finally finished rinsing Kara's hair, wrapping it in a towel. "Sorry if I got some of that in your ears. The water should be out, cause we're all done."

"We are?" Kara sat up as the towel fell on her shoulder. Anne wasn't around, but her presence lingered thanks to the missing pieces coming in. "Right, I almost forgot where I was!"

"Yeah, we gotta finish fixing that hair of yours. Come on back to my station." The girl led her to the chair while Kara checked the other areas. No one resembled Anne here. No one else spoke to her but the girl, an innocent person who had no idea about Kara's dark secrets. Once they got settled in, the girl began to comb Kara's hair out. "You have to be more careful if you cut your own hair. It's not that easy."

"Tell me about it." Kara grumbled as the haircut began. This girl didn't tremble like Thomas. Her hands stayed still as she gathered Kara's hair, cutting it bit by bit. "You're really good at this."

"Thanks. It takes a lot of practice to get a haircut exactly right. It's even harder when you try doing it yourself. You can't slip up or move around too much, or the whole thing comes undone."

Listen carefully, Kara. Pay attention to her words and movements. Anne whispered from behind. Kara stared into the mirror to find herself and the stylist, but no one else. *Don't waste time trying to find me. I'll help you with whatever I can on my side. It's all I can do right now.*

Kara held back tears as more of her hair fell to the ground. This time, she wanted it to fall, but Anne's words hit harder. She failed another person that people hadn't discovered. She couldn't fail anymore. The next time Thomas sent a message, she'd pack up the notes and rocks for rescue. If she could alert someone, anyone, then maybe this nightmare would end. *Thomas said I keep trying, that's the only reason he didn't hurt me. Well, that's all I can do too. Try to save the next victims. No promises to do anything but try.*

"Hey, you okay?" The hairstylist sat her up as the tears rolled. "What's wrong? You don't like what I did?"

"No, it's not that." She sniffled. "The hair looks great. Really. You're doing a good job."

"You don't have to lie to me. If this isn't what you want…"

"This is fine." Kara wiped her eyes as the girl slowed down her cutting. "I'm not upset over this. It's just…my hair wasn't supposed to be like this. It was…I just made a stupid mistake and then it…"

"Hey, it's okay. It happens." The girl squeezed her shoulder, which Kara allowed. This girl's body was warm and friendly, not the cold creepiness that Thomas dripped off. "I have had clients who have done a lot worse to their hair. And yeah, a lot of them accidentally burned their hair too. You don't have to cry over that. You shouldn't be embarrassed."

"I am though." Kara admitted. "I'm just so…I was so careless. I didn't really think about it at all. I was doing what I normally do."

"We all get careless, but that doesn't mean your life is over."

The poor girl couldn't pick it up at all. Kara went on about her work, picking up Thomas from the airport. She drove him to that house in McIver Drive believing she wouldn't see him again. Oh, she was wrong. She ended up completely wrong. Why him? Out of all her riders, why was he the one she got stuck with? Why did she ever agree to him? Then again, if she didn't say yes, some other poor soul would. They'd get dragged into his game. Worse than that, if they screwed up, he'd kill them.

The girl continued to work away on Kara's hair. "This is tough, but this will work. In fact, I think it's gonna show off those cheekbones. You'll be a new you."

"A new you." Kara repeated. That's all she wanted, to become a brand-new person. If no one could recognize, she could get a new life altogether. Her hair looked so much better now, still long enough to use her hairbands and no longer appearing jagged. No one could complain about this look. "Thank you so much. It looks great."

"I'm not done yet. Let me take care of a few things here..." The girl continued to snip the cut off ends, combing and straightening Kara's locks. After ten minutes, she stepped back and handed Kara a mirror before turning around. "Here, let's take a look. Tell me if I need to do anything different."

Kara checked out her locks, now even and short. This would work. "I like them. This is as long as I'd like."

"I figured as much." The girl took off the cloak and helped her step down. "Thank you for such a great customer! You look so great!"

"Thank you for being a great stylist." Kara reached into her purse, taking out a few dollars. Many other people didn't think to tip stylists, but her mother always reminded her to do so. These people did her a service. The least she could do was thank them with a little extra money. Putting the bills on the counter, she grabbed her purse and waved as the girl went to get a broom. "See you next time!"

"Likewise. You look fantastic!"

Kara left the salon, taking one quick glance at her phone. Her happiness dissolved at the sight of Thomas' number popping up. Go figure he'd pick this moment to send a message. He didn't want a ride now, but his message still made her quiver in disgust. She deleted it, shoving her phone back in her bag. If he didn't need her, she didn't need to stare at that creepy message. It would stay in her mind for a long time. Even if she ignored him from now on, she wouldn't stop seeing it.

You look good.

Chapter 12

As suspected, her parents were fine with the new haircut. Her mother approved of the style being manageable than her previous hair. She only wished Kara had some time to touch up her roots, but Kara cut her off by pointing out the lack of funds. Getting her hair dyed meant taking up a little more time.

Her first three rides went smoothly. One person needed a ride to the Amtrak station, another person needed a ride to the Mint Museum, and a third person wanted to be dropped off at a restaurant. As long as they didn't need a drive down a long stretch of empty road, she accepted them. For the most part, her passengers remained pleasant with them being mostly families and young women needing help getting around. The only time it became a pain was when the family leaving the station needed help with their car seat. Kara helped them out as she had other riders who often bought babies and toddlers along with their car seats and strollers, yet she struggled. For all the straps and buckles, she prayed she got them locked in properly.

Yet she'd still take struggling with car seats over another day with Thomas. Whenever her phone went off, she nearly jumped out of her seat to check it. Most messages were the usual coupons for buy one, get one free item and the occasional political ad. She blocked the latter ones before putting the phone away. As much as she wanted to mute it, common sense told her not to. Thomas' glares bore into her even when he wasn't there. She drove down the streets of downtown Charlotte pretending he was right behind her, waiting for her to run a red light or miss a turn. The moment she turned into a bad driver; he'd have his reason to kill her.

Is that what you want? Him to kill you? Anne's voice kicked in. By now, Kara no longer feared it. Anne kept the little bit of sanity inside of her, a reminder of lives at stake. She talked to her like they were friends for years, not strangers who knew of each other until now. *I know you're stronger than that, Kara. You wouldn't crumble to him.*

"Yeah, well, he's not going to crumble to me." Kara slowed down at the red light as several pedestrians started crossing before her. "He came this close to cutting my neck last time. He was shaking so hard..."

Do you know why he was shaking? Not out of fear.

"No. Not out of fear." Kara drummed her fingers against the steering wheel more people passed in front of her. For seven in the evening, the crowds didn't die despite a curfew three hours from now. Everyone acted like this was a normal night, no killers out there. A part of her struggled not to yell at them to go home. How could they be so happy and carefree when The Traveler stalked people here? He was still around. He still lingered and stalked the victims he wanted to kill. As soon as the light turned green, she pumped the gas and drove away before she rolled down the window to scream.

They wouldn't believe you if you yelled. Anne pointed out as Kara drove away from downtown. *You must be more careful. If you want to get the upper hand, you must be stealthy.*

"Yeah, because if there's one thing I'm known for, it's stealth." Kara flicked a strand of hair falling on her forehead. Her phone reminded her of one more pick-up she needed to do, take someone from a hotel to the airport. Accepting that right, she made her way towards that hotel, still praying Thomas didn't send a message. "Maybe he's gonna get tired of this place and get out of here. He might go somewhere far from Charlotte. Hell, he should get out of North Carolina or even the United States."

And then what? He kills someone in another state. He starts the cycle up all over again. Now Anne's sweet voice turned dark and upset. *Is that really what you want, him to leave so he kills people somewhere else? You want to live that?*

Kara turned the corner towards the hotel, pulling up to the curb where her rider waited. No, she couldn't live with that. She couldn't sleep again if she let Thomas run away and kill someone else in another place. She needed him here. As her rider began to load their bags in the trunk, she stared down at her phone. No messages from Thomas, but a travel agency sending her a deal for a trip to Europe. After this ordeal, if she survived the ordeal, a trip was all she wanted. Somewhere far away where no one could find her.

Not yet. You can't go anywhere while you're under his thumb. You're still working too.

Her rider got into the back, an older woman heading off to the airport alone. "Hey, thanks for picking me up! I thought no one would show up given the whole curfew thing."

"Nah, we're still running for as long as we can." Kara shifted gears and headed towards the airport. "Granted, we can't take anyone in the late hours until the curfew is lifted. Not that very many people want rides in the middle of the night."

"Oh, I'm aware of why. I hope they find this guy soon. Everyone's so rattled. I'm amazed you're willing to be out so late." The woman moved her bag to the side. "I'm glad I stayed close to the city. From what I heard, this guy goes after people who live far away."

"Really?" Kara faked her surprise. "I guess he's smart not to kill anyone in broad daylight."

"Either that, or he's got another motive. I wish I knew what it was." The woman leaned back in her seat. "It makes you wonder how long he's been doing this. What does he get out of it? I'll never understand people like that."

"Me neither." Kara put all her focus on the road. The woman meant no harm, but she didn't care to discuss Thomas with strangers. Glancing at her rearview mirror, she slowed down for the next stop. "So, do you have any plans for later?"

"Not really. I'm going to stay in place and pray nothing bothers me. I miss having quiet times, you know. These days, so much is happening around the world. We never get a second to stop and breath." She inhaled as Kara hit the break at the next stop. "You take some time for yourself too, dear. I bet you don't get much rest either."

You don't know the half of it. Kara opted to keep the conversation at a minimum. The old lady rambled about other things, which she murmured in agreement with. The woman had a point. Kara needed to do something for herself. Get something sweet to eat. Drive places she didn't visit often. Stop at a bar for some food and maybe a drink after her shift. Go to the library. Go to concerts. These were the things she did when she was younger. Back then, even with her struggles at school, she found time to enjoy the little pleasures. She went to the clubs and concerts when nights were free. She enjoyed the company of random strangers all enjoying the same thing. She loved to try new food, visit a brand-new place, or experience something she never did before. She wanted that thrill back.

Maybe I can get it back. She plotted everything she wanted to do once she got away from Thomas. Go to another concert and stay out late. Discover new artists. Read new books. Visit the museums on their free admission days. Take her parents out of the house occasionally and go to a new restaurant to eat. Go to the park. God, there were a million other things she could do besides drive. *Yeah, I can start on that now. Get something I want.*

Upon dropping off the last fare, Kara took a quick break at the nearest shopping center to get some ice cream and rest for a few minutes. She calmed down at all the cars parked around as well as the people still walking outside. She even got comfort from the security cameras hanging above. Even if Thomas or anyone else wanted to try something, they couldn't do it. They'd get caught. Thomas was too smart for the cameras. He wouldn't kidnap or kill anyone in a place where the world could see. He did his best work when no one watched.

Hopefully, he won't call me for a ride tonight. My time is almost up anyway. As it was now 8 PM, she parked close to the ice cream shop and headed towards it, glad to find a whole group of people inside. Most were children and teenagers struggling to decide on what they wanted, so she stood back and stared at the menu. Then her eyes fell on the glass covering up the different flavors. From rainbow sherbet to butter pecan, plain vanilla to rocky road, she couldn't make up her mind. No wonder the kids squabbling up front hadn't shut up yet. The poor father at the front of the line wanted to crumble in place. Kara forced herself not to smile. It reminded her of the days when her father took her for ice cream. She never could decide what flavor she wanted that day. They'd spend a few minutes in line before her father decided for her. Not that it mattered. She loved it all the same. It was with ice cream that they tried to solve math problems together. While she rarely got an answer right, at least the reward tasted sweet.

"That's enough, you guys!" The father in front snapped at the complaining kids. "Pick something now! I don't want to be out while that lunatic is still around!"

That lunatic. Those words didn't really describe Thomas. He wasn't out of his mind. Everything he did, he had his reason. Sick, twisted reasons, but they made sense to him. It wasn't a messed-up mind that made him commit murder. Hatred did. His hatred towards anyone who appeared better than him drove him to kill. Unfortunately, no one else got close enough to him the way she did. No one dug deep into his psyche for the source of his pain. Even though he hadn't revealed everything, she began to put pieces together. His hatred steamed from the dark parts of his life. Whatever happened back then influenced everything going on now. Worse than that, he dragged her into his world. She kept secrets, she drove him to places for killing, she covered up her messes. He was not just a rider. Instead, he became some dark passenger settled in the back, letting her take him around town to get his kicks.

So, how can I get rid of my dark passenger here? She glanced up as the father with his squabbling crew moved away. The girl behind the counter smiled at her as she changed gloves. "Hey, there! Do you guys have any specials tonight?"

"We have our new flavor, salted caramel. Also, milkshakes are half-off tonight." The girl tugged on the gloves. "You can also try any flavors here to see if you like one."

"Then I'll do that. I'll try your salted caramel." Kara pointed to the flavor behind the glass. "And could I also try your vegan chocolate?"

"Sure." The girl handed her two small spoons with tiny scoops of ice cream. "Tell me what you think of them."

Kara tasted both, nodded in approval, before tossing the used spoons in the cup on the counter. "Can I have both of those in a cup please? Medium size."

As she walked down, she caught sight of Anne standing by her. Anne didn't stare at the menu or the ice cream before her but the young girl behind the counter. *She's about my age. That's how old he usually likes them.*

Kara didn't reply until she paid for the ice cream and left the store, Anne in tow, looking for an empty table to sit at. Once she found it, she dug her spoon in. "I know that's what he likes. I wonder if he thinks she's wasteful too, working at an ice cream store."

I hope not. She's doing nothing wrong with working here. Everyone needs money.

"Don't remind me. I survive off tips on my rides." Kara glanced around to make sure no one else listened in. With most people either far away or in the store, she could still have this odd conversation with Anne's ghost. "I hope we can help her if he does target her. I know where she works."

Do you even know her name?

"I...uh, crap. I didn't even pay attention to that part." Kara couldn't even remember if the poor girl had a nametag. "In any case, I remember what she looks like. Brown hair, brown eyes, very young either in high school or maybe college. If I can describe that, they can probably lead me to her."

Anne furrowed her bloodied brow. Another droplet rolled down her cheek as she scrunched up her nose. *Do you know how many brown-haired, brown-eyed young girls are out there? You know how many get abducted and murdered on a regular basis? That won't help anyone.*

"I, um...oh fuck me, you're right." Kara dropped the spoon into the cup. "I gotta stay one step ahead of Thomas if I want to save anyone. The problem is I'm not sure what his next step is going to be. He calls me for rides at random times and to random places. The only place that appears constant is McIver Drive. I'm willing to bet that's either his home or where he's making his hideout. I've never been inside of it though..." She swallowed. "Was that...did he..."

Only for a while. Anne gazed down at the half-empty cup of ice cream on the table. *He kept me in that house only for a day or two. I can barely remember much, but it was a short time. I kept praying for him to come in and kill me. The darkness, the loneliness, the starvation, the cold. I'd take a swift quick death over those.*

Kara finished up the ice cream, tossing into the trash behind her. "I'm gonna get justice for you. I don't know how yet. I don't know when, but it will happen. First though, I have to finish up..." Her phone went off for more rides. "I think I can squeeze in some more rides tonight. I should get them home. If they live close enough, I'll drop them off."

Make sure you stay until you're certain they're safe inside.

"Of course. I'm not leaving their sights until I know they're okay. It's the very least I can do." She headed to her car. "Let's do this again. Just a few more rides before I call it quits."

She continued to drive her riders around, dropping them right at the door and waiting until they went inside before leaving and completing her ride. Most of them appeared grateful that someone out there kept an eye on them. It didn't matter how crowded or well-lit their destination was. Kara never drove off before they made it indoors. Prior to picking up Thomas, some riders told her it was okay to go ahead. They were here. They'd be fine. Now, she couldn't listen to them. Even if she drove a few feet away, she was close enough to drive back and help them if needed. Not that she could fight back, but at least she could try.

"Oh, who am I kidding? I can't fight anything." She waited till her last rider got inside the house, greeted by another family member, before driving away. At nine PM, she decided this would be her final ride of the night. The next few were too far away, and she'd end up missing the curfew. When she tried to accept some, another rider got to them. Breathing slowly, she put the phone down. "Okay, they'll be fine. If someone gets them, they'll be fine." She checked some of the names and Thomas' didn't pop up. "He may not need me tonight. I think I might rest a bit before heading home."

As she drove down, she turned towards a local bar and began searching for a parking space. She wasn't much of a drinker, and usually didn't like drinking anything before driving. Yet with all the secrets weighing down on her, the temptation grew. Her good conscience warned her not to do it. Thomas was a cruel killer, yes, but she didn't need a DUI in her life. Happy Riders didn't appreciate anyone who drank and drove on the job. Those who were caught drinking alcohol the first time around were suspended from driving for two weeks. If it happened again, they would lose their job. If anyone got a DUI while driving or caused any harm to their riders or others on the road, that could lead to possible charges and even jail time. No, she wasn't an idiot, and the parking lot had no space for her. Thomas warped her mind up to the point where she almost caved into drinking.

"What am I doing?" She finally found a spot far from the bar, and right in front of a coffee shop. Coffee held a lot of caffeine, but she could drink that. It could lift her spirits. With the air cooling now, it made more sense to drink coffee instead of a cold beer or cocktail. The tickle in her throat grew, reminding her to drink something warm before catching a cold. It would keep her awake through the night, but she'd survive it. Happy Riders didn't mind anyone drinking coffee or tea while in the car. They only requested their riders keep their cars clean and know their limits with caffeine. Kara shut the engine off and headed into the store where three people stood in line ahead of her. Each time, she checked her phone for any texts. No Thomas, no new riders. She got a few more five-star reviews, much to her delight. They complimented the clean car, which unnerved her. There was a very good reason her car smelled lemony-fresh, and the seats didn't reek of rotten food and dirt. Thomas got her to clean it after many years. If only she cleaned for a good reason.

Upon getting her coffee, she sat down and kept reading the reviews. They liked her. Every rider that came with her praised her for driving the speed limit, keeping plenty of snacks and water, and found her a good conversationalist. Above everything else, they loved that she kept an eye on them as they went inside. Most other drivers drove off, but Kara made them safe. Seeing those words only dug the pain deep in her heart. She made them safe. She watched after them. Unfortunately, it only lasted if they were in her car. If another driver got them, she couldn't guarantee they'd stay safe the next time. She sipped up her coffee and bit into the lemon cake she also purchased. Driving around this late with multiple riders often made her hungry. Since she missed dinner, this would keep her fueled for the next hour.

By now, more customers came in, all chatting about one thing: The Traveler. None of them feared him. They wanted to see his next move. They wanted to guess the next victim. They glued themselves to their phones, talking and scrolling down the screens. They didn't bother looking up to give their orders, just shooting them off for the barista to make. Kara shook her head as they handed over the money, gushing over the possibility of a new true crime. Her throat burned at a desire to yell at them. How clueless could these people be? Every single moment with Thomas was déjà vu for her. He won the people over by killing someone. Who could find any excitement in that? They wouldn't think this if they'd been victims. They'd never film him for their TikTok videos or interview him for podcasts. He'd slit their throats before they got a chance to speak up.

"Oh man, the police sent a warning!" One of the girls waved her phone around. "They really don't want anyone out after ten. They're gonna be all over the place, warning people. Apparently, he's nearby and he might be stalking a new victim!"

Kara cringed over the excited chatter before turning to her phone. Sure enough, a police bulletin came out as a warning for everyone in the area. They got word that The Traveler was still in the area, so everyone needed to stay on guard. No picking up people they didn't know. No getting into cars with strangers. Avoid anyone they didn't recognize. Kara hated herself for reading the last one. She couldn't do it since being a driver meant helping strangers. She couldn't avoid new people while trying to do her work. The one thing calming her down was the number of police who'd be out at night to help anyone in need. Hopefully, they'd do their jobs and keep people safe. If she got lucky, they'd take him down for her.

Driving down the road, she spotted all the bright red and blue lights blinking ahead. The police stopped people on the way, so she slowed down and fixed her hair again. Not now. How could there be cops out on the street when she wasn't breaking laws? She checked the speedometer, which was at the correct speed for this area. She also had the lights on, her registration was up to date, and she didn't carry anything in this car that wasn't her own stuff. What could they stop her for besides being nervous? No one deserved to be harassed for having anxiety.

"Stay cool." She breathed out. This was the last thing she hoped for. However, it did provide a tiny glimmer of hope. If she could get the cop on her side, maybe she could lead him to Thomas and any victims who were still alive. This was a chance to get out. "Stay cool, Kara. You didn't do anything wrong. He's not here."

As she slowed down, a cop approached her while she rolled the windows down. "Yes, officer?"

"Good evening, ma'am. We're here to remind you about the curfew. Are you aware that it's almost nine-thirty PM?"

"Yes, sir. I work for a rideshare company, and my shift just ended." She pointed to the yellow sticker on her windshield. "I dropped off my last rider, so I'm heading home."

"Well, that is good. We're here to remind you that The Traveler is still very much at large. We want everyone driving on these streets to be on high alert for him. And given that you are a rideshare driver, I need to be careful who you pick up."

It's a little too late to tell me that. Kara nodded at him as he handed her a piece of paper with several rules on it. The same talking points printed down on it, she folded it up and put it to the side. "I'll be sure to be careful and..."

Splat!

A small drop of blood landed on her window. Then came another drop of blood. Then another splat slowly swirled down towards her door handle. She squinted into the dark to find he was no longer there. Peeking her head out, she called for him. The police car was parked on the side, but he wasn't around. "Uh, officer? Is everything okay?"

With no response, she slowly rolled the window back up as the blood drops smeared across the glass. Her scream stuck in her throat as her brain processed the scene before her. Blood again. That couldn't be. The officer was right by her side, talking to her and warning her of danger. He handed her the piece of paper only seconds ago. He couldn't run off that quickly without saying 'good night' or 'be safe' or something of that sort. She grabbed the steering wheel again, ignoring the blood rolling down the window. Another lit area. She had to find another empty area to clean those windows and_

THUD!

A body hit her windshield as she hit the brakes. She screeched with the tires as her hands went up to shield herself. More blood gushed out, covering the glass as it dropped down. Gasping for air, Kara parked the car before jumping out to see what it was. She didn't drive far or fast enough to hit anyone.

"Oh my God!" She shrieked as she found the corpse. The cop that spoke to her a few seconds ago lay there in that pool of blood, no longer moving or breathing. "No no no, what the hell?! Oh God! Oh, what do I do?! What am...he...mmpfh!"

A cold hand clamped over her mouth while the other hand dragged her back. Her heels skidded across the pavement as this person pulled her away. She clawed at the arm, trying to bite down. It wasn't until the voice behind her snapped "Calm down!" that she finally put it all together. He found her and took her from the scene. Until she stopped thrashing around, he didn't let her go. Kara calmed down though couldn't stop shaking as he pushed her away.

"You shouldn't scream out here, Kara." He leaned in, smelling of cheap cologne and pine needles. Great. He came when she never wanted him. "People could hear you. After that scene, do you really want any more cops coming here?"

Kara swallowed and quieted down. She wanted no more commotion even with that strong smell of blood reeking in the air. He did it. He found her, and took care of this cop. "Why though? Why did you..."

He pulled her back and turned her around, grabbing her arms and pushing her to stay in place. Breathing in, Thomas locked his eyes on her, daring her to make a move. He wanted her to say something stupid or try to fight. His hands and shirt bloodied, he narrowed that blue gaze on her. Kara couldn't speak, but she still shook as he slowly ran his hands down her body. At this point, Kara prayed someone would come save her. She prayed to every deity out there, even the ones she didn't believe in. As late as it was, she wanted one person to find her. The moment they slowed down, she'd run to them and yank that door open. She had strength in her legs to bolt to another person.

Please come by. Please come and take me away.

Instead, the entire road remained silent except for Thomas breathing hard. He approved of her appearance as her hair came undone, revealing what the stylist had done. The curls bounced on her shoulders while he nodded.

"That new hair is good on you."

Kara gulped to return that nod. It didn't matter now. No one was coming to her rescue tonight. With the curfew creeping up, she had to deal with Thomas alone. She had to face him, ask him a million more questions. All the while, a dead cop lay on the ground and her car reeked of his blood. Clutching her chest, she closed her eyes to keep the tears in. The same tears that kept falling after every shocking moment. She cried every single time she got near Thomas, and he killed someone around her. He destroyed every bit of normalcy in her life. She couldn't go back to concerts or clubs anymore. She couldn't hit up new restaurants and museums while acting like everything was fine. Her world shattered the moment she brought Thomas into her life. Her present, her future, all she ever wanted...her grandfather was right. The stars wouldn't get into her favor until she did something about them.

And one way or another, she had to get away from Thomas.

Chapter 13

It took a good few minutes for Kara to calm down. Her heartbeat came down to a normal rate and her breathing returned to normal even if it sounded a little ragged. Her eyes darted from the cop's dead body to the smear on her windshield then back to Thomas again. The past few minutes went too quickly for her mind to process. The police car stood off in the distance, still blinking bright red and blue lights. No one else drove by, so she finally picked up her feet and walked around the car, surveying all the damage. Aside from the blood, her car would be fine with a quick wash. The vomit in her throat surged up and fell as she struggled for words. Thomas stood behind her, silent and waiting for her next move. He wouldn't say or do anything until she did. He drummed his fingers together, wanting some reaction.

"Well?" He prompted. "Don't you have anything to ask me?"

"Why...what..." She managed to get out before walking over to him. "What was..."

"He wanted to hurt you." Thomas sneered over at the corpse. "He stopped you on purpose."

"Yeah, he stopped me to give a warning. That doesn't mean he had ulterior motives! I told him the truth. I'm just out here trying to finish up my shift!" She ground her teeth as Thomas gazed down with that cold glare. He didn't lash out at her for her anger. Instead, he took a step back and let his arms fall to his side.

"Normally, I'd believe that about any other person but not the police. These warnings are just the start, Kara. He'll find out all about you. Everything you've done. It always starts so innocently, but I know people like that. They give a small warning before escalating. He wanted you to loosen up your guard before he struck. I only helped you out."

"Yeah, but things didn't escalate. I was going home and now..." Her vomit sunk back into her stomach at the sight of the blood. "What am I going to do?"

"Oh, please. You cleaned up the car last time, you can do it again. This time, it's just blood on the outside. Rinse it out, no one will know what happened." Thomas patted her on the shoulder, leaving no blood smudges this time. "And look, you don't have to change clothes now. Keep your little mouth shut, you'll get through another night."

"Speaking of that...I'm gonna get home after curfew! Oh shit! Shit!" She gasped, covering her face and walking away. "What am...why did you..."

"To keep you safe, Kara. There are so many terrible people out there. I would hate for you to trust the wrong ones." He led her back to the car. "You should get home after washing that car."

"Wash it where? The car washes are all closed. I..." Kara moved away from her car, wishing she didn't have to go back. At the very least, she could send them a message. "Why? He's not the same as the others."

"Oh, he's exactly the same as the others." Thomas grimaced. "He's just like those who lie about everything. How safe you'll be. How wealthy you'll get it. How healthy you truly are. Then you find out what's going on, how they've turned on you and ruined your life. They destroy everything."

Kara saw that moment to press on. "Someone ruined your life, huh? Is it regarding your wealth or..." His fingers twitched as the light bulb came on in her mind. "They lied about health. Not just anyone, the doctor lied to you!"

"Said everything would be fine. Said I'd be okay in a few years, that I'd be healed. He wanted me to stay positive. He believed everything would be okay. How could I believe that when the tests told me otherwise?" Thomas waved at the road behind him. "How can anyone be positive in this world, Kara? Day and night, all you hear about is corruption and violence plaguing it. Not just here either. I bet you've heard a lot about dangers in other countries."

Kara couldn't argue with that as she went to the trunk and got out all the cleaning products. Thank God she kept a few of them around for situations like this. Granted, she never had to clean up blood before, but it would a little cheaper over driving to a car wash. "What are you going to do with the body? Someone might try to find him."

"I'll handle that part. You fix your car. After all, I may need you soon. I'll need a lot of rides in the future." Thomas let her get into the driver's side before taking his sleeve and wiping some of the blood off. It smeared farther down as he yanked away. "Those cleaning products won't work."

"I'm sorry?"

"The stuff that you have won't clean much up. It'll take the blood off for now, but the stains will remain. You need something else." He wiped his brow, flicking the sweat off his face. "I know of a small place that's closed, but anyone can use the hoses over there for a small rinse. If you got a credit card, you could use it. No one's gonna check on you."

"Still, I..." Before she got a word in, he handed her a card. "What is this?"

"Use that. If you're so worried about anyone finding out, use that card and clean your car. Be quick though. It's almost ten." He motioned her to drive. "Go! Get out of here, Kara, before you get caught!"

"Where do I..."

"Straight down, take a right at the end of the road, car wash will be on the right if you go down one block. Can you remember those directions?"

"Yes, but..."

"Then go!" He slammed the side of her door. "Get a move on and stop asking stupid questions! Some of us don't have all night!"

The last sentence stuck with her as she peeled out of the area, hands slipping up and down the wheel. He didn't explain much, but she got something out of his words. Something was wrong with Thomas' body, something he refused to divulge into. He wanted a cure. He went to get a cure. He got told that everything would be all right. He got the positive news every patient wanted. Then reality hit him. The doctor lied about Thomas' health. Either that, or he didn't know all the facts. He couldn't admit he knew nothing, so he lied to keep him on the positive. As soon as Thomas learned the truth, he struck. He gave up all hopes of being cured by killing the doctor. That was only the beginning. He got nothing from that death, but the satisfaction to getting rid of someone.

So where does everyone else fit in? Most of these other victims aren't doctors. Most aren't even in the medical field. Why attack them if they're not involved? Some of these victims would be too young when he was diagnosed. Kara pulled into the empty wash, grabbed the card Thomas gave her, and used it to access the water hoses. He wasn't wrong about everything being available for her. The best part was the lack of people to ask about the blood. It washed down the drain as Kara aimed the hose at the bloodied parts, hiding her sobs and disgust. Even in the moments when she was, she couldn't escape Thomas. *How did he even know where I was? He never called me for a ride. I checked my phone a billion times, and he never asked for me.*

As the watery blood pooled around her feet, a horrible thought gripped her. Thomas found her driving down this road that she had never heard of. He knew she'd be stopped by the police, something that no one else informed her of. He got there before she got a chance to react. He knew too much about her. She splashed through the water, cut off the house, and opened the back of the car.

Well, the nice thing about this place is that I can get a quick vacuum in and clean up the inside. She wiped some dirt off the mats. *Maybe, just maybe, I can find some clues here.*

Now, you're thinking in the right direction. She gazed up to find Anne sitting on the passenger side, the cut on her forehead still gushing blood. *The quicker you clean this, the quicker you'll get your answers.*

"I didn't expect to wipe my car down so early, but..." She silenced herself right then. *Somehow, he's figuring out where I am. If I talk too much, he'll know what I'm doing. I gotta pretend that all I'm doing is washing this car.* Anne continued to watch her, slowly nodding as she vacuumed the bottom of the car. "Okay, I should be done and it's..." She stared at the clock on the dashboard. "Five more minutes till ten. I'll make it."

Of course, you will. Did you find what you were looking for?

Kara's hand rolled over something under a mat, the size of a small rock, something she couldn't find until now. Carefully, she pulled up the mat and found the little black thing hiding there. A recorder. She saw this when she watched videos on the latest technology. The users showed off how small and invisible it was, a recorder that could go anywhere. The only thing that could disrupt was being put in a box full of other things. That way, it could not tell what it needed to focus on.

This was it. He knew her moves through this thing. Well, she could deal with that. She needed to get rid of it, but throwing it away wasn't an option. If Thomas couldn't hear her, he'd know she found it. However, she could hide it somewhere else, something that would make it hard for him to hear it.

I have no idea how to fix this stuff, but maybe...just maybe... Her eyes fell on the box of snacks in the corner. If it stayed buried in that and hidden in the trunk, he probably couldn't track her as easily. Gingerly, she opened the box and buried the little black thing into the box. Hopefully, this could hold Thomas away for a bit. Now that the car was cleaned, she got in the driver's seat and headed towards home. Gazing down towards the break, she found it. A white wad of tissue dotted in red.

"What the..." Getting out of the car again, she picked up the tissue. Blood. Someone bled in her car, leaving wads of used tissue on the ground. She continued to search around, gathering more bloodied tissues. These didn't come from any of Thomas' victims. She didn't recall any of her other riders having an injury. That left her with one option. Thomas bled in her car. She didn't see injuries on him, yet he left all of this.

"When did you start bleeding, and how come I'm just finding this now?" She collected all the tissues, gathering them in one corner. This didn't all happen during his last trip. Some of the blood turned darker than others. "How did I notice this? You never said a word."

Is it making sense now? Anne stared down at the wads. *Not that this would help me. He's bleeding for some reason.*

"No one attacked him though, did they?" Kara racked her brain for all the information on The Traveler's victims. No one ever found any self-defense wounds on the victims. Not even Anne, kneeling right by her, had anything on her hands save for the rope burns on her wrists. "Is he attacking himself?"

If that's the case, wouldn't he have wounds on himself?

Kara got back in the driver's side, ignoring all the tissues, and revved up the engine. Thomas never had injuries on his body, not even a scratch. He sniffled a lot and she caught him coughing on occasion. Still, that didn't prove anything. "No way. I don't think the guy has tuberculosis now. I don't know anyone who does."

Her head throbbed during the entire drive home. Thomas stalked her after all. He listened in on her rambling to herself, talking to other riders, and even calling home from time to time. She took care of this recorder, but what if he had something else? All her thoughts of escape needed to stay locked away in her mind. Hopefully, her room remained free of his bugs. Thomas didn't know where she lived. He only listened to whatever happened in the car.

Then again, he knew where I'd be. What if it is tracking my moves? He might know where I live too. She remembered the house alarm. If there was one thing she figured out about Thomas, he didn't go into houses with alarm systems. Anne didn't have one. Many other victims didn't have one. Her parents set the alarm every night, so Thomas wouldn't be stupid enough to break in. No, he took his time. If he wanted to hurt them, he could do it. She believed all of this during the entire drive, up until the moment she pulled up to the driveway. Her mother's car sat outside of it and the lights glimmered inside. That didn't mean much, but she held onto that hope as she opened the door and got inside. The house stayed clean and quiet, not a spot in sight. So far, so good.

"Karishma?"

"Hey, I'm home." She took off her shoes and hung her jacket in the closet. "I know it's..." She never finished the sentence as her father rushed out of the living room and scooped her into an embrace. He even lifted her a few inches off the ground as he rocked her back and forth, head buried into her shoulder. "Whoa! Whoa, Baba! Calm down! I'm here! I got back!"

"You are home after ten!" Her father exclaimed. "Don't remember that there's a_"

"A curfew? Yeah, I know. I'm sorry." Kara rubbed her forehead. "I, um...I..."

"Oh, Karishma, tell me you didn't forget to take your medicine." He led her to the sofa. "You come home past your driving time. Now, you're coming home after a curfew is set. This isn't you! We've done everything we can to help you stay focused!"

"This isn't about my ADD, Baba! This is..." She took a deep breath. The image of the dead cop flashed back to her. One second, he gave her a warning about the dangers on the street. The next minute, he lay in a pool of blood and Thomas hovered over her like some evil angel. With his little recorder hidden deep inside her snack box, it gave her a little time to plot things out. He wouldn't hear her talking to herself anymore. He couldn't trace her as easily. He couldn't make a move until he called her. "I'm having a hard time lately.""Because of the job?"

"No, it's not the job itself. It's…I can't take these curfews. I don't know if they're helping." She gazed down at the floor, grateful to see something that wasn't blood on the pavement or the mats on her car. "I'm glad to be home now. You guys still set the alarm before you go to bed, right?"

"Of course. It's dangerous to keep them off with some maniac lurking around." He joined her on the sofa. "Is he the one that's scaring you? I don't blame you for that. I do think I could follow you around. I know you said no, but_"

"No, Baba. I mean it." She sniffled. "I don't want you getting into trouble as well."

"Why would I get into trouble? I would only be following you from a distance. I wouldn't even be right behind you. If it will make you feel better, I'll let a bunch of cars cut in front of me. It'll widen the distance." Her face continued to droop over this solution. "You really don't want me to go?"

"Baba, I wish I could tell you why." She inhaled. "This is something I must handle alone though. It's a big thing. I just…" She yanked on her collar, waving her hand in front of her face. The temperature rose inside of this house. Coupled with her nerves, she burned up on this couch. "Jesus, does Ma put the cooler at 80 degrees or something? I'm sweating!"

"Your mother was feeling cold, so she raised the thermostat. Still, it's only 76 degrees. It can't be that hot." He pressed his hand against her forehead. "You're warm, but not sick. You don't feel sick, do you?"

"No, I'm not sick." Her stomach gurgled as she stood up. The whole ordeal threw off her appetite, and now it returned in full force. "I'm a little hungry though. I know it's late but…"

"You can have some cereal. Nothing too heavy though. You know how your mother feels about eating anything after 10 PM." He warned her. Kara winced at her mother's reaction to anyone eating after 8 PM. She launched into lectures how unhealthy it was, how everything that she ate at night got stuck in her body, how people gained weight from eating in the late hours. Kara tried countering the fact that some of her classmates ate while studying into the late night, but they were fine. Most didn't gain more than a pound. It never worked.

"I'll get something a little later." She decided as she headed to her room. "I'm gonna go get changed, maybe take a quick shower. It's been a long night."

"Go ahead. If you need to talk though, I'll still be up and in the living room. I need to watch the news before bed." He waved her off. "I'm here for you, Karishma. Always."

"I know, Baba. Good night." She left the living room and went into her bedroom to grab her pajamas. She couldn't sleep tonight, yet she didn't want to wear these clothes all night long. They still smelled like that cop's blood and Thomas' breath. He got too close to her recently.

Her phone went off constantly though there were no messages from Thomas. She got plenty of updates regarding the curfew in town and more information about Anne. The police could not retrace Anne's last steps with co-workers mentioning her being friendly with many customers. One older gentleman appeared very friendly with her though they saw no threat in him. After all, plenty of other customers were kind to them. Anne treated them all the same way.

"It can't be." She shook her head. "That's too much of a coincidence. I mean, there are plenty of older men out there who are friendly at fast-food places. She couldn't run into him, right?"

I did. Anne peered over her shoulder at all the articles. Without blinking, she nodded in approval. *They're on the right path. Still too far away though.*

"How can we get them closer to finding the truth?" Kara scrolled down her phone. "I mean, your coworkers are describing a lot of old men this way. You probably ran into a lot of guys like that."

That's true. There are a lot of guys who are very charming. Very rarely did I get some guys trying to cross the line. Anne pointed out a new article. *This one just came up.*

"What did?" Kara tapped on the article.

New articles popped up on her phone over another missing girl. The curfew remained in place, yet Sara Murphy, a college student who lived on campus, was no longer around. Her roommates claimed that she went to dinner with them but opted to stop at the library to do some research for a class project. Like everywhere else, the library closed at ten. Yet no one over there saw her around. None of the librarians noticed her come in or leave. No one heard from her after that.

"Another one. Oh God, another one." Kara covered her face. She didn't know when Thomas went after this girl, and she never noticed it. He gave her no clue about hunting someone else. Still, a small glimmer of hope burned inside. Thomas was always clean when he rode with her. The only blood he spilled recently was that of the cop and Anne. If Sara just went missing, then there was a good chance she was alive. No blood. If he didn't bring blood, it gave her time to find Sara.

Look at me. I'm relieved at how little blood there is. The more she thought, the harder she coped with it. The blood washed all over her car wasn't a comforting thing. No matter how much she cleaned it, she couldn't remove it. She couldn't stop picturing it all over her seats and dashboard. Even as she took other riders around, she always saw them sitting on those blood-stained seats. They never commented on her nervous behavior though many couldn't stop talking about The Traveler. The majority were nervous about him as they should have been. A few were too excited to meet him.

"You know, if I ran into him, I'd like to do an interview for my podcast...provided he doesn't kill me, that is."

"He's kinda mysterious, don't you think? It's like Ted Bundy. Somehow, people are drawn to him. He's got some charm. He could win anyone over."

"I wonder if I ever got a selfie with him. Who knows, maybe his face is all over Instagram and TikTok and no one knows! Can you imagine what that's like?"

All those poor excited souls didn't know what it was like driving The Traveler around. They didn't know how quickly he got angry, and his unpredictable voice changed. They didn't have those blue eyes piercing the back of their car seat. She wanted to scream at these riders, lash out at them for lionizing him. A serial killer wasn't someone they needed to get close to or care about. Somehow, not even one of them recalled that a woman died recently and there were many more victims prior to her. He wasn't charming or mysterious in a way that people would love. He wouldn't sit there for podcast interviews or take selfies. No, he wouldn't waste time on these things. He'd kill these people and move on. Her blood boiled each time they gushed about Thomas like he was some rock star or actor they had a crush on. They truly had no idea.

Yet every single time, Kara held her tongue. These poor kids truly didn't read all the information. Even if they paid attention to TikTok, they'd get only some of the facts. They wouldn't know the hatred Thomas harbored towards their kind. They didn't know about his issues with people. They never knew that the person driving them around met The Traveler. Not only did she meet him, but she also took him around everywhere he wanted to go. Like a good rider, he tipped her handsomely, but the money no longer mattered. Between his extravagant tips and the cheap asses who barely gave her a dollar, she preferred the latter. At least she didn't fear her life around them. She could give them a quick side-eye as they left, and she could drive off in one piece. Thomas didn't want her to check anything out. He didn't want anyone to get close to the truth. He wanted her all to himself.

Then on the flip side, there was Anne's ghost still tagging along. She spoke whenever needed but remained monotone and lifeless with her words. Anne could provide some advice. She understood all the danger they were in. At this moment, Anne held Kara's sanity together. She always kept her on alert, reminding her that Thomas was a monster. He'd been a monster for decades. No one would change him or turn him to the side of good because he didn't want to go there. Not even Kara had the power to turn him into someone he wasn't. The only thing that comforted her was finding his little recording device and hiding it in a place where he couldn't trace as easily. No one dug into those boxes except for her.

"I wonder if I can crush that." She held up her thumb and index finger, pressing them together. "It shouldn't be hard to squish."

If you break it, he'll know. The moment he can't track you down, he'll forget all about his own rules. It's not time to set him off. Anne warned her. *He's a time bomb ticking away. Don't light the fuse before you have a plan of escape.*

"Time bomb is putting it lightly. I did notice one thing though. He hasn't asked me to take him to the airport." She went back to that night when he rolled up her car door with very few bags. "How long do you think he wants to stay here? I mean, is McIver Drive really his house?"

I'm not sure. If it is, how does he pay for it? Who keeps it clean? I don't think he's hiring anyone for that.

"I don't think so either. Give me a second." Kara picked up her phone to read up on the other cases before Anne's. Not all of them were in Charlotte, so she went looking for something to tie them together.

As it turned out, there were plenty of missing people who ended up dead in the end. Plenty of cases that left law enforcement baffled. The biggest case overseas was in Paris, France over a decade ago. A young student left her university one night to meet up with friends and never showed up at the club. Her body was discovered three days later floating around in the Seine. That didn't mesh well with her. Why would he fly all the way to France to kill one girl? Then she read further and learned that the girl had been an art student at a prestigious university. This was the case with three other victims as well, all art students and all studying painting as their medium. "He's killing painters?"

I used to paint as a hobby. But that was years ago. I gave it up once I had to go to college. Anne pointed out. *Do you think that's why...*

"Possibly." She continued reading and found a few victims who worked in art supply stores or the painting section of home improvement stores. "He really hates painters of all kinds. Either that or he hates anyone tied to them. It doesn't explain the doctor though. Was he also a painter?"

He could be. What did you find about him?

Kara checked out Dr. Moseley's obituary, running down the paragraphs until she zeroed on one sentence. "He was a kind, hard-working man who loved fishing, reading, and painting in his spare time. Painting! There it is again! Maybe it isn't about young people wasting their lives away. Maybe it's about people who paint!"

Anne shook her head. *I don't think that's the only connection. He hates young people who waste their lives. He hates people who paint. We're missing a piece.*

"Yeah, we are." Kara put the phone away. "I wonder if I can ask him about some stuff. I can bring up art with him, ask him if he has any favorite artists or artworks. I can dig into his life, get him to talk about something besides death and killing. He's got to have passion deep down."

So, you're going to talk to him about his passion?

"I'll work my way into the conversation. Mention something about the Mint Museum or any art festivals nearby. I can engage him with what I know about local artists. There's got to be another connection between all of you and the painting. Did he hate them for being painters?"

Well, by technical means, I wasn't a painter when I died. It was a hobby once upon a time. I think the last time I painted anything was... Anne fell silent as footsteps came down the hall. Kara closed her phone down as her mother entered, holding out the landline phone.

"Your grandfather wants to speak to you. It's urgent." She waved the phone "I told him you went to bed, but he insists on speaking with you. He says it's very urgent that you take his call. If you don't want to_"

"I'll take the call." Kara held the receiver close to her ear so her mother couldn't catch bits of the conversation. "Hi, Dadu. How are you?"

"Oh good, Karishma. You've come home." Her grandfather coughed on the other end. Over the past few years, his health has plummeted. He got sick from the smallest cold draft. Despite all this, he tried to call as much as possible. He wanted to hear from his family in case it was the last time they ever spoke. "I've been worrying about you since this is a frightening time in your life."

"I've been working a lot lately." She refused to confirm his worries. It was true, of course, that she worked a lot. "Everyone's needing a ride these days."

"Well, you must be very careful out there. I keep seeing those clouds over you. They block out the stars and moon. Are you sure you're not in trouble?"

Every part of Kara wanted to blurt out that yes, she was in danger. She was now in some twisted ride with a serial killer. He held her very existence in his hands. Those clouds her grandfather spoke of were now clouding her entire life. At this point, she didn't know if there was a future in sight for her. "I'm okay, Dadu. Really."

"I don't know about that. I keep praying that you'll get out of your problems. That the sun will break through, and you'll be happy again. I want you to have a better life than this. So far, I'm not seeing it."

"Is it because I'm driving people around? It's tough to find work, Dadu." She struggled to talk about her problems. Her grandfather wasn't a fool. He caught on that she was in danger. He knew that her issue wasn't something her parents could get her out of. It wasn't something he could do beyond warning her. However, he was doing his best to give her a little bit of confidence. He feared for her life. "It's a crazy job, yes. I do meet a lot of strange characters. None of them ever hurt me." *Not yet.* She added to herself. God, she prayed her grandfather couldn't spot the hesitation in her voice.

"Still, this job of yours...it's not the safest job. I'm not talking about the odd strangers you run into. There's something sinister in the air. One of these riders...you shouldn't take them on any more rides."

"Really?" She cursed herself for not speaking with him earlier. If he had given her this prediction ahead of time, she'd never have run into Thomas. "The worst I've seen so far are three-star reviews for my rides, Dadu. They're usually for the stupidest reasons. I either don't have their favorite snacks, or I took the longer route to get them to their destination. They still made it on time. That's it."

"No, it isn't. This isn't over, Karishma. You want to be careful whenever you go out. Drive as much as you need to. Only watch where you're driving. Your life is going to change soon. It'll be up to you to decide whether you want to change it. Make it for the better or worse."

The words didn't comfort her, but they confirmed everything. The only one who could get out of this situation was her. As she said good night to her grandfather and gave the phone back, she plotted on how to escape him. She could try driving off while he made a pit stop. This was her gas money that she wasted, not his. She could take the few minutes he went off to zoom off and head to the police station. He couldn't chase her there.

The police? You really think they'd believe you? You're in the same situation as I am. You're as guilty as me. Thomas' voice rang in her ears. He taunted her when he wasn't around, and the worst part was him being right about it. No police officer would believe that she was trapped by The Traveler. They'd suspect her of being the killer and throw her into a jail cell before going after him. If he found out about them, that was the end of her. No police. No one else could get wrapped in this.

"So how do I take control of my future now?" She stared at the cellphone in the corner. "What do I do?"

She got no answer there, which was fitting. Her future remained unseen as long as those clouds hung over her. Her grandfather didn't say it, but he was aware that Thomas was the big giant cloud who loomed over her life. That was what he feared. That cloud got into her life, messing everything up. He was worried they'd stay, but he also knew that she'd be fine. She was strong enough to break out.

They'll get out of your way. Those clouds will dissolve. It'll just take time.

Hopefully, it doesn't take forever.

Chapter 14

Kara couldn't cry anymore. She couldn't be honest with anyone, not even herself. She couldn't laugh or enjoy the small things in life. She didn't love anything. No matter where she went, Thomas would be right behind her. He haunted every second, taunting her in her dreams. If that wasn't enough, Anne popped in now and then to creep her out. Her ghost wouldn't rest in peace until Thomas was gone. Kara tried not to dwell on her though the image of her bloodied face never left.

Her grandfather was right to worry about her life. This little adventure with Thomas went beyond her control. He didn't see the future for her because she couldn't sort out the present. Kara struggled to focus on other things. Only a few things got her attention: Thomas' messages, his stalking, him getting closer than she wanted. She struggled not to stare at her phone in fear that he'd call her out. That was no longer an option.

"He knows everything." She tucked a few strands of hair into a small bun. "Well, not anymore. I can play your little game too. I'll get you."

Not that she had a clue on how to play the game. She followed Thomas' directions out of fear. He chopped off her hair. The next time, he'd go for a body part. Getting ahead of him would require a lot of thinking on her part.

She tried coming up with various escape plans, each one getting more ridiculous than the previous. Running, calling the police, escaping to Hawaii, faking her own death, faking an illness. All those ideas ran through her head as she crossed them out. Thomas was twisted, not stupid. He'd hunt her down if she tried escaping. Every option led to death, either her own or someone else's. By the time she got to the end of her list, she had nothing but crossed out words.

Well, that's a bust. I'm getting nowhere with my escape plans. She closed the pad, tapping her pencil on the table. Her mother found her right there, eyes staring off into space and hands fidgeting. Somehow, she saw this as a cue to give Kara a little work, so she grabbed a notepad from the counter and scribbled a few things down.

"Is everything all right?" She touched Kara's shoulder, bringing her back into reality. Thank God the pad was closed, or she'd have questions on all the things crossed out, questions Kara wasn't ready to answer. "You look a little pale."

"I'm okay, Ma. It's just been rough lately. I'm having a hard time sitting still." She forced her hands to stop fidgeting. "See? Even when I'm trying, I'm moving. I need to get my mind off things. Of course, I still pick up and drop people off today. That's not a problem. It's just being in the house and waiting for my shift to start...yeah, that's the tough part."

"Maybe this can help you out." Her mother handed her a piece of paper with a list of items. "I know you're busy today, and you'll get a lot of rides. But whenever you get that free moment, can you pick some milk and eggs for me?"

"I'll try." Kara folded the list into her pocket. "I mean, do you need it right away?"

"If you get a chance, then pick it up. It's not something I need immediately. If you can't, just let me know and I'll get your father to bring it." She untied Kara's hair, letting her new hairdo come down. "About time you cut this! It was getting so dry!"

"Yeah, well, it's time for a change." Kara sipped the last of her coffee. "You were right about the bottom part looking like a bird's nest. It's about time I got rid it."

"Well, next time, make sure you get your nails done too. Look at them! They're so short since you keep biting them."

Kara stared down at her fingernails, knowing her mother was right. She always had that nasty nail-biting habit but after picking up Thomas, it intensified. She sat at traffic lights and parking lots chewing away at her nails. She tried to keep them long, yet the nerves kicked in and she bit away. Now all she had were stubby nails. She wanted a manicure, but it would have to wait till her next free day.

"Maybe later, Ma. When I get a chance...and that's very rare." She turned her gaze to her toes, the toenails growing out. The last time she went in for a pedicure was two months ago. Since she didn't have the best grasp with toenail clippers, she let the people at the nail salon take care of them. Of course, she hadn't stepped into one of those in weeks either. "I'm telling you, Ma. I can barely do your errands. With the curfew in place, I'm only able to drop off a rider and then come straight home. No store runs or anything."

"I know. I'm just saying if you don't have too many riders, you can get this." She stroked Kara's arm. "Be sure to take care of yourself."

I wish I could. Kara twitched harder over the idea of driving again. Even if it was just to get her mother's things, she couldn't stop being nervous. A part of her almost considered calling in sick to Happy Riders. She was sick deep down with a headache and upset stomach. She was only going through all this so no one else worried about her. Every time anyone asked if she was okay, a pain shot through her as she lied to them. She forced herself to smile and tell them she would be fine. Whatever she dealt with, it would pass.

As her shift began, she got a message from the one person she expected. Thomas needed another ride, waiting outside of a restaurant in downtown Charlotte. Hopefully, he wasn't planning to hurt anyone tonight. Downtown Charlotte was full of people. If he wanted to kidnap anyone, someone would see him. This restaurant was situated well in view of others. She caught the name, remembering that she took a lot of people over here and picked up many. Apparently, it was a Brazilian steakhouse that had many good reviews. She never went on the basis that it was expensive, and she didn't eat meat that wasn't fish or chicken. A few people that she knew went there and loved it. They said it was somewhere they went to on special occasions, not a place to eat out every day.

And here I go again to pick him up. She flipped on the air conditioner and let the radio play. All these old songs were the best distraction right now. They kept her mind right on the road. She hummed the melodies to herself as she checked her mirrors before changing lanes. Downtown Charlotte appeared within seconds, the bright lights and tall buildings welcoming her as she drove in. A part of her wished she was stopping her for a few minutes, hitting up a bar or walking around. If Thomas wasn't gonna make her drive around town, and she didn't get many riders afterwards, she'd come out here to take in some air. This kind of nightlife was the one she wanted. Even as she rolled down the streets with the AC blasting in her face, she glanced around for some free parking. It would be impossible to find a place close to the restaurant. Most of the parking decks were completely full as well. She wasn't sure where else to park.

I might have to come here later than most people leave. She finally spotted him waiting outside of the restaurant. She pulled up the curb and unlocked the door, preparing for the next long night. *Oh, I hope he's in a good mood tonight. God get me through this.*

"Good evening, Kara." He got into the back seat as she accepted the ride. "Right on time as always."

"Well, if I'm late, I lose money. I got to save every bit I get." She waited till he settled in before pulling away. In the corner of her eye, she caught the name of the restaurant along with the long crowd waiting outside. "I've never picked you up in front of this place. Is the food any good?"

"Eh, it's typical of a Brazilian steakhouse. Have you ever been to one?"

"No, I don't really eat much meat so it's probably not my thing. I wouldn't want to spend money on something I don't eat." She glanced once more at the growing crowd before driving off. "I guess other people really like it though. It must be a little expensive."

"It is, but if you have the money, I see no harm in trying it out. That's the thing; try the new things in life. Don't worry about how much it will cost in the end. If you get the moment, seize it. Remember that Latin saying? Carpe diem?"

"Seize the day." Kara's shoulders tensed up at his latest words. Thomas didn't sound like himself tonight. He didn't have that killer lust lingering over him. He left that restaurant like he was any other patron: happy and full. Even as he stared out the window, he smiled as they passed by several streets. He wasn't bloodthirsty right now. He enjoyed his night in the restaurant. Kara took his advice and seized her moment to ask more. "So, did you go out with friends or by yourself?"

"Eh, these days, I don't have time for friends. They don't have time for me. I know it's more to visit these places with people, but I can't wait for anyone anymore. That's why I went by myself. I wanted to treat myself."

"You got a table to yourself? That's impressive."

"More like they asked if I was okay sitting with a group. I didn't mind it, and I don't think they did either. They didn't really notice me though. They were too busy with their own lives." He scowled for a second, before noticing a little dog in the corner and waving at it. "It's fine. If the food and service are good, I'm not worried about the company."

So, he eats alone. I guess that's not too shocking given his extracurricular activities. He didn't appear angry at the other group either. He didn't have that anger he had towards his victims. Maybe he realized that he intruded on them, not the other way around. *All right, Kara. Keep pressing. He's still in a good mood.*

"I'm assuming there are no vegetarian dishes there."

He scoffed. "Why on earth would a vegetarian go to a steakhouse, Kara? I'd expect them to be a little bit smarter. It's like saying you can't eat chocolate, yet you order a chocolate cake for dessert. It doesn't make sense to me."

"Me neither." Kara ran out of questions then. Her mind turned towards the road, now building up with more traffic. She groaned internally as a giant group of pedestrians crossed in front of her, several holding out their hands to stop traffic. For ungodly reasons, they decided to cross here instead of the crosswalk where it would be safer.

She waited patiently for the large groups to move, her foot pressed on the break. None of them knew of the danger lurking in her backseat. Even if he was happy now, he wouldn't stay that way if she didn't get him home.

"I see you were able to get your car cleaned out last night." Thomas rubbed his hand up and down the seats. "Not a wet spot in sight. I hope you were able to get home before curfew went up."

Kara gripped the steering wheel to slow down at the light. She couldn't take another second of him doing this anymore. "How did you know I'd be there? You didn't ask me for a ride last time."

"No, I didn't. I wasn't ready for a ride. However, I knew you'd still be driving out there in the dark. It's like I told you before; you can't really trust anyone out there. The nicest people might end up being your worst enemies. You don't understand that because you're still very young. The world just opened to you. You have opportunities that someone my age won't get again. That doesn't mean you can't be vigilant."

"So, that's what this is about? You're being vigilant?"

"I'm protecting you." He inhaled as she turned on the next light. "I can't let anyone else lay a hand on you. The world isn't evil to you yet. Because you're young and free, you can do as you want. You have your whole life in front of you. That's the beauty of being in your early twenties: the world is yours until the moment you turn thirty."

Kara listened carefully as she drove on. "Did something happen at thirty?"

Thomas leaned back in the car with his head tilted towards the window. The coldness evaporated right then. "My life ended then. At that point, no one wants to help you. They think you know everything. You can do everything. Once you go past that point, you can't return. You can't go back to being young and healthy again. You lose your options."

As the traffic slowed down, he also changed the chilly tone in his voice. Something got to him now. Something deep down ate away at him, the same thing that ate him several years ago. She didn't know how old Thomas was but suspected him of being somewhere in his fifties. No wonder he talked about losing options now. Her father mentioned years ago when he struggled to find work. Back then, no one wanted someone who had education and experience. They wanted someone young, someone they could mold and change. She spent days watching her father pour through his own resumes, get ready for interviews, nail them, and come back with no job. Whenever she asked why, he told her the same thing.

"I'm just too experienced, too old. They need someone who's just starting."

The reply never made sense. "But wouldn't it be better for you to get the job? You'll learn it faster than the new person does."

"Maybe. But let's be honest with ourselves. I'm older. I don't look as good in the company as someone younger would. I wouldn't fit in."

"Fit in?" She still couldn't wrap around those words. "Why are you making it sound like you're back in school and you got to fit in?"

He chuckled on that question. "Well, in a strange way, the working world is a lot like school. You may not be in class anymore, but you're still fighting to find your place in it. It sadly doesn't end in school. You fight like this your entire life."

She couldn't grasp his analogy back then, but it made sense the moment she started applying for jobs. She didn't fit into anything. Even retail jobs couldn't see any use for her. She couldn't be molded to fit in. The younger the model, the more likely they were hired. It hurt now whenever her father pressured her to find work. He forgot how hard it had been for him. Then again, not long after that conversation, he was hired by a good company and kept them afloat. Kara couldn't do the same. She figured that her father probably had a little more charisma than she did.

He found the tissue box in the back, a brand-new pack she laid out after the last one vanished. "Are these for passengers too, Kara?"

"The tissues? Oh yeah, that's for my riders. Anyone can use those." She waited until the first car turned before making her move. During that wait, she checked the address to drop him. McIver Drive, her new hangout. "You're going home tonight? No other stops?"

"Not tonight." He closed his eyes as she drove on. "I don't have the will to do anything tonight. That's a good thing for you. You can get home early."

"I don't know. If I get another rider close by, I might pick them up." She couldn't shake it out. Thomas was being a little too normal and kind over here. He acted like this was the first time they rode together, much like at the airport. He didn't go for any of her water bottles or snack packets in the back. He didn't try to ask about her this time. He rested while she drove, which alarmed her. "Are you okay, Thomas? You look exhausted."

"Oh, you don't know half of it, Kara. I spend most of my life exhausted." He didn't bother opening his eyes. Glancing back, she caught how white he turned and his slow breathing. That breathing came from someone who ran multiple errands and spent most of their time on their feet. It didn't come from someone who ate at a restaurant. "You don't have any idea what it's like to burn out before you're thirty-five. To be told there's nothing else for you. You better give up any dreams you had because they won't come true. They'll go to someone else. They'll live the life meant for you."

"Is that true?" Kara's stomach churned. The calmness was replaced by bitterness; she began to peel away Thomas' layers. His motives started to come into light. He had hatred for the younger generation. He blamed them for taking away opportunities, no matter what they did. "Did someone steal something from you?"

"Not just something. They take opportunities, only to squander them. So many young, idiotic people get the prizes deserved for others." He started snarling, breathing in and out. "They get all the opportunities in the world! They get everything! All they need is one job, and they're set for life! When you're older, nobody cares about your life skills! Nobody cares if you live or die! Nobody is_"

"Then why go after twenty-year olds with nothing to do with you?"

"Because they're invincible, that's why!" He snapped as she hit the brakes. Grabbing the back of the seat, he went on as she stood at the light, tapping her fingers on the wheel. "Twenty-something year olds don't fear anything. They're so sure they're going to be that way forever. I know. I was there once upon a time. I was reckless and carefree, not thinking about what could happen to me. I didn't feel vulnerable and weak then. I was strong. I was wanted by the whole world."

Kara moved her foot from brake to gas as soon as the light changed colors. "That's what you think of your victims? They were invincible?"

"They were...until I proved that they weren't." He laughed as he tapped his hands against the seats. "I reminded them why they shouldn't have squandered all their chances. Fast-food, retail...those aren't stable careers. They can change at any moment. They have that ability to move forward, and they don't. The worst part is that they're not being held back."

"Held back in what way?"

"Their abilities. Their wealth. Their skills. There are some people who are truly stupid, who get whatever they want. They don't do much. Everything they wanted is handed over. Then there is the small fraction who aren't idiots that don't try hard enough. If I had their bit of luck, their youth, their health..." He coughed onto his sleeve. "I couldn't stand to see that any longer."

And that's why you started to kill them. You didn't think they tried hard enough. Kara finished off in her head. By now, she had arrived at the exit for McIver Drive and began the long dark drive towards Thomas' house. "And you're sure a twenty-year old took your spot? What evidence do you have of that?"

"I don't have to get the evidence. It's everywhere I go." He sniffled as he grabbed her tissues from the backseat. "Everywhere I turn, I see some young person living life to the fullest. They don't know what dangers lie ahead. They don't know how quickly their health will deteriorate."

Kara pulled into the driveway, shining the headlights on the front porch. "Your health's deteriorating? You...you seemed okay to me. You're able..."

"No, I'm not." He got out of the car, still wiping his nose. She spotted red all over it. More blood. His nose bled while she drove him around. "My health isn't the same as yours, Kara. It's never going to be. I'm coming home for a good reason."

"Which is?"

He stepped away from the car. "I think you're smart enough to figure all this out. You're getting warmer, but you're not there yet." He slapped the side of the car, careful not to smear blood this time. "Get home safe, Kara. You know you can't be out too late."

She didn't reply as he went up to the door, but she checked her back seat. Sure enough, a huge wad of bloody tissues lay on the floor.

Thomas' blood. He used up her tissues the entire time she drove. He became careless tonight due to being so calm and quiet. Now she knew he wasn't well, struggling with something that made his nose bleed and his body shake. A little more research at home could get her straight to the answer. She understood his motive a little better. He hated his victims for being young and getting good opportunities. He hated them for not taking their lives seriously. He saw them as something he could never be. He hated himself for growing older and weaker.

"He hates young people for being reckless and carefree. He hates himself for being old. I don't get it." She slowed down her driving, careful not to hit anything that crossed her path. So far, she was lucky that the only critters running on the roads were squirrels. She didn't want to run over them as they darted across the street. Yet as she drove on, she spotted a hunk of something lying out there. Her lights shone on it with its fat tongue rolling out of its mouth. A deer lay dead on the side of this road. She slowed down for a better look though didn't shut the car off.

"I don't fucking believe it." She shuddered as something crawled over the deer's body. Bugs. Fantastic. Not only was it dark, but insects also feasted on this deer's carcass. Still, how did a deer die out here? As far as she knew, she was the only one who came down this way to drop Thomas off. Did Thomas have other rideshare drivers come here? She never saw anything on Happy Riders forum boards that suggested they picked him up. Although she hadn't checked it in a while, nothing seemed out of the ordinary. No one mentioned giving a ride to anyone who matched Thomas' description. Everyone was on edge because of The Traveler, hoping they didn't run into him. Yet no one claimed to come down a strange road or hit a deer. No one admitted to seeing one running across the streets.

It could be him. Anne sat in the passenger seat, not caring about the dead animal devoured before her. By now, more flies and black bugs crawled over the deer's head, covering its face with small bodies. *Thomas hates anything that bothers him. I don't know what this deer did, but he took care of it.*

"It doesn't look like his handiwork though." Kara drove from the scene, wiping off any bugs hitting her windshield. "There are no cuts on the body. Something clearly ran over it. I just don't know if it was me."

If it was you, you would have felt it. Your car would have been damaged by it. Anne turned towards the body once more before turning to the dark road. *As far as I see, you don't have any damage. Right?*

Kara couldn't argue there. Her car had plenty of mileage on it, yet it drove smoothly. There were no dents on the sides or issues inside of it, no specks of dust on the hood or paint chipped off. With all the blood washed off, it appeared brand new. The air fresheners worked overtime to mask every bloody scent on those seats. With each inch cleaned, no one suspected a thing. No one knew of the police officer's body slamming into her car. No one knew about Thomas cutting her hair. The clumps he dropped were long gone. Every rider who got a ride remained blissfully unaware of the dark secrets Kara held.

She drove down the street, keeping her focus on everything ahead. Nothing crossed before her as she got onto the road. Even when she came here around daylight, she never saw many animals outside of squirrels. Not that a deer was shocking to find, yet why now? Why didn't she notice it on the way towards the house? It didn't drop out of the sky while she was dropping Thomas off. Nothing made sense.

An omen. It's a sign of things going from bad to worse.

Dead deer. If this was an omen, it arrived a little too late for her. She swallowed the bile forcing its way up her throat. While burning, she pulled away from the deer carcass and drove off. It would haunt her nightmares anyway. No need to keep staring. She couldn't bring it back to life from watching it. She couldn't stop it from dying. She couldn't fix what was already done.

And that's why I gotta get rid of these storm clouds in my future. She peeled out onto the highway, rolling the windows down and letting the wind blow through her hair. There came that freedom she loved with driving. No riders in the back, no worries about staying out too late. No one was threatening her life or planning to hurt others. This was the life she longed for.

Sooner or later, she'd get it back.

Chapter 15

Once again, Kara spent another sleepless night that led to an early morning. Her parents slept while she got up to prepare for the day. Grabbing her clothes, she headed into the shower to wash off last night's strange ride. Thomas behaved well while in the backseat. He didn't grab her forcefully or make any thinly veiled threats. He acted like any other rider coming home from a restaurant. Still, his conversation about not being able to do art didn't leave her. He held something back. He didn't go to Paris, yet he went to Japan and other countries in his older age. If he told the truth that night, then he had a passport to travel. Why not go to Paris and fulfill the dream now? The exact same dream couldn't come back, but a new one could replace it. Was it the money holding him back? No, that couldn't be it either. He had money to travel elsewhere.

"He must be hiding something deep down. Something even I don't know about." The water ran long enough to steam the bathroom mirror. Then she stepped in and lathered up with cherry-vanilla soap her mother got her. The heat mixed in with that cherry-vanilla scent cleared up all the dirt on her. She couldn't remember the last nice, long shower she took. Usually, she showered at night after getting home from driving. Her mother left food on the table for her, while she showered. Shaking her hair out, she cleansed her face and stood in the warm water, spitting out anything getting into her mouth. Once every bit of her cleaned up, she turned off the tap and grabbed the towel as water drained out.

I wonder if I can press him a little more about his past. She patted herself dry with the towel before going to the mirror. Now all foggy, she wiped it clean and stared back at her reflection. Her eyes now red from no sleep, she rubbed them and turned to the little bits of fog on the sides of the mirror. Her memory of Thomas drawing all over them came back. Using just his finger and the fog on the windows, he created beautiful patterns. He didn't stumble even when she drove over bumps or made sharp turns.

Kara got Thomas' message as soon as she stepped out of the shower. He didn't call for a ride, but a little reminder. *Hope you rested well last night. We have another run to make this morning.*

"Oh, fuck." She took the towel off her hair, letting her wet locks hit her shoulders. She rarely cursed herself, especially with that word. Given all the hell he dragged her through, the hell he still pulled her into, the f-words built up inside of her. "Fuck fuck fuck fuck…"

Stopping herself, she went through the rest of her phone for any replies. No one except for Happy Riders, who congratulated her for another good review. In the past, those kept her going for the next few days. The good reviews gave her that little burst of serotonin that lifted her spirits. They reminded her that yes, she did have a job and there were perks. It was not some massive job of importance like a doctor or engineer, but it gave her a pleasure that an office job would never give.

She had gone through the websites of former friends and classmates to see how people reviewed them at their work. The results always varied while she remained highly reviewed and recommended by others.

Her heart sank at the reminder of everything else. Thomas planned another run with her, so she had to prepare. Maybe he found someone lonely at the Brazilian steakhouse. Or worse yet, he targeted one of the poor waiters there. She didn't know anyone who worked there that could fit his description of a lazy, carefree young person. In any case, she was ready to stop him from killing tonight.

As she dressed up, she spotted Anne sitting on her bed, legs crossed and head still bleeding. Anne's eyes glanced all around the room before locking on Kara again. *You will have to be very careful around him. If he spots you, he won't hesitate to kill you.*

"Tell me something I don't know." Kara grabbed the hairbrush, running it through her hair. This hair, the same one Thomas chopped off, grew a few inches in the last few days. Holding out a bit of it, she ran her finger down the ends. "I gotta be faster than him. My biggest problem is him finding me before I find the next victim."

It will be difficult, but it must be done. Anne pulled her hair back, revealing more gashes on her neck. Those knife slashes ran deep into her flesh, even making a hole in the side. Kara tried her best not to throw up at that sight. *Use what you know and get control. It's the only way you're going to come out of this alive.*

"I somehow doubt that." Kara finished brushing her hair before sitting in front of the mirror and grabbing her makeup. After running around with Thomas and driving her other riders, she forgot to put on makeup nowadays. She didn't have the time or will to sit down and blend anything together. She didn't remember her favorite lip liners or eyeshadow. Now that she had all the brushes and kits out, she went through them, trying to match each color with the right brush.

Eventually, she settled on some soft, subtle pinks and light browns for today. The less makeup she got on, the easier it would be to get rid of.

"I'm not sure why I'm bothering with it." She started to put on her foundation. "I end up crying and sweating up a storm. I look like a clown on acid now."

That's not true. You've got a lot on your mind. Anne touched the gash across her neck, trying to stop the bleeding. The blood poured between her fingers, running down her hands. *You will look fine no matter what you do.*

"It's not my looks I'm worried about. I just want some bit of normalcy back in my life. I want to drive people around without worrying what they'll do next. I want my next passengers to be regular people like me. People I'm dropping off or picking up at the airport. People who need rides to work or the store or their favorite eating place. People who just want to get home after a long day. Why can't I have that?"

You can still have that. You'll always have that. The moment you stop him from killing, you get your life back. Be grateful for that.

There it was. Anne reminded her that she was still alive, yet Kara couldn't be grateful. She hated all the secrets she kept from people. It was easy for Anne to say that life would come back because she no longer had a life. If Thomas didn't kill her, the police would catch up to her one day. Be it tomorrow or several years down the road, they'd find her. They'd learn about her part in all this. How long did an accomplice to a serial killer stay in jail? The court wouldn't believe that she got roped into this. If they did, they still wouldn't let her go free. If she killed him, she ended up in jail. If she didn't kill him, she'd be in jail. No wonder her grandfather talked about dark clouds over here. He didn't see her future as bright.

"Oh God." She put the makeup away to stare at her face. Instead of her reflection, she saw all of Thomas' victims glaring down at her, empty eyes and bleeding bodies galore. She no longer screamed or shrunk away at them. She pitied them, wishing to help them out sooner. "I know what you're going to say. Go after him anyway. Forget what the police say."

They'll never believe you, no matter what. The voices chanted before her. *They'll never accept you as an innocent party. You might as well throw it all on the line.*

"Yeah, but my family…"

They'll be in more danger if you let that man go. He knows about them. He knows you. He'll get to them before you can. Stop him. Stop him. Stop him.

"Okay, I get it!" She held up her hands. "You want me to stop him, I'll stop him. I need a plan though. It's obvious he goes one step further than his victims. He tries to get ahead of them." She snapped her fingers. "He's not well. I can't figure out what is wrong, but he's not well. I know there are some illnesses where you shake…like chronic fatigue syndrome."

Moving towards her laptop, Kara began to search for everything regarding chronic fatigue syndrome. For a disease that sounded like someone was on tired all the time, there were far too many symptoms with shaking being one of them. But Thomas didn't appear to have the other symptoms. Her head spun at all the information, needing a quick break in between. Getting up, she ran to the bathroom for her medication. Her mind couldn't focus on anything anymore. With how much Thomas invaded it, she wanted something to calm her.

"Come on." Taking her pills, she swallowed them and closed the cabinet door. A blue glint bounced off the mirror, causing her to choke on the water. No need to turn this time; he wasn't there. He never lingered around her at home.

The story about Thomas the artist wanted her to dig a little deeper. None of the reasons he gave made sense. He could still draw if he wished to. He might not study in Paris anywhere, but he could still go and admire all the art there. He could try all over again. He admitted that he could still wield a brush even if the strokes weren't the same. If he could hold a knife, why couldn't he paint anymore? What happened to him? Then her mind went back to how he talked about his father. That evil father who didn't give two craps about his desires or wellbeing. If he didn't nurture that artistic gift, he sure as hell wouldn't pay for any schooling in another country. Her mother went through something similar as a girl. After getting into a prestigious school in England, she almost said yes. It was Kara's grandfather who warned her not to. He'd seen the premonitions of terrible things to come, telling her to wait till marriage to leave India. Maybe it turned out for the better, but Kara always wondered if her mother resented her grandfather for it.

Thomas was the same in that regard. He held a great deal of resentment towards his father. He talked about him with a deeper hatred, a bigger disgust towards him than towards the youth. She couldn't blame him for hating an abusive, uncaring parent. She also didn't blame him for thinking she didn't get it. She didn't have that situation. Her parents took a while to accept dyscalculia, but they didn't hate her for having it. They only wished she was better with numbers like all the other Indian children.

Oh God, why did I have to remember them? That memory opened a flood of other memories at Indian functions. Whenever they went to any pujas or festivals, her parents ran into other Indian parents who bragged about how great their kids were. She'd learn about the kids who got perfect SATs scores, the ones who ended up as valedictorians of their class, the ones who went onto Ivy League schools, and the ones who just wowed the whole goddamn world with their existence. For her part, Kara remained polite and congratulated those who did well. Her parents did the same, taking it all in stride and making small talk with everyone. Deep down, she knew they craved the same things. They wanted their moment to brag to other Indian parents. They wanted Kara to be as great as the others, go to those Ivy League schools, become a famous scientist or lawyer or do something incredible. They wanted her to be great enough for them to talk about.

"And I'm nothing but a rideshare driver right now." She chuckled as she got up and paced around the room. This was the one place she could retain a little bit of sanity. Her parents didn't change much while she stayed in college. The only difference was the bed sheets her mother put out almost every week. Now that Kara was home, she changed the bed herself. Her posters of old Broadway musicals and favorite bands still stayed tacked on the walls. She even had pictures of the family along with some fake paintings by Monet hung up. The room came from five years ago, and seemed stuck there, but at least it provided a little quiet and comfort. Here, she could arrange all her thoughts.

"No wonder he hates his life. It's not what he wanted either." She threw her hands in the air. "Granted, I didn't get angry enough to kill anyone but...oh God, what's wrong with me?" She flopped down on the bed. "I'm showing compassion to a killer. What is wrong with me? What the fuck am I doing?!" On her nightstand, she found that familiar sheet of paper waiting for her. That same paper she forgot to grab before heading out. "Damn it! I knew it!"

Kara gazed down at another list her mother gave her. Eggs and bread. Somehow, she forgot all about running those simple errands between dropping off and picking up riders. Her eyes twitched over the growing list that included fruit, milk, muffins, dishwashing liquid soap, tissues, and AA batteries. Her mother even marked not to bring in store brand products despite them being a little cheaper. Crumpling up the paper, she shoved it into her purse and stared into the mirror. The old Kara no longer existed. A new Kara, one holding so many dark secrets, emerged here. She thrived in this world, being one with a serial killer. She was just like him now. Even if she didn't wield the knife, she carried the killer around and dropped him wherever he wanted to go. She was guilty too. She was part of it.

"No no no!" She shook her head, letting the tangled locks fall on her shoulders. "You aren't him! He's making you think that."

You're right. Anne stood behind her, brown hair covering some of her cuts. *He's in your head now. He wants to tear you apart.*

"It's a little late to tell me that now." She curled up in bed, hugging her knees. "He's already screwed up so much of my life. I don't know what else he could do."

It's not about what he can do to you. It's what you need to do for yourself. You want to be free, don't you? It's high time you broke free.

She couldn't argue with that. The drive at night was a painful reminder of what she missed. Going down that highway, the speed slowly going up and pushing the pedal to the metal. Driving between shifts, not checking her phone every second, being free. Anne was right. Her life was what she would do with it, not Thomas. The answer to her future was up in the air, but she could take a few steps closer to a better life.

A knock on the door sat her right back up and let go of her knees. "Come in!"

Her mother entered, waving a college course catalogue in her hand. "Are you free right now, Karishma? I found the next semester course list."

"Next semester course list?" She covered her face. "Mama, we've been through this. College was hell for me. School in general is hell for me. I don't even know how I survived it the first time around! Why do you guys want me to go through it again?"

"I didn't say that." Her mother opened the course catalogue. "I brought this for you to look through. See if there's anything you like. It doesn't have to be math or science or any class with numbers in it. I know it was hard. I know you had a bad time there. I just wanted to see if you were interested in going back one day. It doesn't have to be this year. If it's taking a long time getting a job..."

"Ma, I started looking for work three months ago. Some people are still hunting for a job after three years, maybe longer." She shrugged. "I mean, I'm trying whenever I get free time. I don't have that much free time, I might add."

"I know. It's just that you appear more stressed doing this."

"I was stressed in school too." Kara shuddered over the idea of going back to school. Long nights studying, eyes blurring while trying to read, trying to fit into more groups. Her current job offered enough adventure and stress. School would be another pain in the ass she wasn't ready to deal with. "Ma, don't you remember all the meds I was on during that time? I was on the highest doses possible of everything."

"But then you got better and..."

"Whoa!" Kara held up her hand. "Who said anything about me getting better? I still have A.D.D, Ma. I'm still an anxious mess. I'm only a little calmer than before, and that's all because I'm not in school. I'm not sure if I want to go back."

"Can I leave the book with you?" Her mother put it on the nightstand. "Look through it. Read it. You don't have to decide right now. Think about it for a while. When you decide, then you can tell me. Okay?"

"Okay, Ma." Kara nodded as her mother left the room, wishing she could think about something so simple. Her head said no. She didn't have the time to go through this again. She couldn't put herself through the same pain. Her heart held a desire to try though. Maybe this time around, if she didn't have to take math, she could get through it. She'd just take the easiest bunch of courses. That couldn't hurt. It did cost money, but maybe she could think about it.

Besides, it would be an excuse to drive less. Maybe then... She gulped as her phone revealed another message from Thomas. She didn't need to look at the message anymore since it was clear: he wanted her to come now.

Maybe then I'd finally be free.

Chapter 16

After fifteen minutes, Kara picked Thomas up from downtown Charlotte, not bothering to ask why he was down there. At this point, she figured out his routine and could drive him anywhere blindfolded if necessary. He nodded at her while she checked the GPS and the air coming from the vents. Once he got in, she took a deep breath. "I take it that you're going to one of your usual places."

"You know me all too well, Kara." He patted the seat before closing the car door. "You got here with plenty of time to spare."

"Then let's get going." She didn't glance at him as she set the GPS and began to drive around. "I'm sorry if I didn't answer right away. I was trying to escape my parents."

"Oh? Were they bothering you?"

"Not really. Mom just wants me to go back to school." She wrinkled her nose. "I've gone through this with her before. I told her that I don't want another degree because the last one was hell. It took forever for me to complete it, and my mind was frayed. I don't want to endure that again."

"So, tell her that."

"Easier said than done." Kara slowed down with the traffic. "I think she's doing that whole trying something several times and expecting a different result. I haven't moved from my spot yet. I did think about it though. No guarantees I'll go back to school, but I promised to think. Nothing more."

Thomas said nothing about that, but she knew he heard everything. He always paid attention to her words even if it was simple complaints. As she eased down the road, watching out for pedestrians darting in front, he checked his phone before gazing out the window. His eyes shifted a bit, losing some of his cold nature at the giant murals they passed. Local artists often created art on the buildings, leaving behind their messages and standing out among the dull colored buildings. He nodded as they continued to drive on. He approved of this art. It wasn't being in museums or being sold in auctions. It came straight from the artist's soul. If he wasn't so gross deep down, Kara would be impressed with his fascination. Like a kid, his eyes brightened at all the big colors and shapes forming pictures around him. The artwork was nice. She almost said something but drove on, letting him take in all the colors.

He's gone all quiet right now. That's a good thing. Hope he stays that way. She drove out of town, leaving behind all the giant murals and got on the main road. No longer avoiding pedestrians, she picked up the gas and hung onto the wheel. Things were going fine right now. If she stayed within the speed limit, they'd make it there in one piece.

"I know you have your share of issues, Kara." Thomas began. "You hide your problems because no one else understands. How long did it take your parents to finally believe you had struggles? What did they tell you when you first went to them?"

Kara gulped. "They told me it was in my mind. There's no way I can do that bad at math. Math is easy. Everyone else can get the answer, why can't you? They didn't accept that I was having problems. They didn't believe the teacher when she said I struggled in class. Apparently, I was just too lazy. Maybe I was too dumb."

"You're neither of those things. You struggled like a lot of people. Math doesn't come easily to everyone. When did they finally believe you?"

"When I made it to high school. I couldn't keep up with algebra or any other math classes. I couldn't understand any of the equations. I kept bombing the exams, no matter how much help I got. In the end, it was my math tutor who brought this up with my teacher and they did some tests. And...well, that's when they finally believed it. Not me, not my teachers, they believed the tests. It's a miracle I survived college. I guess that's the good part of studying humanities: less math and science classes."

Thomas sat in silence for a bit. Then he leaned in as she got on a new road. He wasn't going to McIver Drive yet. "They still don't believe you, do they? Even with all the results in their face, they don't believe you."

She didn't want to answer him, but shook her head no. "I guess they don't want to believe what they can't explain. The important thing is I know that I have dyscalculia. It's who I am. It explains a lot about me."

"Yes, it is. It's what makes you who you are." He waited until she slowed down in front of the house. "Stay here. I won't be too long."

I hope you are. Her mind began ticking away at a plan. He came home often, yet she rarely found the lights on, the garbage cans out during garbage pickup day, or all the mail and packages lay on the porch. If he didn't live there, why not clean up his mess? Instead, he went to someone else's house for a few seconds. He stayed at his house for a short time. The only thing that made sense was that he had someone hiding in this house. That someone wanted to get out, so maybe if she made her presence known, they'd realize hope was on the way. She failed before. Not tonight.

Kara waited until Thomas left her sights before taking her car keys out and unlocking the driver's side. She grabbed the bag of rocks and messages, tucking them under her arm. Déjà vu hit her as she snuck around the car. Much like last time, she got the chance to save the occupant in the house. Hurrying towards the house, she stood a few feet from the door, grabbed a rock, and threw it. It hit the front door. Then went another one.

"Please give me a sign. Do something! Show me you're okay!" She pleaded as the lights came on. Thomas went around but these lights went on in the front. A figure that didn't match his appeared behind the curtains, which gave her comfort. This person was able to move around and turn on lights. They weren't dead yet. "Yes! Someone's there!"

She darted back towards the car, running away from it. If Thomas heard those thuds too, he'd run to it to stop her. No, this time she had to lose him in this wilderness. Zig-zagging down the path, she jumped over several branches and stumbled on the giant stones. A rustling behind her signaled something there. Thomas or not, she didn't turn around to find out. Weaving between tree trunks, she ran down the slope, trying to keep her balance.

Keep running! Move! Anne's voice along with all the other figures yelled at her to push on. Her calves burned as she neared the bottom of the slope, running right into a fork. Left or right, where did she go next? No, she didn't see a road leading to civilization. Taking a second to check behind her, a squirrel darted away but no Thomas or any other person. She was now at the bottom of the slope which led one of three ways: left, right, or down. Inching into the road, she stared at the slope below this one. Deeper and longer, it would take a while to get down there, yet the leaves and branches created the perfect hiding spot. If she could hide out here, he wouldn't get to her.

"Kara! Kara, where did you go?!" Thomas yelled. This wasn't an angry yell, but one of confusion. "Kara! Get back here! I need help!" Then came a bunch of loud coughs. "Kara, help...I can't...I don't..."

A trick. He wanted to drag her back to get her in his grasp. The ragged coughs weren't faked, but she refused to move back to the car. Inches towards the other slope, she grabbed a tree branch and started to lower herself. Maybe there'd be some help at the bottom of this one. At the very least, she could find the highway and flag someone down. Getting someone to help her was better than going back to Thomas.

Please don't find me. Oh God, please don't come down here!

"Kara!"

CRACK!

Her foot slipped on the wet leaves below and she slid onto the ground, rolling down to the bottom of the slope. She shrieked as she covered her face, avoiding all the sticks poking out of the ground. With nothing on the side to slow her down or stop her, she rolled all the way to the bottom, still crying out. Her body weight crunched several leaves and twigs as she went over them. Her knee ached the moment she came to that stop, rolling right into the first rock sticking out of the ground.

"Oh shit!" She winced as the pain shot through her knee. "Shit!"

"Kara!" Footsteps grew louder and closer as the person she didn't want approached her. "Oh shit, Kara! What the hell are you doing down here?!"

"I, uh…" She grabbed her knee as she tried to sit up. "Damn! I think I…"

"Sit up, sit up!" Thomas sat her up to get a better look at the damage. Aside from a few scrapes and cuts, she survived the fall. The knee pain got worse as soon as she tried straightening the leg out. Crying from the burning, she kneeled over to rub her legs. Thomas stepped back and started to get her onto her feet. "Goddammit, Kara! How'd you end up here?"

"I, um…I needed…" Kara stammered as she blurted out an excuse. "I needed the bathroom!"

"The bathroom?" He put her on her feet as the pain subsided. "You came out here for a bathroom break?"

"There's nothing here for miles. I didn't want to…I didn't know where to go." Slowly, she moved her leg forward, relieved that it wasn't broken. "In India, I couldn't find many public restrooms…well, nice public restrooms…when we were traveling from place to place. It's hard to go in them sometimes. They're usually crowded and not the cleanest. So, my mother suggested that if I need to go, go out in the field. It's not ideal, but it's easier to deal with. That's kind of what I was doing here."

"Maybe so, but you're not in India. You're trying to pee in the woods…I assume." He gazed at her, realizing there was more. "Is that the truth, Kara? You needed to pee so badly that you came down here?"

"…I didn't want to pee in a person's yard." The excuse fell out of her lips like a whimper. It wasn't the best one she ever came up with, but it was the only one that made sense. "I didn't think I'd...I didn't want to..."

"Your leg isn't broken." He cut her off as he got her to the top of the slope. "It's not even sprained. The worst you'll get is some pain, which you can heal if you have any of those creams. I've used tons of them over the years. They'll remove pain for a short time."

"...You've hurt yourself like I did?" She wiggled her toes, finding them still bending and moving with ease. By now, her knee didn't ache. She could still walk, but running needed some time. No use in escaping him. Hopefully, she distracted him from his future victim. Even more, she hoped the victim would get out on time. She focused on other distractions, keeping him from his job. "I'm taking it you weren't trying to pee in the woods.'

"Oh no. These pains started well before I..." Thomas caught his breath as she slowly pulled up. Despite her chance to escape, she didn't run. She wasn't physically ready to run. Her knee could give out any second. "You would never understand. You're so healthy and young. Yes, you do have your disabilities. I know you probably take medication for that ADD and you struggle with numbers. It's not quite the same though. You wouldn't get it until you're in the same position."

"You still won't tell me what that position is. Are you angry because people are young and healthy? Is that what this is about?"

His face contorted, scrunching up his handsome features. "You think I'm angry at people being healthy? No. I'm not mad at them for that. I'm not blaming them for that, nor am I blaming them for being young. This goes well beyond that."

"Then what is it?" She grimaced as she walked towards the car, each jolt of pain running up her body. Walking on a bad leg hurt, all right, but walking next to a psychopath hurt more. Her brain yelled at her to walk away. Call for help. Do something but hang around. "If you're not jealous or angry, what is it that you want from them? There's got to be a reason you're targeting certain people. Why not go after some assholes who are destroying the planet? Why not people who've gotten away with crimes? Believe me, plenty of those exist."

Thomas didn't answer her. No big deal. She'd get him to spill something. "Don't those guys make you angry too? Don't you ever watch the TV and wonder why they get so much attention? Why can't they solve problems instead of creating them? Why can't they just_"

"Kara?"

He cut her off as something sharp slashed into her arm. Kara shrieked from the pain, her free hand grasping the new bleeding wound. She gazed down at the blood seeping between her fingers, the pain burning while he stared down, completely cold. "You really talk too much sometimes. You make a lot of sense, but you talk too much."

"What the hell did you do?!" Kara hissed as she rolled her shirt sleeve down. "What the...why the..."

"It's just a tiny reminder, my dear. You and I aren't friends. You can't talk to me like you're sharing your deepest, darkest secrets. Your job is to drive me around, pick me up, and drop me off. Nothing more than that. You can do that much, can't I?"

"I..." She grabbed her arm. "I...my arm..."

"It's nothing more than a mere scratch. The bleeding will stop eventually. I do advise that you keep it covered up though. Find some bandages or cloth to wrap that. The quicker you stop the bleeding, the better."

She noted that he didn't move or offer to help clean the wound. The blood oozed out between her fingers as he moved back. "What do you want with me? I know you want me to drive you around, but what is it really? I know you want something deep down."

"What could I want from you? I don't drive. I need rides. It doesn't get simpler than that. For now, you tie that arm up and drive." She sat still, which only agitated him. "What are you waiting for, Kara? You're still on the clock. Clean that up."

She almost argued that her first-aid kit was in the trunk, so going to get that would burn up time. No, he was already late. Wasting more time by opening the trunk would get him angrier. He made it clear the next cut would be in her neck. Gazing around the car, she finally zeroed in on the glove compartment. If there was anything that could clean up her wound, it would be in there. She kept all the important car insurance and registration papers along with the last car inspection form and some extra emergency things. On a rare occasion, she kept makeup and hairbrushes, which then gave her an idea.

Maybe these will work. They're not much, but they'll do. Going through the compartment, she found a thick piece of cloth and some headbands. She kept them there on the days she forgot to do her hair and needed something to hold it back. Granted, with shorter hair, she didn't use them as much. With no bandages or other first aid things in sight, she attempted to tie the cloth on with the headband. Her left hand didn't have the same coordination as her right one. She often cursed herself for not being ambidextrous. Her parents told her that the left hand wasn't supposed to be strong, never the dominant hand. People used that one to clean themselves with. It was always the weaker hand, the less important one. Given that she couldn't even tighten a simple piece of cloth angered her. She needed it to work as well as the right one. Given the pain in the right arm, she had to rely on it.

"Oh, for the...let me do it!" Thomas pressed the cloth down on her arm and tightened the headband around it. "I forgot that you're right-handed. You probably have no strength in that left hand. Anyway, the bleeding is going to stop soon, so you won't have to see a doctor for it. Keep that arm hidden though. If you know what's best, you won't show it to a soul."

Kara ignored that as she wiped up the drops of blood on her arm. There he went with veiled threats. She never intended to show the wound to anyone. If the pain shot through, she'd take some aspirin and pray that it would die down eventually. Thomas moved away from it and nodded towards the road ahead. Her cue to drive on. With the blood no longer running down her arm, she revved up the engine and continued her way according to the GPS. That cut came quickly and without a warning. All Thomas said was her name and slashed her to shut her up. She focused on the directions, using the left hand to drive most of the way. Her right arm burned when she turned into McIver Drive, the blood pulsing through her veins. Once she got a moment to herself, she'd stop off somewhere and clean up the rest of the blood.

Blood. In the past few days, she saw more of it now than in her whole life. The only time she got it drawn was for doctor appointments. She couldn't bear to look at the needle going into her vein or use knives properly. She got plenty of complaints about nurses having difficulty finding a decent vein because she squirmed over needles too much. Yet she was here, cleaning someone else's blood out of her car and covering her own wound. Thomas didn't flinch at the sight or smell of it. Of course he wouldn't. It wasn't his blood pouring out. He wasn't the one crying in pain or getting his life drained out. He tied that headband well enough to keep blood flowing, but her arm still ached. Once she parked the car, he flung the car door open and got out. Before he left, he poked his head in and nodded at the wound.

"You should clean that up and get a stronger bandage on it. It'll sting, but that pain won't last for long. You should be fine to drive anywhere else. Keep it always covered even when you're showering."

He reminded her. "It'll go away soon. I promise. If you're careful with it, it won't open again."

She didn't reply but nodded as he closed and walked to the house. She didn't wait for him to get inside before checking on the GPS. Putting in the directions for home, she drove off without checking to see if he followed. He had no reason to follow her now, since she did her job. Everyone over at Happy Riders would remain satisfied with her work. Thomas hadn't put up new reviews since the original one, but they knew he was a satisfied repeat customer. That's all they wanted; a rider that got home in one piece and was willing to use their services again. Kara struggled not to tell her boss about her situation. She was trapped with this maniac. He dragged her in, and now she couldn't get out unless someone helped her out. They'd never buy it. They wouldn't buy that Kara, their reliable driver, drove a maniac from town to town. She took him to those victims so he could stalk and murder them. If they believed her, then Thomas would find out and hurt them too. While her bosses weren't perfect in any means, she didn't want them to die by his hand.

All right, Kara. He's been telling you for a long time who he is. You can't keep pressing him for answers. You must be stealthy. She got on the highway, the numbers on the signs blurring together. That blood gushing from her arm never left her sight. It didn't pour out anymore, but the image bothered her. A small cut could cause that much damage. The pain went from her arm through the rest of her body. Now her head wasn't acting right. She couldn't read anything and almost took the wrong exit out. Fortunately, the GPS reminded her before she made that move and she moved back into the lane on time. Her mind raced as she made her way back home, trying to focus on the road. The relief of getting into the neighborhood and rolling into her parents' driveway kicked in. Without their car sitting there, she calmed down. Thank God. She came in, and they weren't there. Her mother sent her text earlier saying they were going to shop for groceries but were waiting for her to get back first. Good, they weren't going to stay too long. The less time she spent explaining things, the better for her.

At home, she slipped through the living room and ran towards her bathroom, flinging the door and lights open. Her arm ached as she fumbled around for some bandages and ointment in the medicine cabinet. The pain, God, the pain got worse during the drive. She winced every single time she took a turn or jerked the steering wheel around. Locking the bathroom door, she slowly unwrapped her arm and grimaced at the ugly, jagged scar. He cut her so swiftly, yet this mark appeared to dig deep in her. The blood dried off even if the pain intensified. She found some Indian ointments, squeezing them on the wound. The cool aloe would kick in quicker than most medicines here did. Her family swore by them, and after a few tries, she did as well. Boro-Plus was the preferred ointment in this household. She rubbed the white ointment on herself before grabbing the bandages.

"Fucking hell." She grumbled as they came undone. Bracing herself on the toilet, she wrapped it up to the best of her ability. With the jagged scar now hidden from view, she pulled on a long-sleeved shirt and gazed at herself in the mirror. Her eyes red from pain and crying, she hated her appearance now. She no longer laughed or smiled or did anything to make herself happy. Thomas sucked out any comfort in her life. Maybe her mother had a point. Maybe going back to school would be better. It wasn't her favorite choice, but it was far safer than driving him around.

"What would I major in though?" She washed her face and untangled a couple of knots in her hair. "I mean...I want something with almost no math, which will be impossible. I don't know if I have the will to concentrate and study stuff again. I can't write papers or take exams. Not now."

The other option was finding another job, even a retail job. Her parents wouldn't be thrilled, but it would be more money. If she saved up enough of it, she could finally move out and get a place of her own. Maybe she could save up money for something fun such as taking a trip overseas or even driving cross country. She'd be glad to have enough money to pay off her student loans. Behind their backs, she applied to these other jobs with the hope that they'd call her. She didn't have much experience in the retail world though she knew what it entailed. She'd have to deal with all kinds of people, which she did when it came to her riders. She'd have to learn to cook some food if they put her in the kitchen. Maybe she'd have to practice balancing trays, pouring drinks, and working cash registers. As tough as that was, she'd take it over driving Thomas around.

Grabbing her phone, she sat on the bed and began to search for various fast-food locations. They were always hiring with their big posters plastered on the windows. They always advertised paying up to $15 an hour, but she knew there were catches to that. The few people that she knew who worked in these areas never earned that much. Even when they got raises, which often took months, it was usually just a dollar or two more than their normal pay. It wouldn't be enough to pay for gas in the car, let alone a month's rent in an apartment complex. Biting down on her pride, she still managed to open three applications and began filling them out. Low pay or not, she'd take it. She'd be a good, quick-leaning employee. All they had to do was hire her.

Come on, give me a chance. She plugged in all the usual information for them. Her personal information, education, and employment information went in thanks to memorization. By now, she learned how to write on her phone and double-checked everything before sending the application out. That's how her next thirty minutes would go. She'd find a place, fill out the application, and hope for the best. A call, an interview, someone to give her a little bit of their time and attention. She even made herself available for possible days to show how flexible she could be. She'd take that late night shift or early morning hours if it meant less time driving people around. Well, not just people. Only Thomas.

He hadn't sent any messages since cutting her arm, which calmed her down more. He knew what he did. He knew she'd take care of it without anyone checking on her. Leave her alone for the rest of the night, she could sleep well. The multiple applications she sent out provided a small glimmer of hope. No matter how stingy the application process got, someone out there could use her. Her lack of experience only meant she could be molded into a good employee. That's what they all wanted in the end: good employees who did everything that was asked of them. Happy Riders followed that same structure. If they could turn someone into a good driver, they would be happy.

To pass time, she began to apply for more jobs around the city and neighboring towns. Plenty of places opened for new hires as she scrolled through the web. Whoever had a job available that wanted her qualities, she tossed her resume there. Someone would see it. Someone would call her to set up an interview. She'd go through interviews before getting hired. That would slow down her work at Happy Riders. It would keep her away from men like Thomas.

At the final application, her mother knocked on the door and came in with a plate of fruit. "You're back?"

"No, Ma, this is my evil twin sitting here." Kara rarely answered with sarcasm, but sometimes the temptation became too much.

"Yeah, I came back a while ago. I've been sitting here and searching for new jobs."

"That's good. Did you get anything yet?"

Kara gritted her teeth. "Ma, I just sent the applications out! I doubt they're going to call me for an interview today, let alone hire me on the spot! I'd love that, but it's not possible."

"You know what I mean. Anyway, I'm glad you're looking for work, but it's going to be hard." Her mother set the fruit down. "Did you give more thought to school again?"

"A little." That wasn't a lie. School did waft in and out of her thoughts if only to make her forget Thomas. "I need a little break from stuff though. Maybe go somewhere before tackling this."

"Where do you want to go? India?"

"Oh God, Ma! Why is India always the answer whenever I want a vacation? India's not a vacation. It's never been a vacation for me. We're just going there to visit people! We don't even go to see anything cool there, just our relatives!" She regretted her snappy behavior. Being around Thomas kept her from acting like a normal human being. She also didn't hate going to India even if the journey was rough on her body. She liked visiting family. For now, she wanted to be anywhere else but there. Holding up her hands, she relaxed her shoulders and let out a deep breath. "I'm sorry, Ma. I'm just...I'm under so much stress. I think Dadu's right. The clouds are all over my life."

"Try to relax then. You don't have to stress yourself so much. Your father and I are going out soon, but if you want us to bring anything, we can..."

"No, Ma. It's all good." She shooed her away. "You guys get what you need. I'm sorry I haven't gotten your groceries yet. Maybe you can do it."

"We'll try. Get some rest, Kara. Don't think about anything important now." She patted Kara's good arm, far from the mark. "We'll come home soon."

Once she left, Kara regretted her behavior. The stress around Thomas now warped everything she said. She never got irritated with her parents. Even when they didn't understand a thing about her, she tried her best to be calm and explain things. She didn't hate them. She didn't want to hate them for the simplest things. As bitter as Thomas was with his family, she couldn't allow herself to become like him. Her heart wasn't twisted.

I'll make it up to her somehow. Maybe I can pick up some extra groceries even if she gets the stuff she needs. I might even ask for a little time off so we can do something as a family. She hated that their last time out was at the Chinese restaurant. Since then, she stayed away from home and did her best to survive. The least those two deserved was another night to eat out. This time, she'd pay for everything. She had enough money from all the rides she gave. They'd go the moment she got rid of Thomas. One way or another, she'd lose him.

Her arm now wrapped up to the best of her ability, Kara dragged herself out of the bathroom and headed straight for her room. A nice warm bath called to her, but that could wait a little bit. Her head needed to stop spinning for five minutes. She plopped down on her bed to stare at the ceiling fan and light. Every day, she thanked random deities for bringing her home in one piece. She always suspected the next night would be her last one, yet that didn't happen. Thomas still needed her to drive him around. He didn't want any other rider. He wanted her alive and willing to take him everywhere. The alive part, she wanted that as well. She wanted him to leave town and never come back. Never bother her or anyone else.

"Oh, what am I thinking? He'll start this up in another town!" She rubbed her head. "Come on, Kara. Don't send the maniac to another town where he'll kill more people! That's not who you are!"

The storm clouds are rolling in soon. You won't stay under them for long, but they will not leave so easily.

Her grandfather's warning came back then. He saw this danger before she did. He knew that every move she made was a crucial one. Thomas was that storm cloud lingering over her. He was the rain about to pour and lightning ready to strike. Her grandfather promised he'd go, but when would that be? He wouldn't leave easily so that left Kara with the obvious clue: she had to chase this storm cloud out of her life. Maybe it was time to stop being a good little chauffeur. Show him that she wasn't going to do as he wanted anymore. Grabbing a notebook and pen off her desk, she began to draw out the map to the house McIver Drive. The first time she went there was from Charlotte-Douglas airport. The traffic slowed them down but without it, the drive was only fifteen minutes. The drives to and from shopping centers took between 8 to 10 minutes provided there wasn't much traffic. Even downtown Charlotte took little time to get there, a fifteen-minute drive on the highway. The times also mattered because between 5 and 7 people were heading home from work. He almost always wanted a ride either early or late in the day, as either her first or last rider. If he was her first rider, he took a longer time doing anything. If he was her last, he wouldn't waste time with her.

"So, if he is stalking people, he'll do that earlier in the day." She scribbled down. "And if he's done for the day, he won't get out of the house. He doesn't like being out in the dark too long. The curfew works for him too. He doesn't have to stay out."

Finding victims was easy. Charlotte was filled with all types of restaurants and fast-food joints along with a variety of shops. He only needed to target one person in these places, someone working in the evening shifts. While there were people out and about in the evening, the darkness could make it easier to move through places. It didn't matter how well lit any parking lot or shopping center was. He could get anyone in darkness quicker than in broad daylight. It was even easier if that person was the last one leaving the place. With less people around, the less likely anyone would come for the victim.

"Okay, he stalks people near his house." She read the list out loud. "He prefers either being my first or last rider of my shift. This usually depends on who he's planning to stalk and where he's stalking them. Now, I don't know how he gets to them if I'm not driving him around. But..." She checked the times of some of these places. "This sounds crazy but is it possible he's walking over to these places or even taking public transportation? McIver Drive is far to do that unless..." She flipped the page and started to draw the house along with surrounding areas. All but one part seemed to be closed off to the public. She never went down there, but it did answer her question. "He might take this path." She drew the arrow down. "If it leads to the city, then he'll have no problem getting around."

The front door slammed as she quickly shoved the notebook and pen under her bed. Her parents came in as their feet shuffled around. "Karishma, we're back!"

"I figured that out from the door opening, Ma!" Kara yelled from her room. Damn, they hadn't gone too long. Glancing at her clock, she gaped at the hour and minutes ticking down. One hour. How did they get done in one hour? She had no concept of time. "I'm chilling out back here! Do you need help putting stuff away?"

"If you can come here, that'll be nice. Keep your father away from some of these snacks."

"Oh, brother. He's at it again." Kara put on her slippers, covered up her bandage, and headed into the kitchen. With her arm throbbing, she opted to pick up the lightest things she could find first. Her parents laid everything out on the counter, already putting away what they could. "Yeesh, did you guys buy out the whole store? Do we need…" She frowned at the giant tub of yogurt in the corner. "Who's eating all that yogurt, Ma?"

"I eat yogurt. Your father eats that yogurt. Sometimes, I use it for cooking too. That size was the smallest one we could find." Her mother nodded to a bag of snacks in the corner. "If you could start putting those away, that would be nice. Do it before your father opens them up."

"A little too late for that." Her father sheepishly held up a bag of crunchy cheese snacks. "I'm sorry, Rishi. They're too good."

"What am I going to do with you?" Kara took out some chips and pretzel bags to put in the pantry. Her arm ached as soon as she flung the door open, but she hid the pain behind her teeth. "Oh good, you got those pretzels shaped like boxes. A lot of my riders love that one."

"I also got the pretzel sandwiches with the cheese in the middle. You told me you needed more nut-free snacks."

"Yes, I need those! I've gotten a lot of people with nut allergies as of late. They're always glad when I have something for them."

"Speaking of which…" Her father grabbed a small pack of pretzels. "You know, these snacks cost a lot of money. It's good you're thinking about the other people but…I don't know how long you can keep doing this."

"Why, because of the snacks? It's not a big deal, Baba. Not everyone eats them. I keep them in case they want them, that's it." Kara snagged the bag from his hands. "And these are also for them. Didn't you eat before you left?"

"I wanted to stop and get some sandwiches, but your mother said no. She's worried about the things that are in lunch meat. Apparently, they recalled a lot of those meats, and she doesn't like greasy, fried food much so here we are. Did you eat anything?"

"Not yet. I'm trying to rest." She stuffed a pretzel in her mouth. "I'm so exhausted. I need a long vacation. And please don't mention India. I already told Ma that's not where I want to go. I want somewhere new."

"We'll think about that later. Vacations are nice, but we must check our bank balance and see where and when we can go. In case you get a new job or something else happens, we can't plan for anything. Thinking about it won't hurt though." He waved her off. "Go get rest. We'll talk a little alter."

Grateful for the exit, she thanked him as she walked off with the pretzel bag. She flipped through the book, all the words meshing and turning into a giant black blob. "I don't know what classes I need to take to get a good job. It seems like they keep changing stuff on me."

"Well, if you want, you can get another..."

"No!" She dropped the book. "It was hard enough to get one degree, Ma! I struggled in every class. I got out by the skin of my teeth. How can you even suggest going back to get another degree?! And even if I wanted to do that, I don't know what to get the degree in."

"Well, you should know that_"

"I'm not going into medicine, engineering, or law. Just because someone else is studying that doesn't mean I should do it too." She lay down on the bed, grabbing the book again and trying to read it. "Maybe...I might think about it. Right now, I don't know if I'll have the time. I accept so many rides whenever I'm out there. Everyone needs to get around, especially with that creepy guy on the loose..."

"That's all the more reason that I want you to do something else." Her mother took the book, checking out a few classes on the front pages. "I know you finish right before 10 PM but...it's still dangerous. You've come home late a few times. These days, you're forgetting to text or call us when you're going to be late. What is wrong?"

Kara gazed up at her ceiling, wishing to spill everything right now. So much went wrong in her life. It started well before she picked up Thomas, and even before he killed Anne. She didn't have any sense of direction for someone who drove people around. Her life came undone with more things being revealed about herself. Sure, the medication helped with ADD and calmed her down, but it didn't fix any problems. They wouldn't get rid of Thomas or stop him from killing. Her mother couldn't get wrapped up in this now. Thomas left that scar on her arm. As he vowed, the next time would be on her throat.

"It's just...these past few days have been crazy, Ma. With all that's going on, my mind's got a lot of stuff in it." She began with a partial truth. Her mind raced with a million things, her mother now adding going back to school as another headache to deal with. "I just...I never get a chance to rest, you know? I got out of college in one piece. Now, I have to find a better job without sacrificing too much of my sanity. Not only that, I have to find a job that looks at my skills. That's the hard part. There are too many nepo-babies taking up big jobs."

"Nepo-babies?" Her mother frowned. "How do you become one of those?"

"Just by being related to someone important. We don't know anyone important. Trust me, Mama. They're not getting the job for being good at it. Maybe one or two of them are, but the majority aren't. I don't fall in that group, so I gotta try it all the hard way." She stared at her phone which kept beeping away with messages. "At least I get a break tonight. I need a long one."

"You don't have to take every ride. Take the ones you're comfortable with. That's what all the other riders do. They accept what they can."

Now you tell me. Her headache forced itself back in. Her poor mother really couldn't see that Kara had no choices now. Comfortable or not, Thomas wanted her at his side all the time. "I wish it was that easy, Ma. With the creep on the loose, more people need rides around. Let's be honest, cars aren't cheap. Not everyone lives close enough to public transportation. And gas costs a lot of money too. So, I might as well do my part and help them out."

"Helping people is fine. I see why you want to get them home safely. However, I would like you to come home safely too. If that means going to school and driving at an earlier time, so be it. Now, you don't have to make that decision right away. Think about it at least. Spend a lot of time thinking about it. And if you need help, we're still here for you."

"I know, Mama. You're always here for me." She reached over and squeezed her mother's hand. "I'll think about all of it."

Once her mother left, she rolled up her sleeve to check her body out. That scar, bright red and thick, stood out though the blood dried up. She touched it, winced upon the pressure from fingers, and pulled away. It took a long time for that scar to close. Until it went away for good, she'd have to always cover it. The way Thomas switched moods, the way people switched lights on and off. One minute, he talked to her like they were chums. He smiled and joked around, went deep into his past, and shared moments with her. He became trustworthy for a few seconds, the only person who truly understood Kara. Then he'd switch and slash her arm.

That's probably what he did with Anne and the others. He switched modes.

That was what she needed to get the best plan. Get him when he was in a better mood. Take him out before he had a chance to shift into his dangerous form. She had to attack before he attacked her. Get him when he didn't anticipate it. If she failed, she'd get more than just a gash on the arm. The next victim could be saved.

Checking her phone for the time, her stomach dropped. Time was running out for everyone. All she wanted was one more ride with him. One final ride through Hell. She'd pretend everything was good, take him where he wanted to, act like they were buddies. Then during the ride, she'd strike him down.

On that ride, she'd bring everything to an end.

Chapter 17

Kara couldn't sleep all night as the nightmares of Anne's murder played in her mind. She had never been in the same room, but the screams rang in her ears and pain ran through her body. She put herself in Anne's shoes, terrified and alone, wondering when Thomas would let her go. The poor thing never knew that she wouldn't see another day. She wouldn't live to fulfill her dreams. She'd die screaming in terror, praying that someone could solve her case. That very same fear kept Kara awake and staring out her window.

He's thinking of me. She lay in bed as the ceiling fan whirled above her. No doubt she filled Thomas' mind the way he filled hers. He dreamed of her too, of their next ride together, and how it would all end. He waited for her to make one wrong move. He wanted her to screw up so he could get rid of her too. Those thoughts alone were enough to keep her looking over her shoulder. Giving up on sleep, she opted to get up early.

He wants you to do the wrong thing. Don't do the wrong thing.

With another day of driving ahead, she tried passing the time by looking through the course book. Her parents had the right idea. As it turned out, there were a few degrees that appealed to her. She left with a degree in liberal studies, but upon finding the degree in psychology, she wanted to try it. Maybe she could focus on children with ADD and ADHD. Probably even help those with dyslexia and dyscalculia as well. If anyone could understand that pain, she could. She'd be the person that the kid needed to get through these struggles.

The more she pondered over it, the more she wanted to go. Her parents couldn't figure any of this out when she was a girl. She could be that person for other kids in similar situations. Give them the support they didn't get at home or school. That's what so many children lacked: support from adults.

"Just like Thomas." She flung the book to the side. "There might be a lot of kids like him out there. What if it's already too late for them?"

She pushed the thought away. She couldn't think about the future children like Thomas while the real one still haunted her. When the time came, he'd send her a message for a ride. Maybe this time he'd ask for a ride from another restaurant or a different store. Maybe this time he'd go to the airport, fly far from the country. Maybe he'd get lost out there, forget about her, and spend the rest of his days fulfilling whatever dreams he had. He'd realize there was a place for him. He could start brand-new somewhere else. New identity. New life.

In that same regard, the idea of taking classes couldn't hurt. It would be a new start. This time, she'd take classes that she'd enjoy and hope they'd lead to something. Who knew? She'd find something less dangerous than driving strangers from place to place. She scanned the coursebook, making notes of interesting classes. These didn't have any prerequisites. None of them required her to take math to get in. She could handle them.

Maybe I could start this later in the year. If I get enough money saved up from all the rides, I could pay tuition. It should cover some of it. Maybe it's something I could do in between drives. I guess Ma does have a point. This may not be a terrible idea. I might give it a try.

She took off her pajamas and changed for another day. She got so wrapped up trying on outfits that she missed her mother entering. Fortunately, she came in as Kara got into a shirt and zipped up her pants. She missed out on the jagged scar, which would take its sweet time healing. Thank God for that. Thank God she didn't need to explain herself.

"I see you were going through the book again. After you fought with me about it, you're looking at it." Her mother held it up. "Did you find anything you like? Do any of the other programs sound good?"

"Not yet. I only looked through it because I was bored." Kara rolled her sleeve down to hide the scar. "I might look through it a little later. There could be something that might be easy for me. If I don't have to take any math classes or anything super hard, I might be able to do it. Especially if it won't take too long to finish."

"You'll have to check with admission on that." Her father sipped his tea. "I know that some students...if you already fulfilled the general requirements...you won't have to do them again. Just take the classes needed for the degree."

That bit piqued her interests a little bit. Given that she finally took care of that one math class she needed to graduate, she could do another degree. "As long as they don't add more classes with numbers to confuse, I think I'll live. Anyway, it's something I'm going to need some time to think about. I wish I had that time right now."

"Well, the next semester won't start till fall so you have some time to decide. In fact, if you want to start next spring, that's fine with me too. Whatever you decide."

Her arm still ached as she backed out of the driveway. Neither her mother nor father asked about the pain in it. Of course, she kept that scar always covered up, so they couldn't see it. The less marks and changes on her body, the safer they all stayed. Thomas left a very shallow cut on her, not deep enough for stitches, but he caused enough pain with it.

He doesn't need to cut deep into you. Anne leaned back in the passenger side, rubbing her wounds. They no longer gushed blood, yet they weren't healed. *Just one swipe and that's it. You're very lucky he didn't get your throat. Your arm will heal one day.*

Kara got onto the road, checking her mirrors and fixing the air conditioner before driving on. The GPS came along with a request from her first rider. Thankfully, it wasn't Thomas but a young woman needing a lift from the mall. She could take that on. The girl didn't want to go anywhere too far, just to a hotel in downtown Charlotte. These days, most people want to be downtown. They wouldn't stray too far from it. She couldn't remember the last time she got on the highway with someone who wasn't Thomas. Everyone else took a ride to places full of crowds and noise. The farther they stayed from quiet, empty places, the safer they all were.

Kara didn't bother holding conversations this time around when she picked up her rider. The young girl was quiet, focusing only on her phone during the drive. She didn't lift her head until the moment Kara approached her destination. Mumbling a 'thank you,' she got out with her things as Kara accepted another ride nearby. No Thomas yet. She could live with that.

Maybe he'll finally get tired of me. That thought disappeared as quickly as it appeared. Thomas wouldn't jump onto another rideshare driver. He got her where he wanted her. When the time came for another ride, he'd call her. She drove off to get her next rider, hoping they didn't talk about The Traveler or his victims. Sara Murphy still needed rescuing. *If I can take him to his house, I can search for her. He must have something with the victims in there.*

Her mother called her at that moment. Knowing she had a few minutes before work started, she went ahead and picked it up. "Yeah, Mama? Is something wrong?"

"I know you are at work right now, but have you decided what you want to study? If you haven't, that's fine. I picked up a few more books from my friends. It's a longshot but I think you can try to go for a better school. Maybe UNC-Chapel Hill. Or if you really want, we can try and see if you can go to an Ivy League school. Your father and I still have a lot of money saved up. We can try..."

"Really?" Kara cut her off. "You called me to tell me you want me to apply for school again? Not just any school but an Ivy League school?! Mama, I can understand wanting me to go to a school in North Carolina. Anything in the UNC system, I'm good with that. I'm good with NC State or ECU or Appalachian State. But an Ivy League school? I didn't do well enough in high school to get into a decent state school. What makes you think I can go to a place like Harvard?!"

"I know you had a hard time. I understand why it was hard when you were in school. But now that you're older and you know better, you can try again. It might be easier. Plus, you take the medicine to help with your attention, right? It could be different now."

Kara sat in the car as she processed these words. No, her mother didn't get it. She praised her before for understanding dyscalculia.

She should have understood it. This conversation went in another direction, one Kara didn't want to go in. Her mother expected the dyscalculia to go away now that Kara was older and knew her problems. She thought the medicine would get rid of the ADD in a few days. No matter how many times doctors and therapists explained this, it didn't sink in. "I can't believe you, Mother. You think I'm cured or something?"

Her mother fell quiet. She had called her 'Mother.' Kara only referred to her as 'Mother' when she became frustrated with her. The frustrations mounted with each little memory of the past. No wonder Thomas got it in a few seconds. He figured out no one else figured out for ages. Kara's struggles went beyond simply not getting math or staying focused. Going back to school wasn't the solution. There was no guarantee she'd have an easier time despite knowing about her learning disabilities. Yet her mother stuck with this idea that it was good for her.

Then again, I shouldn't be surprised by this. They've done this my whole life. I couldn't go to a puja or any Indian party without someone bragging about their kid. They want the same thing too. Instead, they got me.

The more they pressed her, the more irritated she grew with them. They meant well, of course. Her parents never pushed for anything unless they believed she could do it. She loved them for their faith in her, but the facts never sank in. Kara wasn't like the other Indian kids. She didn't care for them getting into Harvard or earning top SAT scores or becoming incredible in all their hobbies. Every Indian function grew more tedious as she grew older. It got to the point where she no longer wanted to hang out with these kids. They weren't her peers anymore: just competitors she'd never win against.

"Why do it, Ma? Why do you guys keep pushing for this?"

"You know why. It's because..."

"You want what's best for me, I know. You don't want me to waste my life driving people around. We've gone through this a million times, Mother. Times have changed. You've asked me three days in a row to go back to school. It can be because of The Traveler." *Believe me, I already know his plans. I'm trying hard to break it.*

"Yes, it's true we've been through this a lot. I just worry about you."

"Like always." She rubbed her temples. "I get it. You hate that I'm going out at night so much. You hate that I'm doing something you can't brag about with your friends. That's all it, isn't it? You're not saying that quiet part out loud, but I got it."

"No! It has nothing to do with bragging! We don't care what other people think!"

"Really? Then why do you always look so uncomfortable when people talk about how great their kids are? Why did you and Baba keep telling me about how they make straight As or are in the top of their class? How they're brilliant in everything they do? Well, I'm sorry to break it but no one cares about that in the working world! How did you think it made me feel to hear that? Did you even care?"

"Kara..." Her mother's mouth opened, then shut. It happened. Kara learned the truth behind all of this. "I do care. That's why I say these things. That's why I want a better life for you. I thought maybe if you saw everyone else and what they did, you'd understand why."

"Not everyone is happy with their parents pushing them, Ma. If you ever looked at social media feeds occasionally, you'd know." Kara grew sick over some updates she found of former friends. So many of them struggled to stay afloat. Most couldn't find a job in their field. If they found it, they wouldn't be happy at all. The pay didn't justify the workload. Others struggled with both physical and mental health, unable to get the help they needed. Then there were the ones stuck in awful relationships they couldn't get out of. Her mother never saw any of that on Facebook. The only things she commented on were the happy photos of special occasions. She didn't care about anything else.

"Karishma, I didn't mean to hurt your feelings. Everything I do is in your best interest. It's always been for you. This is_"

"Mother, don't." Kara cut her off. "You trying to make me feel bad about you doing something for my own good won't work. And I..." She squinted at the clock. "Okay, it's time for me to get back to work. It's getting close to it. I'll have to talk to you later. I'll see you at home."

"Be careful driving out there. They still didn't find that man."

"I know they didn't him yet." *I did.* "I gotta go now, Ma. I'll talk to you later."

"Drive safely." Her mother hung up right then, leaving Kara wallowing in more guilt. It hurt to call her out, but her annoyance reached its peak. Every night, her mother bugged her about taking classes again. Every night, Kara told her she'd think about it though she rarely did. Calling her out on the constant push towards education needed to happen. Their previous conversations about her ADD and her dyscalculia didn't sink in. Her psychiatrists and therapists went into it with them. Family friends did their best to explain it. Yet her family still couldn't grasp that this wasn't a problem that went away in a few weeks. It stuck with her. The medication helped her out a lot, but it didn't make everything go away. This really was all about their pride, nothing more.

"God, I hope I get another job soon." She checked down at her phone for another request. There he was, waiting for her at another restaurant. Somehow, he knew she'd be available to get him at this moment. Her mind tense, she accepted the ride and headed towards this new place, a Mexican restaurant on the outskirts of Charlotte. She picked up people from here before, but him being in this area didn't sit with her. He rarely ventured this far out. Why go this far for a victim if this is what he wanted? Who was he stalking now?

Maybe he's going back to his crime scene. Her mind flashed to Sara Murphy who also lived on the outskirts of Charlotte. He wasn't satisfied with having her alone: he wanted more victims. Before heading out, she checked a little bit more about Sara. As suspected, she worked in a restaurant far from where Thomas lived. Coworkers all worried for her since she wasn't the kind to be late or not tell them if she'd be out. A few of them pleaded with The Traveler to let her go if he had her. They'd pay him anything he wanted. All they wanted was her safe return. Kara put the phone away, closing her eyes for one second. Thomas didn't care for any money. He was never going to see their messages. If he did, he'd only sit back, laugh, and plan his next moves. He wasn't doing this for cash, just some sick thrill. Something to make his days go by quicker. He didn't care about anything Sara's coworkers or family said. He'd never return her. Only Kara could bring her back and hopefully get her back in one piece.

"Let's see what you're up to now, you son of a bitch." She got onto the highway, listening to the GPS, and changing lanes when it required her to. Her emotions frayed after talking to her mother, she drove on without worrying about the people next to her. She didn't fear Thomas anymore. She didn't care if he cut her skin, threatened to kill her, or make fun of her. She dealt with him for the final time. If he tried any funny business, she wouldn't flinch or cry out. She lost the ability to do those things the moment he laid his hands on her. "You can't get me anymore. We're done."

Once in the shopping center, she found him waiting outside of the restaurant with no bags or other items. He waved to her as she pulled up the curb and opened the door. "I thought you'd never find this place. It's not in the usual areas."

"It's fine." She put in the address for McIver Drive. "I assume you are going home."

"Yeah, I've done what I need to do." He slid into the backseat, closing the door behind him. Then he frowned. "I realize this is further than you normally drive. The other places we've met have been closer. Will your company allow you to go further?"

"They allow it. I can take on longer drives if I want." That bit was true. Happy Riders were pleased with all the mileage she got along with the extra glowing reviews. They even asked her if she wanted to work more shifts, which she promised to think about. Not that Thomas needed to know this part. His ride was coming to an end. "Are you buckled in?"

"As always. You know I'd never break simple laws like this, Kara. I wouldn't want you in trouble just because I'm a terrible rider. The last thing we need is someone pulling you over because of something I failed to do." He put his focus on what lay outside the window. "We're good to go."

"Then let's go." Kara put the car into drive, trying her hardest not to glance back at him. He was right about that one thing. If he wasn't a sick killer, he was a well-behaved rider. He didn't yell, burp, smoke, or fart while she drove on. He didn't leave a mess outside of blood on her seats. He even threw his bottles away when he was done with them. Still, she couldn't get swept away by these charms. His charms got her in this mess. Her wits had to get her out of it. For now, she'd talk like there was nothing between them. "So, how's that place that you were at?"

"That place?"

"The Mexican place I picked you up from. I see them pop up during Charlotte Restaurant Week, but I've never been there. It's a little far for me."

"Oh, that!" He laughed. "They're very good, Kara. Are you a fan of fajitas?"

"I like chicken fajitas. I don't eat beef for religious reasons." Her mind coached her into saying these words. No beads of sweat formed along her forehead as drove on. "Do they have enchiladas?"

"They have all that and then some. Although if you are a fan of dessert, please try their flan. Oh, and if you like guacamole, they can do it right in front of you!" He brushed some lint off his jacket. "Trust me, it's worth watching."

"I'll check them out sometime." She screamed internally for her casual replies. He didn't suspect a thing as she got onto the highway. Today, the roads remained quiet and easy to go through. With more police officers around, most people were doing their best to stay within the speed limit. She passed by a police car, glancing over at Thomas. He didn't squirm as she picked up speed. He didn't pale or panic at the sight of those blue and red lights flashing off to the side. He truly didn't care about getting caught because he didn't believe in that. He didn't believe they'd come after him after he left no trace of himself behind. Kara bit down on her lip as they passed by a few more police cars on the side. "I wonder what that's all about."

"I wouldn't worry too much. They're waiting for the next idiot to speed by them so they can drop off a ticket. It's funny how they'll target some poor soul rushing on the road, but not the actual killers walking around free. What a sick institution. Who are they really protecting and serving?" Thomas scratched his nose. "Oh dear, it's getting warm here. Do you mind putting on the AC?"

"Sure, I can do that." Kara turned on the air conditioner. "Let me know if it gets too cold for you."

"Will do. Let's just enjoy the ride for now, Kara."

The last thing she could do was enjoy the ride. He didn't have anything on him, but that didn't mean he couldn't flip on her. She never saw the boxcutter earlier when he slashed her arm. Who knew what other tricks he hid up sleeves? She controlled her breathing as they drove on, waiting for him to say something. With his mind on the window, he wasn't opening up.

Don't ask about Sara yet. You want him calm and easy, so he doesn't cut you. Her eyes checked the mark on her arm. While healed, that scar tormented her. Thomas left this as a reminder that she belonged to him. She did his bidding. Cutting her arm took only seconds to do. Cutting her throat would be no different. He didn't have that box cutter with him now, but she didn't take chances. His shift in tempers, the tone of his voice, everything about him stayed unpredictable. Even now, as he drew on her fogged-up windows with his fingers, she expected him to switch gears and yank her hair. Scratch her neck. Snap at her. He stayed calm until he snapped. Given that he wasn't talking, she forced herself to make conversation.

"Sorry about the dew on the windows. I've turned on the defroster to help it out, so you might get a little warm air in." She flipped the windshield wipers to remove the rest of the dew. "I didn't expect it to fog up today."

"Eh, it's all right. Do whatever you need to make driving easier for you. At least you're smart enough to drive with the lights on, and you're clearing up the windows." Thomas pulled away from his artwork, a nice lattice pattern all over. "I haven't done this in ages. I forgot about the joy in that."

"What, draw on the windows? I can't blame you for doing that. We haven't had fog in a while." She took the right turn as the fog started to clear up. At the same time, the car grew warmer, so she turned the defroster off. "I think I'll be able to see in this mist."

"You should." Thomas stared at his handiwork before adding a small TW on the corner. "I used to do this all the time. Draw on the windows with my finger. I drew all kinds of things: patterns like this, trees, houses, flowers, you name it. If the windows stayed fogged like now, I'd sign my artwork. It seems silly, but it made me proud. That I created something so beautiful from nothing but the fog on the glass." He tapped on the window before moving away. "Then my father would yell at me to stop messing up the windows and wipe it clean. There went all my hard work that he couldn't appreciate. So many people don't appreciate beauty before them."

"That's sad." Kara took another turn into the long road ahead. "Didn't you tell him to stop?"

"To stop?" Thomas burst out laughing. "Oh Kara, I forgot that you have family members who care about you. Yours appreciate everything you do. They encourage you to keep trying, be the best you can be. Not everyone gets that. It doesn't matter how talented you are, the parents won't get it. You win a contest? It's a waste of time. You're praised by teachers, called the next art master? It's a waste of time. You even get asked to study art in Europe? What do you do? It's a waste of time according to your parents. They refuse to pay for it because they see no use in it."

Kara took all of that, absorbing every little detail. This hatred steamed all the way from his parents not appreciating him. Clearly, Thomas had something going for him a long time ago. "You're an artist?"

"I used to be." He flexed and curled up his fingers, admiring his shortened nails. "It was the one thing that gave me a purpose in life. As a boy, I went down to the museum whenever I could to look at all the paintings and sculptures. I saved my money to pay for admission since my folks wouldn't give me any. Then I'd go down and spend the whole day in it, learning about all the artists. Whenever local artists came, I'd go and see their lectures. God, I dreamed I'd be just like them. I wanted that."

Kara believed every word as she continued to drive. This Thomas reverted to the boy he talked about. He went back to those days in the museums and lectures, the days of dreaming of his future. Somewhere between then and now, those dreams died. Maybe his father killed that dream or something else, but Thomas no longer liked art in the same way. "It's not too late to pick up art again. I'm sure you can get supplies from any art store and start painting or sculpting. Hell, I think they even hold classes around here if you need a refresher! If you could_"

"Oh, Kara. You're still so optimistic. I like that about you." Thomas began to wipe the lattice pattern off the window. "I wish I could start back again. Go to Europe and learn from art masters. Immerse myself in all of it. Unfortunately, the time for that has come and gone. Even without my father in the picture, I can't go there now. I can't show up and tell them I'm ready to learn. It's over."

"How?" She noticed traffic slowing down in front, worried about another accident. Foot over the brake, she inched forward. "How can it be over? I've seen people well over 100 trying new things! It's not too late for you, no matter what people say! And you could_"

"You're bold to assume I have until 100 to do anything." Thomas waved it off. "I'm shocked I made it this far to begin with. I have tried to pick it up, but to no avail. I can't do it anymore. I can't create beautiful art. I look the same as before, I appear fine, but I'm a different person inside. That wasn't who I was. Just like you, Kara. What people see isn't what is inside."

"What about what you drew on my window? That was beautiful."

"That's just for fun." He peered over her shoulder. "Why are you slowing down? There's no traffic jam, is there?"

"I don't know. I'm checking and..." Her heart sank at what lay right ahead of them. There was no accident or jam, but a biker on the road, taking his sweet time to his destination. He held everyone up. He was the reason the other cars moved to the other side when no traffic came. The biker held them up. "Fantastic!" She threw her hands in the air. "Just what I needed, a guy on a bike!"

"And you can't overtake him? He's just on a bike."

"I'll see if I can get around him." Kara gazed at the other side of the road, wishing she could cross into it. With double lines keeping her from going into the other side, she could only follow the cyclist while doing her best to keep distance. "Maybe if he turns in the next few minutes, we'll be free. They usually do."

Her words betrayed as the cyclist pedaled straight ahead with no sign of speeding up. By now, other cars zoomed by in the other direction while she still dragged herself along. She held in the groan as the cyclist grew closer, slowing down to let him pass by. Thomas gazed out the window as the cyclist continued to pump on the pedals, moving as quickly as they could, yet not fast enough. Kara couldn't overtake him with the traffic coming in the other direction. She wasn't getting her chance to swerve away while the cyclist kept moving forward. "I'm sorry. I don't think he's going to make a turn any time soon. I'll have to_"

"Run over him." Thomas finished off, folding his arms across his chest. "Just hit him and run over him."

"I...what?!" Kara let her foot off the gas to slow down. By now, the cyclist was right in front of her. "I can't run him over! He's got a right to the road too!"

"No, he's taking up your sweet time. He's refusing to let you go past him. Make him pay by running him over."

"What the...I can't do that!" Kara watched another car zip past while the cyclist moved along. "I can't run this guy over! He's done nothing! And even if he did, that doesn't give me a right to kill him!"

Thomas leaned back in his seat with his arms folded across his chest. "So, you are going to be a good little girl and just let him go on?"

"Unless he chooses to turn, or I finally get a chance to overtake him, yeah." She checked the lanes to find it empty. Not giving him a chance to suggest death, she switched over and passed the cyclist. The poor guy focused on the road ahead, not knowing he came inches from death. Thomas glowered at him, knowing he missed his chance of turning Kara into him. Kara continued to drive on, her hands on the wheel but ready to release them at a moment's notice. He warned her last time not to jump out the door. Not this time. If she got the right opportunity, she'd leap out and roll onto the ground, letting the car crash. She'd lose the car, of course, but she'd keep her life.

"You can always get another car." Her father reminded her whenever she went anywhere. "We can help you pay for it if you need that. Don't worry about accidents if the only damage is to the car. There's only one of you. Don't risk your life for something you can buy later."

Those words rang in her ears now. Her hands slowly dipped down the steering wheel, preparing to open the door. "You see that? We passed him. No harm done."

"You got lucky this time." Thomas wagged his finger. "The lane freed up for you. If you still had cars coming, you'd be tailing him the whole way. Don't waste time like that. Take him out and drive away."

Kara shook her head. "You're still stuck on that."

"I can't help it. I see an opportunity and think of different ways to get what I want." He flicked his finger against the window. "I guess you still see the good in everyone. I can't blame you though. You're young. You want to get through life without drawing blood."

"I've done it so far. I don't plan to draw innocent blood. That man didn't do anything wrong. Maybe at worst, he's taking up too much time. And besides," she nodded as the man took a turn, "he's finally gone. We'll make it in time."

Thomas conceded her point. "You got very lucky with him, Kara. He lives to ride for another day."

She cringed when he said those words. Every second of her life in this car, she drove to live another day. Her arm throbbed as she made her way towards McIver Drive. With no more bikers, or pedestrians getting the way, she got into the driveway and drove carefully over the rocky road to that house. The entire drive, she waited for him to do something. He wasn't happy with her choices. He would let her know about it on the next ride.

"Here we are." She parked the car a few feet from the front door. "Do you need help getting anything?"

"No, I didn't bring anything with me this time." He unbuckled the seat belt and opened the door. "Thank you again for another good ride. There were a few mishaps, but nothing you couldn't handle."

A mishap. He called her ignoring a biker and not running him down a mishap. If that didn't prove he was twisted, nothing would. She gripped the steering wheel as she checked her phone. A few requests popped up with most of them being too far away. She'd reject them the moment Thomas left her sights. Instead of going where he should, he walked around to her side and gazed through the window at her. That gaze. Her knuckles whitened as she tightened her grip. When he wouldn't leave, she unrolled the window and quickly glanced at him before turning back to the wheel. "Is there something you need?"

"No, I'm about to go in. That's one thing I admire about you, Kara." He tapped his knuckle on the side of her door. "You won't give up your morals for anyone. Even if your life's on the line, you stay true to yourself."

The phlegm building up in her mouth forced itself down so she could speak. "Not wanting to run people isn't about being true to yourself. I'm not that cold-hearted. I can honk at him, swerve around him, maybe even yell at him. I'm not gonna run over him because I'm running late."

"There you go again. You're refusing to do anything that you think is wrong."

"It's not what I think is wrong. I *know* it's wrong." Kara shook her head as he back away from the window. He still considered her to be like him, slowly rotting away on the inside and growing colder by the second. He figured that she'd get used to these rides. He wanted her comfortable with their conversations, so he'd treat her as an old friend. He didn't go deep inside of her, didn't know that underneath all that talk was a little bit of humanity. Kara wanted to keep hold of that humanity as long as possible. "I still got you where you need to be, and I'm right on time."

"Indeed, you are. You always get me where I need to go, and you're never late. Those other reviewers complaining about you don't know anything." He pulled away from the car. "Well, I'll let you go. I have no doubt there are more people who need rides. They need someone trustworthy to get them home."

I wish I could say that someone is me. Kara held onto the steering wheel as she checked her phone. One rider waited for her only two miles from here. Good. This person would hopefully be no problem. "I will see you later, I guess."

"More like sooner, Kara." He winked. "Be ready for anything."

She didn't need that reminder anymore. At this point, she stayed alert about everything on her rides. Thomas went back to his cool self, but that didn't mean anything now. Given that she refused to follow his order, she expected the next ride to be tense and long. If she failed to answer his call now, he'd follow through on some silent threat. She caught it when they were talking earlier. He gave her that eye, an evil blue eye narrowing down her. He vowed to make her pay though she couldn't figure out what he'd do. Without her, he couldn't go anywhere. He'd need someone else to drive him around. Unless he walked close by, he couldn't hurt her now.

Or maybe he can. I shouldn't relax so easily. She accepted her next ride, driving away from the house. In the rearview mirror, she caught Thomas standing on the porch. He didn't wave to her. He didn't open the door. He stood them, staring her down as she drove off. She couldn't read his face, but she found the anger all over his body. He was kind for now. He let her get away with bypassing the cyclist because he brewed something else in his mind. She rubbed her chest to keep it from burning. She didn't want to see him anymore, not tonight or for the rest of her life. She still had no plan on getting rid of him. All she did was sit and wait for his next instructions. *Come on, Kara! Enough is enough! This man won't let you go unless you push him off! What are you waiting for?*

Nothing. She waited for nothing, so her mind focused on letting him go on the next ride. Even if it meant getting hurt or losing her car or getting in trouble with the law. She couldn't keep being a good girl by following all the orders given to her. Maybe it was time to put weapons in this car. She didn't have a gun, but knives or rope could work. Rolling up the car window, she accepted the ride nearby and put all her focus on them. These poor people wanted to get to their destinations. She could do that much without problem.

Her next few rides were quick, quiet ones. They all needed help getting to their hotels, to the train station, or at some restaurant. Not one of them tried to converse with her, which she appreciated. After talking with Thomas, she didn't want to get into deep talks with anyone else. Most of her riders spent the entire time on their phones, either talking or scrolling through it. Not once did they bring up The Traveler or Sara Murphy's disappearance. It ached to watch them go through the ride, comfortable and quiet, while knowing that Thomas wasn't done. Now that she failed to follow one rule, she feared his retaliation. Then again, he preferred that she follow the laws. Running over a cyclist, even if they were annoying and taking up the road, qualified as not following the law.

"God, I need a drink...or some good food." Her mind wafted over to various restaurants she wanted to try. Hopefully, her parents hadn't cooked anything, so she could go out and get something from Aria, an Italian restaurant downtown. They'd only gone there twice, but the food always hit the right spots. They were only open during dinner and getting reservations was tough, yet they'd have something once she got off her shift. Their chicken parmesan and tiramisu called to her as she drove on. At a stop light, she sent her parents a text about eating out. That way her mother wouldn't make food for her later. Maybe she'd get a scolding about it, but she'd handle that. Sometimes, she stopped by and ate lunch and dinner during shifts. It saved her mother some cooking time and it gave Kara some time to herself.

Despite her excitement for Italian food, she expected a message from Thomas to pop up any second. He claimed to be done. He went in the house when she left. He didn't have anything else for her right now. Why would he call her? Checking her messages, she only found one disapproving reply from her mother, several deals from different restaurants, and some more people needed rides though they were in the following town. No Thomas this time. Sending out an apology to her mother, rejecting the rides, and ignoring the deals, she put her mind back on food. The moment she entered the restaurant,

She put in her order and sat in the lobby, constantly glancing at her phone. Her mother did not reply after the apology. Typical. She'd either send an 'ok' or ignored the whole thing completely. Now was one of those latter times. Her mother got angry about her stopping off for food and refused to reply. Oh well, she'd deal with it. Within ten minutes, Kara got her order and headed home. No more rides for the night. No more Thomas tormenting her.

Relax. Focus on what you'll do later. You dropped him off. He can't come after you. That mantra circled in her head as she made her way into the neighborhood. Things weren't right about this place even though she didn't spot the difference. Her neighbors stood out in their yard doing work or chatting around. Kids played nearby. Shoulders tense, she drove into the driveway and found their car outside. They were here. They needed to be here.

"What's wrong with all this?" She got out of the car, checking her phone. Neither her mother nor father replied to her text. It went out ten minutes ago, which wouldn't be a big deal with anyone else. Not getting an answer from them? She didn't like it. They wouldn't leave her hanging. Getting out the house key, she entered the place and found nothing out of place. No sign of struggle, no dirt lying around, not even the TV blaring. Even when they were the only ones around, they still made noise to remind her they were there. Shuffling feet, loud music, talking on the phone. They made their presence known to anyone who entered.

Right now, she received their silence in return. Putting her bag down and getting her slippers on, she walked from room to room. No mother or father was in either one. The TV wasn't on, and no one cooked in the kitchen. Her mother's purse and the other car keys were still on the counter. This didn't make sense. Her parents wouldn't leave without telling her where they went. They wouldn't go without their car unless someone gave them a ride. Even still, they'd let her know who they went off with. They'd give her every little detail: where they went, when they planned to come back, and if she wanted anything from wherever they were. Given that she got none of these texts, her stomach lurched and knotted itself. They wouldn't leave her like this.

"Ma? Baba?" She called out as she tiptoed on the carpet. "Where are you guys? I know I grabbed dinner earlier. I'm sorry about that, but I'll make it up to you! Can we get some dessert?"

Once again, they didn't reply. This was no longer them being angry to talk to her situation. Something else went down here. She stepped out onto the deck in case they were sitting around the garden. Going through the entire backyard, she called out to them. No sign of either. No sign of a fight. No one had come out the entire time she was gone. Sweat rolled down her forehead as her heartbeat picked up. They weren't here. Grass blades tickling her ankles, she ran around the entire area, checking every place they could be. Nothing. She checked her phone for another message. Maybe her mother went out for a walk, or they both went with someone else. Her heart leaped to her throat over getting a message.

"Oh, please, please..." She scrolled through her messages to get nothing back. No one had seen her message after her apology. No worries about when she'd come home. No scolding about her eating out again. They didn't reply at all. She dialed the number and listened as it rang before heading to voicemail. "Come on, Ma! Give me an answer! Say something!"

The dial tone went off then, giving her the answer. The operator came on to apologize that no one was picking up the phone. Her hands went limp as the phone fell from her palm. She couldn't yell anymore because the truth was out. She didn't need to ask what happened. She knew her parents were gone. They were taken away, possibly hurt, tired, and scared.

And Thomas was the one behind everything.

Chapter 18

Kara hated jumping to conclusions, so she gave herself another shot at contacting them. When her hands stopped shaking, she dialed her mother's number again. The voicemail popped back up and told her to leave a message at the tone. Then she called her father and received the same thing. She forgot all about the food she bought and everything she planned to do. They weren't picking up their phones, which only spiked her anxiety. She stumbled back into the house, falling on the sofa. Her parents were gone, and it wasn't because of their own will. He couldn't have come here. She got rid of his little tracker. He wouldn't get here.

Unless he got someone else to bring him here. He'd know where I live because of that thing. She grabbed her head as she pictured what happened. Another ride share driver picked Thomas up from his home and brought him here. He introduced himself as one of her friends, probably told them she was in trouble. Then when they got ready to leave, he got them. How he managed to get them from home to wherever they were now remained a mystery. The Traveler didn't work with accomplices, so he probably roped another poor soul in. When that person had done their duty, he removed them out of the picture. The man worked quickly.

Her phone rang at that moment, which she picked up without checking who sent it. She knew. "What did you do?"

"Oh, Kara. Is that the way you greet your riders?" Thomas clicked his tongue. "You have lost your manners, young lady."

"Screw you. Where are they?" She paced around the room, checking every corner. Not a sign of a struggle. Her parents let this man in since he didn't pose a threat. Then he charmed his way into their hearts, they trusted him, and now he took them away. He pulled this mess off with all the other victims. Now, he crossed the line. "I swear, if you did anything..."

"Relax, they're fine." He purred, which froze her blood. "And you can get them back. If you know where to look, you'll have them back in one piece. Them, and anyone else that's there."

"Anyone else?"

"Oh, Kara. You think I only want your folks? Come on, we've been at this for a very long time. You have a chance to save everyone...if you just follow my instructions. Your first stop is my house. By now, you know how to get there. You can do it without any GPS. Once you arrive, you'll know what you need to do."

"No, I don't!" She raced around the house, grabbing her purse and anything she could use as a weapon. He crossed the line. Throwing whatever she found into her bag, she kept him on the line for any information. "You've been cryptic with me the whole time! You're expecting me to know everything about you by now. I don't, okay? You're supposed to be a rider for me. Someone that I'm not supposed to see again! I never see any of my other riders."

"Ah, but we have a different bond, Kara. We got that bond the moment I stepped into your car. We got it when you started talking to me. I knew you were the one I needed in my corner."

"I don't want to be in your corner!" Kara glanced through the window blinds in case he chose to come over. No one popped out from the bushes or neared the corner. Her neighbors were now all inside. He was calling far from this place. "When are you going to understand? I went along only because you gave me no choice! I've seen what you can do!"

"That bit is true. You finally understand me. Now, I don't have time to waste and neither do you. It's passing by quickly. If you want to save your mom and dad, you know here to go."

The line fell dead at that moment, so Kara pocketed the phone and grabbed her bag. She didn't bother to ask how he got a hold of them because it didn't matter. He didn't give any hint that he hurt them, just to come to his house. If she drove fast enough, she'd get them both out and maybe save whoever he kidnapped. Hopefully, Sara Murphy was still alive down there. She'd get everyone out, no matter what state they were in.

Drive on! Anne appeared at her side as she ran towards the car. The blood trickling down her forehead and onto her face served as a reminder of what waited ahead. *He's not going to wait too long. Everyone depends on you!*

"Yeah, yeah, everyone depends on me. I don't even know why. I'm just a driver." Kara yanked the car door open, buckled up, and brought the engine to life. As soon as she locked everything and shifted gears, her plan went into action. Tonight was the night to hurt him. He gave her the opening to escape with everyone. If she found everyone without drawing his blood, that would be best. That wasn't Thomas' style. He wanted her to come. He wouldn't mention his house and not be there. "I don't know what to do after but..."

You'll figure it out. Anne sat next to her. She was the calm quiet presence next to Kara's stormy side even with blood running down her face. *The first step is to go to his house. He doesn't go many places without help.*

That bit she still didn't get. Who dropped him off at her house? Where did he find her address? More importantly, how was he able to trick her parents into coming with him? He didn't drive. He had no car. From the sounds of it, he didn't use public transportation outside of rideshare and he didn't have friends to drive him around town. Even if he had her address, he couldn't walk from there to McIver Drive. He didn't have the physical stamina to run anywhere. What did he do?

I can't think about that now. I gotta find them. Kara drove through the highway blinded by rage, not bothering to glance back before changing lanes or slow down when the speed limit was 55. Several cars honked at her as she drove on, her heart pounding. McIver Drive. By now, she could get there blindfolded with both hands tied behind her. Not now though. With the clock ticking away, she prayed to every deity that her parents were alive. They had to be. Thomas claimed they were, but his unpredictability told other stories. If she got lucky, she'd find Sara Murphy too.

Come on, come on. As soon as she got onto McIver Drive, she didn't slow down on the gravel. She drove on until she got to that house. Empty and dark as always except he was around tonight. Slamming the car door shut, she jogged around the house for an entrance. Knocking on the door wouldn't do much for her. He knew she'd be coming, and he'd be ready. She wasn't gonna barge in while he had all the knives at his disposal. He'd stab her the moment he opened that door. She wanted to get in from a secret entrance. He had to have one. Every house had another way to get in.

"Come on, come on!" She hissed as she stared at the back. Her eyes dropped down to the crawlspace, her skin prickling. "Oh, fuck no. No! Not there!"

The more she dreaded it, the more she believed it. He kept everything down there. Everyone he wanted to harm and kill stayed there until he was done with them. She backed away for a second, unable to process her thoughts. She couldn't be late. In any case, there was only one person she wanted to throw hands on.

"Thomas!" She ran around the area, her feet crunching all the dead leaves. "Thomas! Where are you?! Answer me, dammit! I know you're out here!"

Remember to stay calm. Anne warned her. *He wants you to lose it. Don't give him that satisfaction, Kara. Never give him that!*

Kara stopped pacing around, controlling her breathing. No, she couldn't lose her sanity on him. She wanted him to find her angry, but not psychotic. She slowed down and got her voice to a normal level. "I'm out here, Thomas! You asked me to come! I'm here! Just like always!"

"I thought you'd never show up." He wiped his nose, the blood trickling like a strip of red plastic. "Sorry for the mess I'm in. I had a little accident earlier. That's why I'm cleaning myself up now."

"Where are my parents?!" She started to stomp towards him but slowed down. This was a killer. She couldn't lash out at him and not expect him to stay still. He waited for her to throw a punch or a kick, something he could deflect easily. Not wanting to give him an upper hand, Kara slowed down though kept the rage in her voice. "Where the hell is Sara Murphy?! Who else did you hurt?!"

"Calm down, Kara. There's no need to lash at me when I haven't done anything." He motioned her to lower her hands. "Hurting me won't get you any closer to them. If anything, you'll end up hurting yourself. Be a good girl and listen to me. For a little while, just listen to me."

Be on your guard. Anne's bloody figure got behind her. *He'll try to lower your defenses. Keep them up.*

"I won't ask you twice." She inhaled the cold air around her. Funny. Earlier it was warm and bright to the point where she had to turn on the AC. Now, she wanted to wrap her arms around herself and run inside the warmest place nearby. "Just tell me where everyone is, and I will forget all about this. I've held your secrets for a long time. However, if you did anything, it'll be the last thing you ever do."

"Oh, Kara. You've learned how to threaten people." He shook his head. "I had a feeling we were getting to this point. You were doing such a good job until now. You were a good talker. A smooth driver. You clearly cared about your riders and gave them free water and snacks. Not only that, but you were also punctual, and you took me exactly where I wanted to go. You're not like others who honk at people going slow or change lanes on time or run red lights. Then you had to go and ruin it all."

"I didn't ruin shit." She stepped back, careful not to break the sticks in the ground. Anne stood by her side, still bleeding from her head and neck, but appearing more defiant. "You dragged me into your life. You made me a part of it. I never asked for that."

"Ah, but you were the one who answered my call." Thomas began to walk towards her. "You were there when I needed you to be."

"Stay away." She warned him. Even without a weapon, she didn't want him to think she couldn't fight back. "Don't get any closer to me. I'm done with this!"

"Come on, Kara. If you knew anything about me, you'd understand why I'm the way I am." He sniffed. "You'd have a little sympathy for the person I've become."

"I doubt there's anything you can tell me that'll make me see you as sympathetic." Kara held her hands out to keep that distance. Thomas shifted back and forth but never lurched forward. He waited just like she did for the right moment. "All you've done is torment me, drag me into your sick game, and kill people while I've had to sit in the car and wait. I'm stuck in place right now. Why would I care for you?"

"Well, I don't expect you to care for me but let me tell you a story. It's something I should have told you from before...or something you could have figured out earlier." Thomas circled her while she followed him. Both wanted the first blow. "Once upon a time, there was a young boy who was a gifted artist. He could have become the next Monet or Picasso or another one of those great artists out there. He got praised to high heavens by all teachers and peers alike. He even got an opportunity to study art in France when he was about your age. He had the whole world in front of him, ready to take over."

Kara turned when he turned, her hands in her pockets. "Then what happened?"

"Well, the young man suddenly started to feel terrible. At first, he thought it was a cold. Then he suspected it was the flu despite getting the flu shot. Then it got to the point where he could barely stand up, let alone create anything. He was too tired, too ill, but did the doctors know what happened? No, none of them knew. They all said he was fine. Whatever bug he had, it would pass, and he'd be able to go on his trip."

"He never got a chance, did he?" Kara fiddled with the rocks in her pocket. One move. One opening, and she could nail him. "He only got worse and worse. The doctors couldn't do anything about it. Not even Dr. Moseley."

"Dr. Moseley kept saying he'd survive this. That one day, he'd be cured. He was never cured of anything. The tremors got to the point where he could no longer hold a brush steady, let alone paint anything without messing it up." Thomas' voice dripped with venom. "The boy had that one disease no one had a name for. Something that less than 1% of the population could get. Hence why there was no cure. No one bothered to look for one. I mean, less than 1% of people get it!" He laughed into the air. "You think I wouldn't be one of them."

"You ended up getting it. And with no cure, no answers...you lost your dream."

"I never got that chance to study in France. I spent days in bed, wishing I could have someone else's body, someone else's life. I saw so many people walking around, happy and healthy, who could have done anything they wanted. Explored this world to the fullest. Yet as I turned each corner, they weren't doing that. They weren't exploring a thing. Just wasting their entire lives on menial jobs and pointless activities. Dr. Moseley said I'd be like them, getting my life back. I never did."

"So, you killed him." Kara's eyes darkened as the truth dawned over her. "He let you down. You couldn't deal with that pain anymore. You had to get rid of him."

"Not just him. Every single person who lives without living." He leaned against a tree branch, his shoulders tensing. "I can't bear to watch it. How can they be so happy in this way?"

Kara went over to another tree, ready to use it as a place to hide if needed. With the distance in place, he couldn't hurt her. Not with his weakened body. "Not everyone gets an opportunity to leave the country though. Not everyone's an artist genius. That probably wasn't the case with Anne or Sara or Dr. Moseley. It wasn't the case with anyone else."

"Maybe not, but they could have tried like you try. Even now, you stand strong in front of me. You're willing to fight back. You haven't given up hope that you'll find Sara alive. I see that fire in your eyes, Kara. That fire burned out of Sara and Anne and all the others before I laid a hand on them. They lost their hope. You didn't."

"Where are they?" She lowered her voice. This banter didn't get her anywhere. "You know I'm not getting out of your way until you give me some clue."

"A clue?" He waved her off. "Baby, I've done nothing but give you clues this whole time. It's not my fault you're not able to put anything together. Now, let's get one thing straight: I don't want to hurt your parents so don't give me a reason to do so. They're not like the others. After all, they raised you. I didn't want to take them but...well, you broke the rules."

"No." She shook her head as she moved from the tree. "I'm not the one who's breaking any rules here. None of your victims broke any rules. You're only killing them out of jealousy. That's all."

"Jealousy?" Now Thomas' temper hit its peak. He stormed towards her as she backed away, using the trees to hide. "You think I did all of this because I'm jealous?! Why would I be jealous of some stupid kid wasting their life?!"

"You just answered that question: they're wasting their life in your eyes. You hate all of them for that." She swerved around as he lunged towards the trees. "You hated Anne, you hated Sara, you hated everyone for having what you could never have! More than that, you hated them for letting it all go! You wanted their youth, their time, their health to pursue your dreams. That's what it's all about, isn't it?"

"Shut up." He whispered as he grabbed the tree trunk, where she last stood. By now, she moved a few feet from him, weaving between tree trunks. "You shut up, Kara."

"You can't deal with it, can you? You know I'm right." She swung around as he tried to grab her. "You can't deal with the pain anymore. I don't blame you for that. No one wants to lose everything they worked hard for. You have nothing else because of this disease. The only way you get satisfaction is by making others suffer."

"Shut up, Kara!" He growled. "You don't know what you're talking about."

"I don't? I see right through you, Thomas. This is just your sick fantasy. This is the only way you feel better." She spotted the house a few feet away, knowing this was her chance. If anyone was around, they'd be somewhere in there. "You can't heal yourself physically. You might as well take care of the mental one. It's why you kill. To feel better."

"Kara, you little..."

"You can't fight back cause I'm right!" She cut him off, now starting to run. "I'm right, Thomas! I've been right about you the whole time! You're not proving anything except what I always knew: you're just some sick, twisted man who thinks he's getting better by killing others. Well, newsflash...you're still the same as you were all those years ago. The only difference is that you're a lot weaker."

"SHUT UP!" He jumped at her, knocking her to the ground. His hands wrapped around her throat as his body pushed down on her. "You shut the fuck up! You don't know anything! You don't know! You don't know what is going on with me!"

Kara croaked as her hands grabbed him to pull them off. The colors changed around, growing darker and fading out. Thomas continued to grunt and growl as he pushed down. Her feet kicked into the air as

Anne's voice yelled at her. *Fight, Kara! Fight him! You were right, he's weaker than you!*

"I...uh..."

"Shut up." His body shook as his nose started bleeding, drops of it landing on her face. At this point, he loosened his grip as color returned to Kara's world. She made out the trees and night sky before her while Anne screamed. *Now's your chance! Bite him! BITE HIM!*

As soon as Thomas took his hand off, Kara lifted her head and chomped down on it, letting her teeth sink into his skin. He howled as he let her go, falling off her body while she kicked him down. Blood gushed out as he rolled towards the slope. Dizzy and reeling from the choking, Kara kicked him again to knock him down.

"Fuck you!" She spat out as he rolled to the side but not down. While he writhed in agony, rolling back and forth, she grabbed a large on the ground and held it above her head. "I'm done with you! Get the hell out of my life!"

"Kara..." He coughed as the blood streamed all over his face. "Kara, you..."

Kara didn't wait for a reply from either him or Anne. She slammed the rock down on his head, knocking him down the slope. His body rolled to the bottom, smacking against the rocks and sticks poking, covered in dead leaves. Her neck ached from the choking, but she watched him go down. Her vision returned the moment he started rolling.

That should do it for now. Anne stood next to her, glaring down at his unmoving body. *That gives us time.*

"For now? He's not dead?"

She shook her head as Thomas groaned from below. *You've only knocked him out for a bit. It'll take him a short time to wake up. So, you need to find everyone else and get them before he starts climbing.*

"Right!" Kara turned her heel towards the house. Thomas didn't drag anyone outside of this area. He kept all his victims here, which made it easy on his body. She got the picture then. He'd coax the victims, bring them to this house, then kidnap them and eventually kill them. That took the toll off his body. He pretended everything was fine, but it wasn't. With the police bringing up Anne's case, he needed to change his methods. He needed to look like he was moving around.

And that's where I came in. She concluded as his house came into view. *The Traveler needed to travel again. With a rideshare driver, his job became a thousand times easier. I take and drop him off wherever he wants to go. He doesn't need me to move bodies, just help him stalk his victim and provide an alibi.*

She ran around the woods, praying he wouldn't catch up with her. She did it now. She got too far to be safe. All their rules were broken. Now she ran around for survival. As soon as she got her parents and other victims out, she'd take care of him. She vowed to hurt him if he did anything. Even if he hadn't, she wanted to hurt him. Make him pay for all the pain he put her through. Hurt him for hurting everyone else through the years.

Gazing at the moon, she let the clouds pass by before trekking to the house, prepared to battle anything blocking her way.

Chapter 19

Kara stumbled around in the dark, her body bumping into tree trunks and almost falling into the bushes. Her body scratched up from everything sticking out, she ignored all that small pain and focused on finding her parents and Sara. If he had any other victims, she'd get them out too. Constantly checking behind her, she fully expected Thomas to chase after her, bloodthirsty and fueled by hatred. Whatever trust she won from him, it was long gone. He didn't want her as his chauffeur anymore. He didn't want her to live.

The house stood a few feet away, yet each step made it appear farther from reach. Her hand stretched out as she gasped for air. Out in nature, surrounded by trees, she still struggled to breathe. Time wasn't on her side tonight. Everyone depended on her to get inside the house and get them out. She inhaled and exhaled as the house came into view, all those white sidings a beacon to lead her. He didn't turn the lights on. He didn't leave any sign of life, but every part in her assured her that someone lived inside. Willingly or not, they were there.

Her grandfather's warning rang in her ears as she checked the stars above. The clouds shifted away from them, revealing the twinkling lights above. The clouds moved away from the skies and revealed her fate. It all came down to her. What she did tonight, her survival, her freedom all depended on her next moves.

That night will tell you everything, Karishma. Do not ignore the warnings.

He didn't need to tell her twice about that. Every step she ran, every tree branch she swung around, she imagined Thomas only a few inches from her. She pictured his snarling red face, his eyes ice-blue and locked on her. How would he kill her? Stab her like Anne and several other victims? Maybe he'd choose a more personal method like strangulation. Or maybe he'd give up all his methods and go for something new. Whatever it was, she didn't want to hang and find out. Any other time, she'd run away. The car still waited for her at a distance, but she wouldn't leave without finding her parents or any other victims.

You must hurry, Kara! Anne ran next to her, not losing her breath. By now, she no longer spoke with that emotionless voice. The danger became real for them. She ran for a life that she didn't have anymore. *Thomas is hurt! He can't move for a while!*

"Is he dead?!" She gasped as she ran towards the door. "Please tell me he's dead!"

I don't know. All that I can say is that you have your chance. Go find them!

"All right, I'm going!" Her lungs burned as her speed picked up. This was it. This was the moment she got to escape him for good. "Come on! I know I can make it! I know I'll get there!"

Hurry! Anne ran beside her, the blood from her head and neck streaming down. *You knocked him out for a bit. He'll take his time getting up here. He's not as strong as you!*

Kara ran straight into the house, flinging the door open, and locking it shut behind her. Staring into it, she found nothing out of the ordinary in the living room. A sofa, table, two armchairs, a couple of plants in the corner. He carried no pictures on the walls, but plenty of artwork adored them. Approaching each painting with caution and amazement, she found the initials TW on them. The pictures depicted human life in both good and bad times. Paintings of people at a party, paintings of war and death, paintings of every place Thomas went to. If he wasn't a psychopath, Kara would have been impressed with his skill. He clearly put time and effort into each painting, his brush strokes thick and bringing scenes to life. As she wandered down the hall, his subjects changed from light and laughter to darkness and death. He gave up painting about happy moments. All he wanted was darkness. More than that, he wanted everyone else in the darkness as well.

"I can't believe he made all this." She strolled through the rooms, admiring everything in them. Thomas filled every wall with a painting he created. Anne followed her, unable to express the same awe. These paintings didn't matter when the man who created them was a killer. "I don't get it. I don't get why he let one thing turn him into this."

He couldn't deal with it. Anne turned to find nothing following them. *Some people are strong enough to endure the pain. He's not one of them. He's not you.*

"I don't know." Kara pressed her hands on the walls, trying to trace the source of the whimpers. With each step, they grew louder. "I'm not strong, Anne. I'm the idiot who picked this man up and threw herself into the nightmare. If I just rejected his..."

She trailed off once she found that hollow spot in the wall. Tapping it, a groan answered her, and she continued going down the way. With each tap, she got closer to them. Yet she couldn't take her time with the taps. Thomas only fell down the slope. The moment he came around, he'd make it up to the house. She pictured his evil blue eyes blazing, ready to shoot her on sight. Quickly, she raced down the hall, tapping each spot.

Please take your time. Take all the time in the world. I know you're ill. You won't be able to climb up as fast.

He wanted to kill her now. She screwed up enough for him. She disobeyed him, went against his back, and proved that she no longer wanted to play this little game. This time, she got inside the house before he could. With no lights on, she relied solely on her instincts. Turning any light on would alert him. First, she had to find her parents and save them along with anyone else he kidnapped. Maybe Sara Murphy was also locked away in here. If he hadn't been in this house for days, she still breathed. She walked sideways, listening closely for anything inside. The floor creaked under her, yet she spotted something out of place. In between each creak came a groan, then a whimper. Yes, someone was here.

"Hello?" She tapped on the wall. "Are you there? Give me a sign."

A whimper came back, confirming her suspicions. Thomas' house was where he kept his victims until he was ready to kill them. He hid them far from the world, so no one could come across and rescue them. Hence the long dark road into McIver Lane, the fact nothing was around for miles, that the nearest way out of here was down a slope behind the house. If the victim never saw that slope, they'd never leave. If she got these people out, they'd be the first victims to survive and make it to civilization.

That was the case with Anne, Dr. Moseley, and the other victims. They breathed around him, healthy and ready to take on the world, while he wasted away. No matter how many times he ran off, he couldn't escape his mortality. His physical strength drained out with each passing day. He no longer drove himself around. He couldn't use a tissue without bleeding into it. He couldn't breathe or stay still anymore. That disease ate away at him, taking him down. Dr. Moseley couldn't save him. Despite all his efforts, he could do nothing to stop it from spreading. He had no cure. This wasn't enough for Thomas, so he took out the only person who tried to help him. It gave him satisfaction for a second, but no cure.

"I guess trying wasn't enough for them, huh?" She tapped her hands down the walls, each part growing hollow and empty. A little muffle sprung out from behind it. "What are you hiding back here, Thomas? What's so important in this house of yours?"

Watch your step! Watch it!

She stumbled in the dark over the giant lump blocking her path. The moonlight shifted through the window and lay on top of it. No, not a lump. Body. Her legs tripped over a dead body, blood pooling all over it. Holding her breath, she zeroed in on the face. Sara Murphy. Somehow, he managed to kill her before Kara got here. Her decaying corpse reeked in the entire room, nearly causing Kara to vomit. The poor girl stood no chance. Given how angry Thomas was at Kara, he was going to take everyone down with him. The smell gave Kara no time for mourning, but she couldn't leave Sara in this way. In the corner, she found several comforters and blankets. Grabbing those, she carefully draped them over the body, giving it something to keep it warm. Not that it mattered. Sara couldn't get warm anymore. She couldn't get cold or angry or worried about anything. She lay there now, bloodied and still. The police would find her soon. If Thomas didn't move her from this place, they'd find her and bring her home.

Anne stared down at the body, shaking her head. *We weren't fast enough.*

"No." Kara closed her eyes to pray to whatever God lay out there. Her family always told her that the human spirit couldn't die; it only moved on to a new vessel. It could take the spirit a while to come back to the world. She always wondered who she had been prior to this life. She heard stories of reincarnation from others but no memory of former lives. Maybe the same thing would happen to Sara once she was reborn. She wouldn't remember the terror and torture of this night. She'd come back in a new life, hopefully sooner than later, to another family. If all went well, it would be a kind family. One that treated her well and didn't force into anything. One that understood her desires and encouraged all the way. One that...

A family that isn't like Thomas' family. She quickly prayed for a quick trip for the spirit before standing up. "Is she the only one here?"

Anne's gaze fell on the window as Kara's stomach churned again. Anne deserved a good reincarnation as well. She deserved a new loving family, and new opportunities to live her life. She didn't need to linger here for Kara's sake. *She's the only one I can see. Come on. We have to find the others.*

"Right." Kara stepped back as the floorboard creaked out. Jumping away from it, she almost fell over the other comforters in the bed. Pulling herself up, she waved her hands in the dark, using the moon as her guide. "Ugh, seriously? How can he be so messy?"

So messy and so clean at the same time. It's incredible how it took so long for someone to find him. Anne pointed to the door. *Forget about everything here. Start looking for your family.*

She didn't need a reminder. Her feet still running across creaky, unstable floorboards, Kara peeked into the other rooms for a sign of life. "Ma? Baba? Anyone? I'm here now. I'm here to rescue you. If you can hear me, give me a sign."

The only replies were the chirping crickets nearby and some hooting. Owls. Fantastic, there were owls out tonight. With them on the prowl along with other nocturnal animals, she'd never know what was making the sounds inside. Step by step, she moved on. She was too late for Sara, but not for anyone else. Hopefully, they heard her. Hopefully, they would...

Something grabbed the bottom of her jacket as she fell to the ground. "AH! Help! Help me!"

As she rolled, the coat rack which caught her by surprise fell on top of her. Groaning, she kicked it off and pulled her jacket from it. "Stupid piece of shit. I really thought..."

He's not back yet. Anne listened to the howls in the distance. *He won't be held back for a long time. Protect yourself.*

"Yeah, I gotta protect myself." Kara grabbed the coat rack, dragging it on the ground. It wasn't the best weapon, but it was all she could carry and use. "Sorry I called you a piece of shit earlier. If you save my ass, I'll never curse out another inanimate object again."

With each foot moving forward, she clung tightly to the rack. It wasn't too heavy to lift, and it would barricade her from Thomas if he showed up. He couldn't come up here quickly. He couldn't make his way over here. *Creak...creak...creak.* Her weight on that floor only scared her. Why didn't he have any carpet in here? Probably because blood took longer to clean on the carpet. A wooden floor took less time. She understood it now after having to clean her car out. With the rack leaving a trail on the dust, her foot stamped on the ground.

Thud!

That wasn't her. She whirled around to face Anne, who only shrugged in reply. Anne didn't make that sound. Once more, she stamped down on the floor, leaving her footprint in that thick dust.

Thud! Thud!

"Someone's alive in here." She leaned against the wall, tapping on that. "Come on. Show me where you are. Hit harder now."

As if on cue, the thuds grew louder and more frantic. THUD! THUD! THUD!

"I can hear them!" She dragged the rack towards the first door on the left. "Okay, I'm coming! Let's try..." She tapped her hand against the door. A muffled cry came from below. "They're in here! Someone's in here!" More rapping led to more muffled cries including one that almost sounded like 'help.' Kara attempted to open the door to no avail. It was jammed. All the dirt and thick paint around it jammed it up to the point where she put the rack down and yanked it. Then she kicked it. "Shit! I'm almost there!

Harder! Anne commanded. *You're almost there! Pull once more and they'll be free!*

"I'm trying to pull! I'm trying! I'm..." The door yanked open with the last pull. "Holy shit! I opened it!"

Then why are you waiting? Go!"

For a ghost, Anne grew more impatient with each passing second. Kara found the light and tried to turn it on. It fizzed for a second before dying. She threw her hands in the air, hoping for another light around. "Great. Nothing here works. All I can do is count myself and brace myself on the..." She grazed the wall for a banister. "On nothing. No banister, nothing to hold onto. What kind of a house is this?"

I wondered the same thing when he brought me down here for the first time.

"First time?"

Oh yeah, he brings everyone down here at least once. It's his way of making sure we never leave him. He doesn't live next to anyone. He's not close to any stores or places. He lives out here with no lights, no sounds, nothing. I'm surprised you weren't aware of that. Then again...

She paused long enough for Kara to make her way to the next step. Finding the wall, Kara used that as her new guide. "Then again what?"

I noticed something when he dragged me. Behind the trees, there's a shopping center. I remember hearing people talking and music and I smelled food of all kinds. Pizza, Chinese food, burgers...I don't know if he knows about it. If he does, he's never gone there. He's never mentioned it anyway.

"Is it far from here?" Kara found the next step, teetering on the edge. "Jesus Christ! If there's only something that can help me find out where I'm going..."

"MMPF!" The muffled cry got her off guard as she stumbled to the next step. Then a few more muffled cries joined in, luring her in. They confirmed what she suspected: he kept people down here. Judging from the sounds, some of them were still alive.

"Oh God, I'm coming." She whispered, hoping someone down there heard her. "I'm coming, okay? I'm on my way."

Slowly, she went down the stairs as the smell of blood grew stronger. Once nearing the bottom, it hit harder while a few whimpers came up. Step by step, a horrible stench filled the room as she finally got to the bottom. Holding in the gags, she choked out. "Oh fuck."

"MMFP! Mmfp!" The muffled cries grew closer now that she made her way towards a closed door. No, not closed. In the corner of her eye, she saw part of it slightly swing open. Thomas didn't lock this room up. He left it open even though no one left him. No one tried to escape through this door. The only way they wouldn't get out was if they couldn't. She pushed the door open and was hit immediately with an all too familiar smell.

There it was. She knew it existed but now she saw it. His secret room reeking of all that blood. Small and dark, her parents huddled up in one corner while three young women huddled in the other. They all tried calling her while she stepped around, attempting to make sense of this torture area. All the victims sat bound and gagged, which explained why no one left. In the corner were more bloodied rags and ropes. Perhaps that's where Sara had been before he killed her. He took care of her and was coming for the rest.

Blood surrounded them, from their feet to the walls and straight to the ceiling. Little by little, it dripped down, some of it drying before it hit anything. None of the girls nor her parents had any wounds on her. These were the other victims who stayed here before death. The chains on the ground revealed how hard they fought to get out. The frayed ropes, the dead plants, bones galore...Thomas didn't clean this place up before he brought someone new. The endless skeletons froze up her insides. He killed more people than mentioned in the news. He killed repeatedly, painting his house with their blood, and decorating it with their remains. That's why he traveled so much; he stayed away from the stench of his own house. He didn't want anyone to find this hideout.

Carefully, Kara kneeled by the first girl and took her gag off. "I need you to keep quiet, okay? I'm not here to hurt you. I want to get all of you out of here, but I need your help. Can you keep quiet long enough for me?"

The girl let out a small gasp before nodding, her lips trembling as she spoke. "What day is it? Who are you?"

"That doesn't matter right now. I know he's lurking out in the back, so I distracted him long enough to get here. I'm getting all of you out." She began taking the gags off the others. "Has he done anything to you guys at all? Hurt you in anyway?"

"I...I don't think so." Another girl struggled to breathe out. "It's hot in here. I'm starving. He comes down here and says...he says..."

"He says our time will come." The girl got out, breathing heavily like the others. She took in all the air like it was the first time she learned to breathe. "Called us bitches when he tied us up. Said we had all the opportunities in the world, and we threw them away. Said we didn't deserve to be on this planet. We wouldn't know suffering if it kicked us in the face. Then he locked us in here."

"That's what I was afraid of." She went over to her parents, taking their gags off. "Hang on. I'm here now."

"Rishi, how..." Her father began as she went around to the back and started to untie him. "Where did you..."

"Don't talk." She silenced him. "We have to get out of here before he comes back."

"He? I thought you were going to get the eggs and bread I asked." Her mother flung off the frayed ropes. "I thought you'd_"

"Yeah, well, things have taken a turn in another direction. I don't know if you've noticed this, Ma, you're in a psycho's house and you were tied up." She pulled her parents onto their feet before helping the girls. They struggled to stand still, weakened from lack of food and sleep. Once everyone got a little balanced, she motioned them to start moving. After a second, they followed her towards the door in the back. That window peeking through gave away her location. "All right, I need you to listen well. Once you get out of that door, you start running. Get the strength you have and run down that path. Don't look back. Don't slow down. I'll take care of him."

"Him?" Her father swallowed as reality came over him. He couldn't stop her from anything this time. He understood she went too deep in this. Only she could get herself out of it. "Are you…"

"I don't have time to explain, Baba! All of you need to get out of here before he gets back!" She pushed them out the door, letting the cool air blow in. "Run, okay?! Run until you see the streets. There's a shopping center so run into any shop and tell them what happened! Tell them to call the police! Just get help from anywhere!"

"But what about you?" One of the girls tried to bring her through the door. Kara planted her feet down to keep from skidding forward as the girl kept yanking her arm. "Come on! You gotta go too!"

"Not yet." Kara pulled her arm from the girl's grasp. "I can't go yet. Not until I finish this."

"Finish what?" Her mother tried to go inside but Kara pushed her towards the door. This wasn't the time for her to argue against anything. Her life depended on everything Kara did from here on out. "Karishma, what are you_"

"I'm telling you now, Mama! Leave!" Kara waved them off. "I'll hold him off! I'm the only one who can! And when I'm done, I'll bring the bread and eggs, Ma! I promise! Just go!"

She slammed the door behind them before running around the empty room, her hands flailing and hitting the walls. Her arms covered in blood and feet crunching on bones, she ran up the steps to hear the front door slamming. He made it.

She began to unite all of them, finding the ropes completely frayed out. They could easily slip through, but not with weakened bodies. More pieces came together as she freed each one. Thomas didn't tie anyone tightly on purpose; he let them believe he had so they'd give up fighting for their lives. He killed everything inside first, before he took them out. With his victims giving up on life, he gained some excitement from their suffering.

Creak!

She froze in place, her courage running away from her. Not only was he here, but he was also close by. Carefully, she got on tiptoes and made her way towards the door. Get out. It was time to get the strength back and run away. Leave him behind. Let him rot in his house forever. Get to a police station even if they did nothing for her. At least she could try and convince someone over there.

It's now or never. Are you ready? Anne stood by her side, eyes on the door.

Kara nodded. "I'm ready."

Then run!

Chapter 20

Running wasn't an option until Thomas' creaking footsteps moved away from the door. She didn't start to move until silence greeted her and then she climbed the steps. With her hands in fists, prepared to draw his blood, she inched upwards. As soon as she had a little breathing room, she quietly pushed the door open and began to run around in the darkness. For a small place, he had a lot of room in it. She couldn't find the front door anymore.

"Kara...KARA!"

He yelled around while she went in the other direction. Not yet. She couldn't fight him with no weapons. The white rage in his voice spelled one thing for her: death. If she didn't outrun, that was it for her. She couldn't run like a lunatic through the house. No, in all her panic, she had to remain strategic. She did exactly what she needed to do tonight.

They're out. Dear God, they're all out.

She didn't have her phone to know where her parents ran off to. Thomas knew they were gone, taking the white car. They drove out of the area and into safer places. Hopefully, they went to the police with all the information on him. The bloody rooms, the broken ropes, the chains...any idiot could see this and claim it was a torture chamber. He dropped all his victims in it first. Poor Anne and the others ended up here until he got tired of them. Thank God she found everyone before he tired of them too.

As long as you're not in the area, you'll be safe. She prayed to gods above for everyone's wellbeing. Let them get to a person. Let them get help. Save them. Someone could save them. *I can't explain much now, but if I get out of here, I'll tell you everything.*

If you get out of her? No, you must get out of here! Anne crept up from behind, peering over her shoulder. She grimaced at the footsteps around the house. Either they were his, his victims, or hers. She couldn't ponder over that. *He won't let you out of his grasp now. The only way to get out is to die or kill him.*

Kara moved away from the wall and then found the curtains, thick and black, with only a small sliver of light peeking through them. Going from ceiling to floor, it hid every inch of her as she stood there. Anne didn't lie about the two ways of getting out, but only one option made sense. If she died, he continued his reign of terror. He'd go after the victims he lost. Death was coming for one of them, but not her. The car. The moment she went outside, she regained control. When her hands grabbed the wheel, she laid out her destiny.

Thank you, Dadu. Those storm clouds are moving away. Hopefully, her grandfather could rest easy knowing she was almost free. She'd be fine after this. Maybe it wasn't what she wanted, but she'd still be alive. She had chances in the future for a better life, whenever that would come. First though, she had to chase those storm clouds away for good.

"Here, Kara...come here, Kara..." Thomas called out, holding in his sneezes. She didn't peer around the curtain, but knew he got closer. "You don't want to do this. Don't give me a reason to hurt you."

Kara held her breath, half-tempted to reply. He knew she was here so there was no point in acting that the room was empty. She shifted from one end of the curtain to the other, careful not to block out the light. He couldn't find her like this.

"All right, you had your little fun playing hero." He laughed as he entered the room. She sunk deeper into the shadows, letting the curtains hide her figure. "You enjoyed yourself. You get to save someone now. But it's all over now. I'm done playing this game. I have no doubt you were done with it a long time ago."

You got that right. As the lift shifted in the room, she did the same thing. Thomas waltzed around the room, checking every corner he could find. From the curtains, Kara shifted away from the moonlight and hid behind the wall, hands pressed against it as he came forward, each floorboard creaking under him. Slowing her breathing, she poked away at him. "Your power is fading, Thomas. You can't do this anymore."

"You don't know what I can do, Kara." He moved in, now stomping on the floorboards. "You're no stronger than the others. The only thing that separated you from them was that you were trying."

"Trying what? Trying to find a job? Trying to fit in when I couldn't even get an interview?" She scoffed. "Your victims were one step further than I am. They had a job. Granted, it may not be what they wanted to do, but they had something. If anything, I'm a failure...just like you."

"Me?!" Now he snapped, slamming his fist into the wall. Kara shuddered but refused to show herself. "You think I'm failing because of a disease? I didn't get this from anywhere, Kara!"

"No, you're not a failure because of the disease." Bit by bit, Kara pulled away from the wall. The door was only a few inches away, slightly opened and begging her to get out. "You couldn't help that. It's all bad luck on your end there. You failed because you thought you had it easy. You got me as your driver."

"And what's that supposed to mean?"

"It means you fucked with the wrong person, that's what." She held back her laughter as the blood dried on her cheeks. "You know, all this time, I was afraid of you. You killed when you felt like it. You thought that if I was your driver, I would take anywhere you wanted. Let you kill and get away with it. Let you take control of me. And in the beginning, that was true. I feared you."

Thomas peeked under the curtain where she had been, then started slashing into them. "You don't know what scared is, kiddo. You don't know how lucky you were that I let you live."

"No." She tiptoed towards the door, slipping through it. "You're the lucky one. I allowed you to get control of everything first. Not anymore. You crossed the line."

He whirled around as she slammed the door behind him, letting out a guttural scream. Kara bolted away from the door as something rammed it again and again. Running down the halls, she heard nothing but Thomas yelling and slamming away. Her family and the three girls left a long time ago. She didn't know what direction they were going, but it was far from here. She wanted Thomas all to herself now. Get him riled up. Get him angry to the point where he had lost all common sense. The moment he lost his grip, she won. She'd have him right in the spot she wanted him to be.

"Get back here, Kara!" He snarled as the door flung open. "Get your ass back here!"

"Come get me!" She turned the corner, grabbing the side of the wall and diving into the darkness again. This time, the bed made for a better hiding place with no light hitting it. Another door on the side waited for her, most likely a closet or a bathroom.

"Oh, Kara. This is where it ends." Thomas sighed. "I didn't think it would be this way. We went on a great journey."

"Journey? It's a nightmare!" Kara shot back. "You...you dragged me into your life! All I wanted to do was to pick up people and drop them off where they want to go. I didn't want to chauffeur you around! I..." Her voice caught inside her throat over at her parents, long gone from here but lost out on the streets. Did they understand her instructions? In any case, they weren't close to Thomas. He didn't want them anymore. Just her. "I should have listened to my father and gone back to school. Maybe then...maybe I'd..."

"You'd what? Struggle through more classes? You said so yourself: school wasn't for you. It took you time to get where you were. Not to mention, you'd still have to work to pay for tuition. We'd still find each other, sooner or later. It just happened to be now."

She flipped over each bottle, attempting to read the instructions in the dark. No use in turning on the lights for this. She'd put things away to the best of her ability. "I wish...I wish I never accepted the ride."

"Wish all you want. This is where we are now, and it was fate. You and I are the same, Kara. You don't see it but here we are. We're two people who don't fit into the world. It dealt both of us a bad hand. Your parents don't see you the way I see you. They'll never get it. No matter how many times you explain it, they won't get it." He breathed out. "It was the same with me. I remember telling my parents about my dreams. They didn't care. Even when those dreams died, they didn't care. They didn't even encourage me to try again, not like you. It was over."

Kara stared down at all the medication on the ground. He wasn't wrong about the pain. Even if no one saw it, it lingered deep inside. "That might be true, but none of that ever made me angry at other people. Jealous, maybe, I never got the urge to kill them. That's why I'm nothing like you. I'll never be."

"Oh, Kara." He peeked under the bed. "I'm afraid you became like me the moment you picked me up from the airport. You took me where I needed to go, and you very rarely questioned it. Even when you learned the truth, you didn't fight back. Why the change now?"

Kara picked up all the pills, unable to read any of the labels. She didn't recognize them by size or color, so she piled everything into one bottle. Whatever he used them for, they weren't working. They didn't heal his mind or his body. The only way to heal him, break him free of the hell he lived in, was to kill him. Her hands trembled as she put the medication back in its place. No wonder Anne and the other ghosts pressured her. They saw this as the only way out. This was the only way to rest in peace, getting rid of him and protecting any future victims. On the ground, she found a few rocks which could hold him back. None would kill him. If the large rock she threw did nothing, these would only give a small cut or bruise. Nothing to hold him back.

"Come on, Kara." He cooed as he got closer to the bathroom. She quietly hid in the tub, holding onto the shampoo bottle. It wouldn't cause much damage, but it would be thick enough to distract him. "Look, I have ways of getting you out of here. You let them go. That's fine by me. There are plenty just like them out there. Everywhere I go, I'll find another worthless young person. So, what if a few are gone? I'll put another one in another place. I'll find somewhere else, somewhere no one will know about. It might take a while but...it'll happen. It's happened before."

Another place? He's not planning to use this room anymore. Kara sniffed the air, catching something strong in the air. A familiar smell that she encountered every time she filled up at the pump. It didn't take her long to add it all together. *Fuck me! He's going to destroy this place too!*

"Now, we can do this the easy way. You walk out now, unlock the door, and things will be good. I will reconsider everything here." His feet stopped right at the door. "Come on, Kara. You and I both know you're not stupid enough to die like this. That's what makes you so special. No matter what anyone else says, you're one of the smartest people I've met. You wouldn't do anything to risk your life or the ones you love. So, make it easy and step out."

Pzzt! The lighting of a match gave Kara all the motivation she needed to move. Carefully, she got out of the tub, still holding onto the shampoo bottle. She sniffed the air for the faint smell of gasoline. He poured it all around the house, most of it outside of her door. One hand on the knob, she leaned in and held up the bottle with the other.

"And you promise you won't do anything?" She tightened her grip. "If I open this door, you won't attack me?"

"I promise. I need you alive, Kara. Together, you and I could drive away from an explosion without looking back. So, don't give me a reason to want you dead."

Kara breathed in as the door grew warmer on the other side. As she feared, he didn't keep the promise. The house was already burning while he waited on her. He had no intention of letting her leave the house alive. Either he killed her, or she went down with the burning house. Holding in her breath, Kara prepared to barge through. Thomas waited on the other side along with the flames. White and hot, they waited to engulf her with the rest of the house.

Well, time to break through. In the corner, she found Anne's ghost nodding at her, giving the signal to break out.

She pushed the door open and flung the shampoo bottle towards his head. He ducked down long enough for her to swerve past him and face a wall of fire. All around her, flames danced while smoke filled the air. In seconds, the roof and walls would cave in unless she got out. Jumping over small drops of gasoline on the ground, she ran to the front where more fire faced her. Blocking that exit, she found the window free of flame and slightly open.

It's now or never! Anne yelled at her, still clinging to her side. *Push that window screen out and go! Get to your car!*

Kara shoved her entire body through the window, falling out with the screen. She rolled across the grass to smother out any flames. Once she got far from it, she crawled onto her feet and ran to the car, fiddling around her pockets for the keys. Her legs stumbled around as she found the keys and unlocked the door. Her arms reached out to open it and threw herself inside. She crawled in with every inch of aching.

Once in the driver's seat, she locked all the doors and brought the car to life, forgetting about her seat belt and lights. Behind her, the house burned a bright orange with smoke reaching all the way to the stars. Thomas. Get away from Thomas. Her brain screamed at her to hit the gas. Her foot went down on that gas pedal, and her hands shifted the gears as she drove away. The only light remained was the burning house. She didn't bother looking behind her. If Thomas survived this, he'd be right there.

Drive, Kara! Drive! Anne screamed at her. *Forget about him and drive!*

The heat of the fire pounded against her back, she gripped the wheel and sped up, tires squealing over the rocks. Her heart raced with the vehicle itself, wanting that stretch of highway. The moment she found the exit towards the center of the city, she'd get on it and drive. Her mind scrambled over all the events as she went on. It was almost over. If he died in the house, that was it. She became free of him, and the whole town would go back to normal. No more curfew, no more pain. She'd drive the night shift again, making sure everyone got home safely. Maybe go back to school like her parents wanted. For now, all she could do was...

BAM!

Her body lurched forward, forehead hitting the steering wheel and the car squealing to a stop. A big blot of blood splattered on the windshield, blocking her view. Regaining control of the car, she pulled it towards the edge and flipped on the wipers. Blood. Dear God, all that blood was raining down on her car. Her heart slowed down as she flipped on the lights, body aching from the impact. Her neck in pain and forehead throbbing, she finally pulled the brakes and stepped out of the car to find what she hit. No doubt it was a deer. The one time she turned off her lights here, she finally ran into one. Legs like jelly, she wobbled out of the driver's seat and stumbled towards the dead body. The vomit finally forced itself out of her mouth when the victim came into view.

Thomas. She never hit a deer in the first place. Thomas survived that fire. He ran after her with every desire to kill, a knife flung a few feet from him. Once she finished throwing up, she wiped her mouth and inched towards the body, no longer breathing or moving. He wasn't faking a death now. He was gone, dead from her ramming into him in the dark.

"Oh God." She spat out the last bit of vomit, unable to focus on anything. "I...I...is he..."

He's gone. Anne stepped up next to her. *You've killed him. The nightmare's over.*

"He's gone." She repeated, letting the events process. Thomas no longer held control over, no longer threatened her, no longer had the ability to kill anyone else. She took him out before he caused more damage. "Oh my God, he really is gone."

The panic soon wiped away over her new and probably short-lived freedom. She couldn't live with this forever. She ran into a man, the same man who held her hostage and dragged her through his crimes. She stopped him before anyone else could. She held all his secrets. She let him get away out of fear. Well, she didn't fear him. She feared nothing. Her body stopped throbbing as she got onto the hood of the car and sat down for a rest. Behind her, the house glowed orange but those flames and smoke no longer harmed her. Let it all burn down but leave Thomas here to get eaten by the wild animals. It was the least he deserved.

So, what are you going to do now? Anne joined her on top of the car, her cuts no longer bleeding. *You can't stay here forever. You don't need to linger around anymore.*

"I won't be here forever. I only want to stay here for a little bit. My feet hurt. Hell, everything hurts. All I wanna do right now is sit. I'm so goddamn tired." She took in the smell of blood stuck on her clothes. A small drop of rain landed on her shoulder. Rain. That would help clean up the car a little bit. Once most of the blood went, she'd hit up that car wash and clean out the rest. Then she'd run to the nearest gas station and get that bread and eggs she promised her mother. Someone out there had to be open now. Not everyone would follow the curfew. She'd find a store or two still open to the public. After she got those things, she'd figure out the rest. She'd decide where to go from here.

Gazing down at Thomas' body, her anger subsided and replaced itself with confidence. No matter what she did next, it wouldn't be his bidding. He changed her. She couldn't thank him for it, but she could rest and reflect for the next few minutes. As the rain came down, she stretched her legs out on the hood, letting the cool water drop down on her body. The blood began to wash off, streaming down the hood and onto the tires. She missed the rain.

"You were right about one thing, Thomas." She gazed over at his body, all scrunched up, bloody, and broken. By now, any chance of life seeped out of him. Just the body remained. A body that could no longer yell, threaten, harm her, or demand anything. From this point of view, he was harmless. "You said one thing that made sense. I'm a fucking smooth driver."

Her eyes closed as she let tears well up behind them. With rain coming, she wept and sat in silence, glad to be outside. Her body healed from the raindrops, each one cleansing her of the sins she committed. She'd sit till the rest of the pain went away. Let it go. Let every bit fade away. Every memory of Thomas, every horrible thing he did, her messy past now replaced with an unknown future. Rest was the only thing that made sense.

When she was ready, she'd get back in the car and drive.

THE END

Acknowledgements

First, thank you to my writing group for keeping me on track with getting this story written. Granted a lot of it was written during the quiet times at work. Though most of your advice has come on social media, I've appreciated it and I'm grateful for you.

Thank you to Tony Anuci at Anuci Press for taking this story and for your patience as I tried to get everything fixed in this novel. Thank you also to Adrian Medina at Fabled Beast Design who made this amazing cover.

Thank you to everyone else who read this book and offered their help to get it shaped into something incredible. Thank you to the ones on social media who have liked or commented on my works. Your engagement makes all the difference.

Thank you to my spouse and my child. Thank you to my coworkers for helping me keep my sanity intact.

Above all, thank you for picking this up. I hope you have enjoyed it.

About the Author

Cithara Susan Patra has been writing for a very long time, dabbling in all kinds of work over the years. Having a degree in Spanish and French (as well as one in Business Management), they've spent a lot of their normal life being very busy learning new things. They've written for multiple zines over the year as well as writing novels in between taking care of their rambunctious child and working for the health department in North Carolina. They've also written plenty of poetry and short stories over the years. When not writing, they are busy taking care of their family, trying to cook new meals, traveling to interesting places, or trying to perfect their French and Spanish speaking skills.

Current social media:
Bluesky: cspatra
Instagram: citharapatra
TikTok: cspatra

www.ingramcontent.com/pod-product-compliance
Lightning Source LLC
Chambersburg PA
CBHW071504110726
47908CB00003B/719